the forever promise

A BILLIONAIRE ARRANGED MARRIAGE ROMANCE

THE FOREVER SERIES
BOOK 2

LEIGH JAMES

GEMINI PRESS

radio silence

"CHLOE, did you see this? Isn't that Bryce's dad?" My brother Noah pointed at his laptop.

I peered over his shoulder at a picture of Gene Windsor, my father-in-law. It was a recent photo that showed off Gene's thick white hair, watery blue eyes, and tanned, deeply lined face. The headline read: *Billionaire Insider Trading Scandal*.

"Let me see that!" I yanked the computer away from him. The article claimed Gene had made a profitable investment that was being investigated by the Securities and Exchange Commission and the Department of Justice. If the accusations were true, Gene Windsor had received illegal tips from his firm, which had resulted in him purchasing a vast amount of real-estate index stocks. Those stocks had earned him over a billion dollars in *just six months!* If he was found guilty, he could be fined up to twenty-five million dollars and spend twenty years in prison.

Gene wasn't quoted in the article. His attorney only said, "My client has no comment."

The internet, however, had a lot to say.

Social media was having a field day with the scandal. The most linked-to article was: *The Rich Get Richer —Until They Get Busted!* The Windsor family was everywhere, all at once. A google search instantly produced thousands of pictures of Gene, Bryce, and his brothers— Jake and Colby—who I'd never met and hadn't heard much about.

I scoured the images, hungry to see Bryce and his family despite the bad circumstances. Both Jake and Colby were tall and handsome, like my husband. I wondered if they were close— Bryce never talked about them. Neither Jake nor Colby was quoted anywhere I could find; they remained a mystery.

But there *was* a quote from Bryce: "We appreciate the gravity of this investigation, and look forward to fully cooperating with the United States government in this inquiry. Thank you to our shareholders for their continued support—our company remains strong because of them."

My heart wrenched when I read the words. It was

the most I'd heard out of my husband's mouth in two long, dreary weeks.

Our wedding photo made it into one of the articles, too—*Second-Generation of Windsors Profit.* I ached when I glimpsed it. Although my gown was lovely, I looked frozen, petrified; Bryce looked handsome in his suit, but his expression was grim. It certainly wasn't the wedding day I'd dreamt about as a girl...

I closed the laptop and shook my head. I didn't want to think about it. Any of it.

"Is Bryce's dad going to go to jail?" Noah asked. He stuffed some fruit snacks into his mouth and concentrated on his video game, something involving a character that looked like a friendly marshmallow.

"I don't know. I don't think he's been arrested or anything." I couldn't picture Gene Windsor being handcuffed and led away; he was an intimidating man who was very set in his ways. I couldn't imagine him cooperating with an investigation, let alone envision him *in jail.*

I wonder what Daphne thinks of all this. But I hadn't spoken to my mother-in-law (oh, how she hated that term!) or anyone else from the island since I'd left. It had been radio silence, and I was too afraid to break it.

My phone rang, and I lunged for it—but it was a local number, not what I'd been hoping for. "Hello?"

"Chloe?" The voice was raspy, familiar, and unpleasant. "That you?"

"*Lydia?*" I sat up straight. Lydia was my stepmother; I hadn't talked to her in ages. "Is Dad okay?"

Noah whipped his head around. We hadn't heard from either my father or my wicked step-monster since Bryce had paid them off.

"He's fine." She sounded as though she were exhaling from a cigarette. "It's *you* I'm worried about."

My heart stopped. "What do you mean?"

"I saw your husband on the news. Looks like his Daddy's in trouble, eh?" She laughed, and it immediately turned into a snarling cough.

"I don't know anything about it. Why are you calling? Do you need something?" I couldn't fathom why she'd bothered to call if there was no emergency. Lydia hated my guts.

"You know what, kid? You're smarter than I thought. I *do* need something." She cough-laughed again. "*Money.* Lots of it. You think you can hook me up?"

My stomach sank. "No, I cannot *hook you up.* Bryce already gave Dad money." In fact, my husband had paid my father one million dollars in exchange for Noah coming to live with us.

"Yeah, but we blew some of it at Foxwoods. Actually,

we blew *most* of it—wasn't your dad's fault, the asshole dealer at the blackjack table had it out for us, I swear to God..." She rattled on for another minute, complaining about their bad luck, how they were tricked and robbed, blah blah blah...

But I knew the truth. Somehow, my father and Lydia had managed to blow through *a million fucking dollars* in the span of a few weeks. Booze and stupidity were *not* a good combination!

"I'm sorry you guys lost, but there's nothing I can do about it," I said, cutting her off. "Now, if you don't mind, I have to go."

"Don't you hang up on me, you uppity little bitch!" Lydia sounded just as nasty as I remembered. "You need to do something to take care of your father and me. Remember how we took you in when you had nothing? You need to help *us*. And if you don't, I am going to fuck your shit up, you hear?"

Hands shaking, I hung up on her.

"What did she want?" Noah's eyes were huge in his face.

I shrugged. "Just to see how we're going," I lied.

"Don't be dumb—I heard her yelling. What did she ask you for?"

"Money." My voice was flat.

"She and Dad haven't even called to check on me."

Disgusted, my little brother turned back to his game. "As far as I'm concerned, they can go jump in a lake."

"Sounds good to me, buddy." It sure did. A freezing-cold lake filled with fresh-water piranhas would be even better!

"I'm going to go to sleep, okay? Don't stay up too late. We can go swimming in the morning if you want."

"Whatever." Noah made his marshmallow character jump onto a cloud. "The pool here is nice and all, but it's not the ocean. I miss Maine."

"I miss it, too." I tucked myself under the covers, not wanting to think about it.

My phone pinged, and I lunged once again. But it was only a text from Elena, the madam at Accommo-Dating, Inc.—the escort agency that had matched me with Bryce.

Elena was *not* happy with me at the moment.

Need to see you tomorrow. Come in first thing.

Okay, I wrote back. What could *that* be about?

I tried to fall asleep. But in the end, I tossed and turned all night, wondering just what the madam wanted with me now.

shambles

IT WAS A SCORCHING JULY MORNING, already eighty degrees with one-hundred percent humidity in downtown Boston. Kai waited for me outside The Stratum. He looked impossibly cool and collected in his dark suit. "Good morning, Mrs. Windsor."

Oof. The name hurt every time. Still, I forced a smile at the friendly driver. "Good morning, Kai."

We drove to the South End neighborhood in comfortable, air-conditioned silence. I didn't take it for granted. We passed by several pedestrians, red-faced and frizzy-haired, as they trudged down the sidewalk; that had been me only a few weeks ago.

That could be me again very soon.

I fidgeted, nervous about meeting with Elena. She'd been none too pleased when I'd called her from Maine two weeks ago and told her I'd been fired. Luckily, Bryce had already arranged for Noah and me to stay at The Stratum; he'd *bought* us a room with an open account for food and drink. Whatever we wanted, he was paying for.

Unfortunately, what I wanted couldn't be purchased with an Amex Black Card.

I sighed as we pulled up in front of the Accommo-Dating office. It was a pretty brownstone with giant planters lining the stairs, the flowers bursting with color. The first time I'd visited the office, I'd been sweaty but hopeful—my life had been a mess. Now I was pulled together but hope*less*. The only thing I had in common with the old me was that my life was still in shambles.

Kai opened the door and bowed his head. "Have a good meeting, Mrs. Windsor. I can drive you back to the hotel when you're finished."

"Thank you, Kai." I took a deep breath and headed for the office.

Elena opened up before I could ring the buzzer. Despite the hot weather, she managed to look refreshed in a black jumpsuit and full makeup.

"Hey, Elena." I tried to sound upbeat.

The madam frowned. "Thanks for coming in."

I followed her inside. "You don't exactly seem happy about it."

She sighed as she clicked through the cool, airy office, bringing me to the small conference room. She shut the door behind her and frowned some more. "I assume you saw the news about Gene Windsor?"

"Of course. It's everywhere."

"It's a disaster." Elena sat down and motioned for me to join her. "There's a ton of press heading up there to cover the family."

"That's not going to go over well." I couldn't picture reporters with their zoom lenses converging on Mount Desert Island, also known as MDI. Located in a remote and pristine area, it was the largest island in Maine. There were also many tiny islands, including the one where Bryce and Gene Windsor had homes. Many locals lived on the smaller islands in the summer and moved to the "mainland" of Bar Harbor and Northeast Harbor during the harsh winters.

Although MDI was a playground for the rich and famous, it was peaceful, secluded, and quiet. People hiked in Acadia National Park, fished in the clear, freezing ocean, and drove their boats to dinner at the island's sole restaurant. Any *one* reporter would stick out like a sore thumb; a large group of them would be like a flock of flamingos, outrageously noticeable and out of place.

"It doesn't help that Caroline's wedding is in two weeks," Elena continued. "She refuses to call it off."

I blinked at her. "Who's Caroline?"

Elena arched a carefully groomed brow. "Do you *ever* go on the internet?"

"Sure." Usually, I was busy googling things like *How to Drive Your Man Wild in Bed*, and more recently, *Is He Still Thinking About You?* But whatever. "I just haven't heard that name before. Who is she? When's she getting married?"

"Caroline Vale is Bryce's cousin on his mother's side. She's marrying a tech CEO on MDI this summer. It's a huge to-do, with over four hundred guests. I'm surprised Bryce didn't mention it."

I swallowed hard. "I'm pretty sure I didn't make the guest list, Elena."

The madam pursed her lips. "The thing is, Bryce needs you to go up there. There's too much scrutiny on the family right now. If you're missing from the picture, people will start to ask questions. The Windsors need to present a unified front."

"I can't go back there." I winced, remembering Bryce's last words to me. *You're fired. I'll see that you receive something for all the trouble.*

"He *fired* me, Elena. And said that he should never

have married me in the first place. It's not exactly an open invitation!"

There was a knock on the door and Anita, the assistant, poked her head in. "Attorney Zhang is here. Are you ready for her?"

"Yes. Please send her in."

"Why is Akira here?" Akira Zhang was my attorney, and she was awesome. But I hadn't expected to see her today.

"Bryce has requested that you return to his estate, and he's sent an updated contract to reflect that."

"That's impossible." I gaped at her as my stomach did a somersault. "He hasn't called me. I haven't heard a word from him."

"He called *me* and sent over the contract last night. He's offering you more money," Elena explained, "but there are several restrictions."

"Oh, I bet." For some reason, my eyes pricked with tears. *He wants to pay me more to come back?* What did he want from me—some sort of paid performance?

Akira Zhang opened the door and sailed through, toting her enormous laptop. My attorney wore an electric-blue sheath and pink eyeglasses, her hair pulled up into a high ponytail. "Elena," she said, by way of a greeting, "you have got to be fucking kidding me with this contract!"

"Good morning to you, too, Akira." Elena scowled at her. "And no, I'm not kidding. May I remind you that Bryce is offering a *lot* more money?"

Akira stuck her nose up in the air. "An additional two million dollars for a short term *is* a lot of money, but it's not just about that. It's about these terms. His new legal team's drunk!"

An additional two million dollars. Maybe *I* was the drunk one. "Akira?" I blinked at her. "What exactly is Bryce asking for?"

"Oh—hey, Chloe." She sat down with us and set up her mammoth laptop. "Sorry I started going off first thing. But this contract is from the Stone Ages! Read this —Section 12-C. You're the *Obligee*, and Bryce is the *Obligor*."

Akira turned the laptop around so I could see the screen.

Section 12-C

- (1) Obligee agrees to not speak to any men unless they are in the direct employment of Obligor, and a third party is present during the conversation;
- (2) Obligee shall sleep in Obligor's bed every night and shall go to bed at the time designated by the Obligor;
- (3) Obligor shall have approval of all clothes worn in public by Obligee;

• (4) Obligor shall have full and unfettered access to Obligee's cell phone and all personal digital devices;

• (5) Obligee agrees to engage in consensual sexual activity at any time as requested by the Obligor; and

• (6) Obligee agrees to review the contract at the end of the term.

I sat there, reeling. *Agrees to engage in consensual sexual activity. Sleep in the Obligor's bed every night. Not speak to any men. Obligor shall have approval of all clothes worn in public by Obligee.* The terms of the contract were possessive, controlling. If I went back, I would be Bryce's prisoner once again.

At least, until he was through me with...once again.

"When's the end of the term?" I whispered.

"*That's* your freaking response to this?" Akira snatched the laptop back. "He's telling you that he gets to pick out your clothes, you can't talk to men, and you have to have sex with him whenever he wants, and you're worried when it's going to *end?*"

"September, Chloe," Elena answered. "He wants you back for a minimum of three months—until the press frenzy around his father dies down, and the wedding's over. He's offered to pay you an additional two million dollars *in cash* if you fulfill these terms. Not exactly chump change."

"You know I want you to make bank." Akira pushed her glasses up on her nose. "But this is some seriously fucked-up shit."

My heart thudded in my chest. "When would I go back?"

Akira rolled her eyes. "Today."

"And what about Noah?" I wouldn't do anything without my brother.

"Bryce is expecting him."

I stared down at the table. "Have either of you spoken with him?"

"I haven't," Akira said. "I think he's probably too afraid of what I'd say."

"I spoke to him last night, right before I texted you," Elena said. "He's not doing well, Chloe. He's very upset about what's happening with his company. You can imagine the sort of pressure he's under."

I nodded. "Did he say anything else?"

"No. Just that there needed to be a specific agreement between you two before you returned. He said he needed it in order to feel safe."

Akira snorted. "*He* needs to feel safe? There's nothing in here that protects Chloe! What about what she needs, huh?"

They both turned to look at me. "What would you need to feel safe, Chloe?" Elena asked. "I want you to do this. It's good for my company, but more importantly, it would be good for you and Noah. It's an amazing opportunity. So how can we make this work?"

My head spun. I needed all sorts of things to feel safe—an assurance from him that he wouldn't stomp on my fucking heart after breaking it would be a good place to start. But how could we put that into a contract?

"I want access to *his* devices." I shuddered, remembering all the texts from Felicia Jones, his evil ex-girlfriend. "And tell him I want three million dollars, not two. And a puppy for Noah. Something huge that sheds." Bryce deserved dog hair on his suit, on all of his suits.

Akira tapped away on her keyboard. "I like it, Chloe. What else? How about a brand-new Tesla?"

"I want the condo at The Stratum free and clear," I said, "in case he's an asshole and I have to leave him again. I should say, for *when* he's an asshole and I have to leave him again." At least Noah and I would have a safe place to go, one less thing to worry about.

"Now you're talking." Akira's fingers flew across the keyboard. "What else?"

"That's it for now. But tell him I'm not happy about this. He needs to know I'm only coming back for the money." I meant it. I also knew, instinctively, that he would say yes to my terms. Desperate times called for desperate measures.

I couldn't believe we were going back. It was all happening too fast. At the same time, it couldn't happen fast enough. *I'm going to see Bryce again.* What the hell was I going to say to him?

Elena took out her phone. "I'll call Dale and let him know you and Noah can fly back today."

I nodded, and a wave of emotion passed through me —*yearning? Excitement? Relief?* But that sentiment, whatever it was, could go die in a hole, where it could join all my previous feelings for Bryce Windsor.

I would never let my husband hurt me again.

THREE

waiting to exhale

"I CAN'T BELIEVE we're going back." Noah sounded excited as he buckled himself into his seat. "I'm going to ask Chef to make me chocolate-chip pancakes every day for the rest of the month!"

"I'm sure he'll be happy to see you." Like the rest of Bryce's staff, Chef loved doting on my brother. That was at least one good thing about our return to the island.

My nerves thrummed as I peered out the window of the tiny airplane. I dreaded flying. More than that, I dreaded *arriving*. There would be a hired car waiting at the Bar Harbor airport; it would bring us to Bryce's yacht. Then we'd leave Northeast Harbor and navigate to his gorgeous ocean-front estate on Somes Island. As it was ninety-four degrees and so humid that Boston felt like a swamp, I should be excited. We were returning, in lavish style, to cool, refreshing, gorgeous Mount Desert Island. Instead, I was filled with dread.

I'd missed my husband, but I didn't want to see him. I didn't want to see him ever again.

Like a cruelly broken record, his last words to me played over and over in my head. *"I made a mistake—I see it now. Marriage was a bad idea. Having a wife makes me vulnerable, and I don't do vulnerable. I'm so sorry, Chloe."*

And as he'd stood to leave, he'd spoken every hired bride's worst nightmare: *"You're fired."*

But there I was, on his private plane, flying back to him once more. What did he want from me? I shivered, remembering the new contract terms. He wanted sex. He wanted submission. He wanted to control me.

Maybe it would be better. Instead of pretending I was his real wife and that he loved me, he was being upfront that I was just his whore. His hired plaything.

Fine by me. Maybe if I could learn to differentiate between sex and love, I might even survive the rest of the summer. My stomach flipped as I remembered our last time together. Bryce was so deep inside me, touching the places only he could ever reach...

Ugh, I'm definitely not going to make it!

"Look at all the trees! Hey, I can see people's swimming pools. Isn't that cool?" Noah stared out the window, narrating the view. He loved flying, he loved Maine, he loved getting the hell out of Boston. We'd be away from sad memories of our mom and the fact that our dad hadn't even called to ask how we were doing.

I shivered, remembering Lydia's call. *"You need to help us. And if you don't, I am going to fuck your shit up, you hear?"* Lydia and my dad were a one-way street, a suck that just kept sucking. Maine might also suck, but at least it meant good riddance to those two.

I took a deep breath. My brother was the most important person in my life. I had to remember that I was doing this for *him*. Three million dollars for a few months' worth of work was *insane*, and it would change our lives forever. We could buy a home wherever we wanted. Noah would be safe, have healthy food to eat, and could go to a good school. I could pay for him to go to college. *I* could go to college—a luxury I never would've been able to afford without this job.

If Bryce wanted to pick out my clothes and set my bedtime, *fine*. I would do whatever he asked for the next three months, and then I would walk away for good. I closed my eyes again and said a prayer, begging God to help me be strong and keep my heart safe.

Bryce couldn't afford to be vulnerable; that made two of us. It was a short-term assignment. If I kept my eye on the ball, I'd get through it. Bryce probably felt the same way.

Maybe we were perfectly matched, after all.

The plane landed ahead of schedule. I saw two black SUVs waiting and three of Bryce's burly, be-suited employees stationed on the grassy tarmac.

"Geez, why do we have so many babysitters?" Noah asked as we climbed off the plane. It was warm but breezy, not a hint of humidity in the gorgeous Maine air.

"I'm not sure."

The men surrounded us as we disembarked. They grabbed our bags and hustled us to the SUV. "Mr. Windsor sends his apologies that he wasn't able to meet you in person," the tallest man said as he tucked me inside the car. "There's too much press around right now. He couldn't risk leaving the island."

"Are there reporters *here*?" I whipped my head around, but the large men obfuscated my view.

"Yes. Please keep the windows rolled up, Mrs. Windsor. We'll be behind you if there's any trouble."

He shut the door, leaving us inside the cool interior. "Trouble?" Noah's eyes were huge in his face as he peered out at the airport, which in Bar Harbor meant a grassy field and a dirt parking lot.

"I'm sure everything's all right..." But as the driver pulled out, I spotted a knot of people with cameras in the lot. Their zoom lenses were pointed in our direction. As soon as they saw us moving, they hurried to their vehicles.

"We might have to drive over the speed limit," the driver said. "Can you two please buckle up?"

"Yes, Sir." Noah and I immediately fastened our seat belts. The second SUV was directly behind us as we peeled out of the airport. We sped down the winding road to Northeast Harbor, the lobster pounds, fir trees, and majestic mountains passing by in a blur.

The driver's phone buzzed, and he answered it through the car's system. "I have you on speaker," he announced by way of a greeting.

"We have a security situation at the dock in Northeast," the man said. "We need to bring them to Southwest Harbor instead. Mr. Windsor has a boat waiting."

"We'll see you there. What about the cars following us?" the driver asked.

"They'll be stopped at a roadblock before the exit. Don't worry—everything's taken care of."

"I can't believe the paparazzi are chasing us!" Noah exclaimed when the call ended. "That is so cool!"

The driver chuckled. "I'm glad you think so. The rest of us should take a page from your playbook—we've all been complaining. They've been out in boats taking pictures of the house. They're swarming the dock at Northeast, they've got helicopters...they're relentless."

"Does that mean I can't go fishing? Or leave the house at all?" Noah wrinkled his nose.

"Don't worry about it." The driver smiled at him in the rearview mirror. "The staff is thrilled you're coming back—I'm sure you'll have lots of fun."

"Cool. Thanks." Noah lifted his chin, and my heart melted a little. The fact that Bryce's employees had taken to my brother and shown him such kindness almost made the whole ordeal worth it.

"Here we are—hang on, I'm going through the checkpoint." The driver sped up, maneuvering past several barricades manned by more of Bryce's staff and several state police troopers. The SUV behind us accelerated, too. We watched through the rear window as the officers quickly moved the barricades across the exit, blocking the entourage of paparazzi trying to follow behind.

One guy got out and started yelling. The officer crossed his arms against his chest and didn't budge.

"The police are helping us?" I asked, confused.

"The Windsors have always supported our troops," the driver said. "Everyone's happy to assist."

Noah grinned. "Bryce is kind of a big deal."

I didn't respond. But inside, I was scowling. Bryce *was* kind of a big deal, but I could no longer let him be a big deal to *me*.

We drove through Southwest Harbor, a cute coastal town. The pretty houses flew by, with their immaculate lawns and flower boxes bursting with color, as we headed to a private dock, the second car directly behind us. "Here we are." The driver parked in the vacant lot, and I let out a sigh of relief. We were safe, at least for now.

We hustled down to the water as the men loaded our bags onto the boat. It was pristine but not as opulent as the *Jules*, Bryce's yacht that he docked at Northeast Harbor. Noah chattered excitedly as we climbed on board. The captain, who I didn't recognize, didn't waste any time—he immediately started the motor and headed out across the clear, blue-green water. It was a color I'd only ever seen in Maine. Gorgeous mountains rose in the distance. Despite the paparazzi—not to mention our destination—a certain peace settled over me; to me, MDI was the most beautiful place in the world.

I recognized several boats we passed, but no one

glanced in our direction. Our anonymity was a good thing. A cluster of paparazzi boats was moored in the harbor in front of Bryce's estate. Several men had their enormous zoom lenses pointed at the house, but thankfully, they didn't look in our direction.

"Please come in from the deck—Mr. Windsor doesn't want them to see you." One of Bryce's men tucked us inside the cabin and closed the door. The captain took the long way around the island, keeping distance from the photographers. We landed at a brand-new dock I'd never seen before—it was further away from the house, virtually hidden by pine trees.

"Where are we going?" Noah asked.

"To the house—we're just trying to be discreet," the guard said.

"Bryce should just get a helicopter," my brother joked.

"They already have one." The guard smiled at him. "But the elder Mr. Windsor's using it today."

I held my breath as we docked. The guards grabbed our luggage and ushered us up the ramp. Two golf carts waited, but there was no sign of Bryce.

"Is the younger Mr. Windsor with his father today?" I asked, careful to keep my tone neutral.

"He's at the house," a guard answered. "He's been in meetings all day."

"Can I drive? This is so *cool*!" Noah hopped into the golf cart, happy as a clam.

"Sure thing." The guard smiled at him. "As long as that's okay with you, Mrs. Windsor?"

"Sure," I said weakly. I'd sworn to myself that I would try to relax; Noah should enjoy himself as much as possible. Besides, you couldn't go that fast on a golf cart, right?

Wrong! Noah floored it, whooping as he crossed the grounds.

"Slow down, or I'm going to take your x-box away!" I hollered after him.

He slowed down, at least a little, as we cruised across the lush grass. The enormous gray-stone mansion came into view. Every time I saw it, it took my breath away. The house soared toward the sky as it simultaneously curved around the circular gravel drive-way. A marble fountain bubbled in the center of the grounds. The whole thing was straight out of a fairy-tale, perhaps the one with the beast who was always angry...

"Hey, there's Bryce!" Noah pointed at the fountain.

And there he stood, The Beast himself—my husband, Bryce Windsor. He wore his customary dark suit, a pair of black sunglasses shielding his eyes from the afternoon sun. His tailored clothes barely contained his muscled frame; I knew all too well what he had going on underneath that suit.

He watched us approach, and I swallowed hard. Why did he have to be so damn handsome? Why did it have to hurt to even *look* at him?

I'm not going to make it. But then I glanced at my brother, and I knew that I had to. I *had* to make this work.

I took a deep breath of clean Maine air—my last opportunity to breathe easy. All hell was about to break loose in my heart.

But paid performer that I was, I plastered a smile on my face.

And went to meet my husband, the man who had forever broken my heart.

essential

NOAH GOT TO HIM FIRST. "Hey, Bryce! Cool golf carts. I heard you got a *helicopter*? And oh man, we got chased by the paparazzi. It was so cool!" He barely hit the brakes before he barreled off the golf cart, talking a mile a minute.

He went directly to Bryce and *hugged him.*

Bryce hugged him back, briefly but fiercely, before releasing him. "Wait, what was that about the photographers? They *chased* you?" There was a dangerous edge to his voice.

"Everything was under control, Sir," the lead guard said. "They were stopped at the checkpoint. We made it to Southwest without incident."

Bryce grunted in response.

"Can I go inside?" Noah asked. "I want to see everybody!"

"Of course." Bryce's voice was gentler toward my brother. "Dale has a surprise for you."

"I can't wait!" Noah sprinted toward the front door. The scene was a far cry from when we first arrived at the island—Noah had been too afraid to go into the house.

It got too quiet once my brother left. To add to the awkwardness, the men took the golf carts and brought our luggage to the house, leaving Bryce and me alone.

Oof. It hurt to look at him. He was as handsome as ever, larger than life. Bryce had either forgotten to shave for several days or was growing a beard, I wasn't sure. For some reason, his scruffy face appealed to me. I longed to rewind my life to Before, to when we were close, so that he could hold me in his arms and I could stroke his scratchy cheeks.

But this was After. I'd do well to remember that.

He pushed his sunglasses up on his head, and for the first time, I saw his eyes: there were dark circles beneath them. "How are you, Chloe?"

I wasn't sure how to answer him. *I'm dying inside? Heartbroken? I've been crying every day in the shower for two weeks straight?*

"Better now—at least I'm being paid properly." I

sounded bitter. "Three million dollars will go a long way toward keeping my brother safe."

Bryce shrugged. "I would've paid more."

I blinked, taken aback.

The muscle in his jaw bulged. "I *need* you."

"You...do?" A stupid spark of hope lit my chest.

"My company's blowing up, in case you haven't heard."

Ugh. He needed me, but not the way I needed him. "You're the one who fired me, in case you don't remember."

He looked past me, out at the water. "Oh, I remember."

Why did he sound hurt? He'd been the one to end things; he'd been the one to send me away. That was the truth, and I refused to lose sight of it. "It doesn't matter anymore—I'm here. You're paying me to be here. What do you need me to do?"

"Honestly, not much." Bryce sounded exhausted. "But it's essential that everything between us look okay."

"How come?"

"Our board might mutiny if there's any more trouble." His brow furrowed. "I can't be having marital problems on top of the charges against my father. The board's aware that our marriage is a stipulation of my vesting. If my stake in the company's threatened, they might try to bring someone else in—or have a vote of no confidence. I can't let that happen."

I nodded. But inside, I wanted to die. I was nothing but a business transaction to him, a way to save his company. All he cared about was how this looked to his board and shareholders. It was just as I'd feared: I was nothing to him, no one. "I'll do whatever you need me to do. I'm sorry about your father."

Bryce snorted. "Don't be. He got greedy, that's all. And it was stupid because he already has so much. He just loves to feel like he's ahead of the game like he's smarter than everyone else. It finally caught up to him."

"Is he going to be arrested?"

"Probably." He scrubbed a hand over his face. "But he's got the best lawyers money can buy, so he has some time. I honestly don't know what's going to happen."

"What about Daphne?" The last time I'd spoken with my mother-in-law, she'd discovered she was pregnant with another man's baby. The father was none other than Michael Jones, who was also father to Felicia Jones, Bryce's ex-fiancée and Bitchface extraordinaire.

"She's not handling this well. She was about to see her divorce lawyer to start proceedings against my father, but now everything's on hold. His assets might be frozen. Oh, and she's pregnant. With Michael Jones's baby."

When I winced, he sighed. "But you already knew that."

"I did," I admitted. "She wasn't exactly hiding it."

He laughed. "She's screwed now. She might not be able to get anything from my father, and Michael Jones wants nothing to do with her *or* this scandal."

"What about Felicia?" I asked. Her name tasted like acid on my tongue, but it no longer mattered. If Bryce was seeing her again, I should know about it now.

He shrugged. "I have no idea."

"Is that because you haven't asked her?"

Bryce scowled, and just as he was about to answer, his phone buzzed. He glanced at the screen. "I have to take this—it's Dale."

He answered it and was silent as he listened to Dale, then grunted. "Tell them we'll be there. Thirty minutes." His gaze raked down me. "Chloe needs to change."

When he hung up the phone, I asked, "What do I need to change for?"

Bryce smiled, but it didn't reach his eyes. "We have a press conference. You're going to hit the ground running, Mrs. Windsor."

"I am so glad you're back!" Midge jumped up and down and clapped her hands. "But we have to hurry—the reporter's already downstairs. And your *hair*." She frowned as she ran her fingers through it. "No one told me you'd be arriving windblown. Gah! Come in here."

She dragged me to the enormous bathroom and stuffed me into the makeup chair. Before I knew what was happening, Midge had fired up the flat iron and was expertly smoothing my unruly waves, talking a mile a minute. "Mr. Windsor said that we were allowed to use your old bedroom as a dressing and changing room but that you were moving into the primary suite. He was *very firm* about that." She waggled her eyebrows. "So what's the deal, huh? No one knew what happened when you left! And then I didn't hear from you..."

Midge pouted as she finished with my hair and moved straight away to my makeup.

"I wanted to call you," I moaned as she applied concealer under my eyes and blended it. "But I didn't think I should. It was all so sudden... What did Bryce say when I left?"

"Literally not one word!" Midge wailed. "We were all *dying*. But he didn't say anything—he just stormed around for the past two weeks like he was on his period, and it was a *bad* one. You know what I mean? And then all hell broke loose with his father, so it's been crazy. Nobody knew what was going on."

"Was Felicia here at all? While I was gone?" My palms started to sweat as I waited for an answer.

"She was here once," Midge said, her voice neutral. Midge hated Bryce's ex almost as much as I did. "I know she had lunch with Mr. Windsor. But she left right after, and she didn't look happy."

"Huh." My stomach dropped. "When was that?"

"Yesterday." Midge frowned. "But enough about her! I was so worried about *you*. Old Hazel kept her mouth shut. We all knew she was the last one to talk to you besides Mr. Windsor, but she didn't say a peep. So we've *all* been worried. And Mr. Windsor's been a *bear*. Literally—like a bear on his period."

I couldn't help it: I laughed. "I'm sure it's been hard because of his father. What a mess."

She started working on taming my unruly brows, no small feat after two weeks away from her ministrations. "There's been reporters in the harbor non-stop. Someone even snuck onto the island in the middle of the night! He hid in the woods, trying to get a picture first thing in the morning. Security got *him*, all right."

I shook my head. "That's awful."

"I know." She nodded, eyes wide. "All of us are on

edge—different news outlets have been calling the staff, trying to get a story. Mr. Windsor is making all of us stay here, and our phones are being monitored. He gave us all raises, though. Like, *big* raises. And it's not like I mind living at a mansion for the rest of the summer!"

"Wow. I can't believe this is happening."

"None of us can." Midge started on my mascara. "Daphne's having a hard time of it. She had to move back into the main house with Mr. Windsor because they can't be having their dirty laundry splashed all over the internet right now. She was just about to file for divorce, did you know that?"

"Yeah, I heard something…"

Midge sighed. "We need to catch up more, but let's get you into your dress. You know what I always say— Mr. Windsor doesn't like to wait!"

My stomach flipped. I wasn't ready to see Bryce again, and I certainly wasn't prepared to be on freaking *television*. "Do you know what's happening? Bryce said it was a press conference."

"I think it's more of an interview." Midge guided me back to the bedroom, and without blushing, she stripped me out of my clothes and started throwing undergarments at me. She rummaged through the wardrobe as she said, "The reporter's the lady from the cable-news network. You know, the famous one? With the blond hair and the legs?"

"I don't know who she is." *Famous? Cable news?* I felt like I might be sick.

"She's terrific. Mr. Windsor agreed to meet with her —he doesn't want to deal with all the riffraff paparazzi who have been spying, but he felt like he needed to make some kind of statement. At least, that's what Dale said." Midge ordered me to step into an emerald-green sheath dress, then zipped me up. "Perfect. I read on the internet that jewel tones work best on camera. You look gorgeous, Chloe—and appropriate. A proper Windsor."

She handed me a pair of strappy sandals, and I groaned. "You know the drill, Chloe! Put 'em on and stand up straight. They'll make your butt look good." Her phone buzzed. "They're waiting—we have to go."

I muttered to myself as I put on the shoes, but as I glanced in the mirror, I knew they were the right choice. The heels made me taller, making me feel more grown up and confident.

Which I needed to feel. Because I was about to go see my estranged husband and smile for a famous cable-news lady and her camera crew. "Do I have to do this?" My voice came out small.

"Windsors aren't quitters." Midge put her hand on

my back and marshaled me out the door. "And you're a Windsor, right?"

"Right," I said weakly. "Right." But as I tottered down the stairwell, I wondered who I was trying to fool. I was Chloe *Burke* from the crummy part of East Boston, a hired bride. I was a fraud.

Still, I lifted my chin as I glimpsed Bryce waiting below. I was a fraud and a no one, but after three months, I would be a multi-millionaire.

And then no one—not even my husband—could ever hurt me again.

strictly business

"CHLOE." Bryce nodded at me. "You look perfect—that dress will work great on camera. Are you ready?"

"Not really." My palms started sweating, and I wasn't sure if it was because I was faced with his handsomeness again or because we were about to be on television—probably both. "I wasn't expecting this. Do I *have* to be part of the press conference?"

He held out his arm for me. When I hesitated, he sighed. "This has to look real. I'm *paying* you for it to look real."

"Fine." I took his arm and steeled myself against the shock that ran up my skin—touching Bryce always affected me.

He glanced at me sharply. Did he feel something, too? But he turned away, a smooth mask of detachment settling over his features. "We're meeting Kysa Reeves in the study. They're almost finished setting up."

I swallowed hard. "Midge said she's famous."

"You've never heard of her?" Bryce sounded surprised.

I shrugged. "I never had much time for television."

"She's good at her job." He nodded. "You don't have to talk—this will be brief. I insisted on firm parameters."

Of course you did. "Okay." But my nerves thrummed as we reached the entrance to the study.

He turned to me. "You'll do fine. You look great."

"Thank you." I melted a little, then chastised myself. *He doesn't mean it. He just wants this to go well.*

A harried-looking production assistant wielding a clipboard hurtled out of the room, his eyes wide. "Mr. and Mrs. Windsor, it's go time. Kysa's already in her chair."

"Fine." Bryce's tone was meant to put the assistant in his place—as in, *fine, but I'm Bryce Windsor, and people wait for* me.

The assistant nodded nervously. "Right this way. Sorry to rush you, Sir. But I'm the one that gets yelled at."

Bryce didn't respond. One thing hadn't changed: my husband clearly wasn't looking to make friends.

All hell had broken loose inside the study. There were klieg lights and video equipment everywhere; at least half-a-dozen crew members wielded cameras as they checked the lighting and different angles. At the center of it all, seated in a rather grand-looking armchair, was a blond woman with impeccable posture. She wore a charcoal dress, and her hair was pulled back in a sleek bun, which showed off her long neck and fine bone structure. When she saw Bryce, she stood, revealing her fit body and long, toned legs. "Bryce, Chloe—please, come and sit!"

I followed Bryce, petrified of talking to Kysa Reeves, who appeared too pretty to be real. "Hi, there!" She surprised me by hugging Bryce, then me, enveloping the both of us in her scent, which was clean and somehow smelled expensive. "It's so nice to see you both!"

Bryce smirked as she fussed over us, ushering us into the chairs facing hers. "Are you about ready to get started? I know you mentioned you have meetings, Bryce."

He cleared his throat. "I do. We only have a small window—I appreciate you coming out and making this possible."

Kysa Reeves leaned forward, big brown eyes sparkling. "Are you *kidding*? This is the scoop of the summer! I've wanted to interview you for years. You've turned me down every time!" She laughed, then turned to me. "I think your gorgeous new wife talked you into it. Is that right, Chloe?"

"Um—"

Bryce reached over and gripped my hand. "Chloe's been by my side through this whole ordeal. She absolutely thought this was a good idea."

I nodded as he gripped. Electricity jabbed through me, straight to my core, making me blush. I hoped Kysa Reeves couldn't tell that my husband's touch made my freaking *vagina clench*—even though I was through with him!

"I'm happy Bryce is making a statement." My voice wobbled. "I support my husband one-hundred percent."

He gripped my hand tighter. My vagina clenched tighter. *For fuck's sake!*

Kysa eyed our entwined hands, her smile broadening. "If you two ever want to do a profile, my network would pay top dollar—not that you need it. Still, it would make a great story. I can just tell."

I wanted to assure her that her instincts were correct; people would love the true story of a virgin from the wrong side of the tracks being purchased by a billionaire. But the truth was more complicated than that. And there wasn't a happy ending...

Bryce checked his massive watch. "We should get started."

Kysa nodded, then motioned for the cameras to start filming. "Let's just jump right in. Bryce and Chloe Windsor, thank you so much for joining me this afternoon."

She spoke briefly about our family and Windsor Enterprises, highlighting the robust past of the company and the Windsor billions.

"I know it's been a tumultuous time for your family," Kysa continued. "Your father's being investigated by the United States government for insider trading, among other charges. How are you all holding up?"

"Of course, what's happening with my father is upsetting." Bryce's voice was surprisingly gentle. "But as acting CEO of the company, I'm focused on our shareholders and the health of our business. My father wants us to put the company first—being a good son requires me to support that."

"So you're saying your father is ready to pass you the torch? Because he hasn't seemed too eager to do that in the past. I'm thinking in particular of his Q1 telephone conference. Didn't he say that he had no plans to step down?"

Bryce nodded. "No one said he's stepping down. But for now, he will concentrate on the investigation, and I will concentrate on running our company. My family is committed to the success of our business. We aren't going anywhere. We intend to come out of this stronger than before."

Kysa Reeves nodded. "I'm not surprised by your stance, Bryce. You don't say much, but every time you talk about your company, it's obvious that you're passionate. Speaking of being passionate..." A small smile played on her lips as she peered past him to me, so help me God. "You recently married. We're so grateful that your beautiful wife Chloe has joined us today. Chloe, can you give us a glimpse into what it's like to be a Windsor? I'm sure our viewers would love a more personal perspective. No offense, Bryce."

Bryce scowled at her.

"Chloe?" Kysa asked. "What's it like to be married to the youngest billionaire in the world?"

I cleared my throat, nerves thrumming, as Bryce reached over and gripped my hand again. Electricity jolted through me—I hoped the camera wouldn't show how physically affected I was by my husband's touch.

"Well, he's not only the youngest," I said, in a joking tone, "but he's the most handsome. And the most intense, in case you haven't noticed."

Kysa threw back her head and laughed. "I love it. So what's it like living with him?"

I straightened my shoulders and clutched Bryce's hand. He looked sour—hell, he *was* sour—but I thought of how he'd hugged Noah. I thought of the last time he'd held me, back when he treated me like I was the most precious thing on earth. "He's very kind and generous. We're all concerned about his father, of course. My husband is very committed to his family."

Kysa Reeves eyed our interwoven hands. "I can see that. Thank you for joining us today, Chloe. And Bryce, thank you for agreeing to speak with us."

"My pleasure." He nodded.

As soon as the cameras stopped rolling, he rose to his feet, taking me with him. "I told you not to ask my wife any questions on camera. That was a dick move."

The reporter smiled at him, flashing her blinding-white teeth. "Our viewers are curious about who you are as a *person*. Your father's in trouble, Bryce—real trouble. Do you want your shareholders to rally around you? Be human." Her direct gaze flicked over to me. "A young, beautiful new bride can only help you. You might want to let her out of her cage more often."

"I'll keep that in mind." He sounded pissed.

"Good!" She didn't match his tone—instead, she laughed. "I really hope everything works out for the best. I'm rooting for you, Bryce. Chloe, it was a pleasure."

"Thank you." It shouldn't surprise me that someone so flawless could be warm and genuine, but it still did.

Bryce took my hand, and again, my traitorous insides clenched. He led me from the bustle of the room. "She shouldn't have put you in that position," he rumbled.

Panic rose in my chest. "I didn't say anything too awful, did I?"

"No, not at all." He shook his head. "You spoke very well. I just didn't want to put you through that."

That *almost* sounded like an apology—which was not exactly in Bryce's wheelhouse. "It's okay."

"Good." His shoulders relaxed. "Are you hungry? I'm sure it's been a long day."

"I could eat." Hope sparked inside me. He sounded so normal, like he...cared.

"I'll have Chef prepare something for you."

The brief glimmer of hope crashed and burned. "Just for me?"

"I have a meeting." He checked his watch. "After dinner, please make sure that Noah's settled. Then it's curfew."

I coughed. "*Curfew?* What do you mean?"

"We're requiring the staff to stay on-campus because of the reporters," Bryce answered. "They have to be inside their rooms by nine each night. So do you."

"I have a nine o'clock curfew?"

He eyed me. "Yes. I expect you in our room at nine on the dot and in our bed shortly thereafter. I'll have your dinner served out on the patio. I'll see you in bed, Mrs. Windsor." Without a backward glance, he stormed down the hall, leaving me alone once again.

What. The. *Hell*. Bryce should patent the emotional whiplash he was so expert at dealing out—he'd make another whole fortune selling it to men aspiring to be a douchebag just like him!

I expect you in our room at nine on the dot.

...and in our bed shortly thereafter.

I'll see you in bed, Mrs. Windsor.

WTF had I gotten myself into? Did he actually expect me to *sleep* with him after treating me like that?

I fumed, hands clenched—but thankfully, not my vagina—as I stormed out to the patio. The sound of the waves crashing against the rocks echoed the feelings inside me; tumultuous, heavy, relentless. Why was Bryce treating me this way? Just when I thought he was being human, that we might do something normal like share a meal, he pushed me away.

Then he dangled the fact that I was his hired plaything in front of me.

When we'd been happy, he'd never made me feel like I was his hired plaything. Now he was treating me like I was a piece of meat—perhaps his favorite cut of sirloin. Something to devour and then, to cruelly forget.

I shivered. *Why* did his words ignite a spark deep inside me? Why did I want him to want me when he obviously didn't love me? I was settling for being needed—in an interview, in his bed.

I was young and inexperienced, but I knew that being needed was not the same thing as being loved. Not even close.

If I'd ever felt like a whore, it was right now.

SIX

curfew

Dinner was delicious—some sort of traditional Spanish dish of chicken with garlic and rosemary, God bless Chef—but I was too pissed to enjoy it. Did Bryce seriously think I was going to have sex with him tonight? He'd fired me. He'd told me marrying me was a mistake. He'd *broken my heart*. And then he'd paid me mega-bucks to return to the island so that I could play the role of supportive wife for the cameras.

And sleep in his bed.

And only speak to other men in the company of a chaperone.

And have sex with him whenever he wanted.

I'll see you in bed, Mrs. Windsor.

Why did that make my insides twist? Why was I clenching when I wanted to smack him for treating me so poorly, for throwing me away like I was East Boston trash?

My vagina was a traitor. I was almost as pissed at it as I was at Bryce—*almost*. I had some empathy, though. I remembered what it felt like to have him inside me, *deep*, stroking the places only he could ever reach. I'd been a virgin when he'd taken me, completely inexperienced. Still, I was alive. I was *human*. Even though I had nothing to compare it to, I knew the sex had been off-the-charts spectacular. Bryce had made me come so hard I'd seen stars. He'd made me come so hard I'd almost passed out.

My vagina clenched again. *Stop it stop it stop it!!!*

Sighing, I picked up my plate and headed for the kitchen. I didn't want to go to bed. I didn't want whatever was going to happen between my husband and me to happen. I was pretty sure I was going to cry when he touched me; it would be awful.

Having sex with him, knowing that he didn't love me? It would break me once and for all.

"Mrs. Windsor, *please!*" A harsh, disapproving voice surprised me. "Let me take that for you. You don't need to clean up!"

I yelped as Hazel sprung out at me from a dark corner of the hallway. The last time I'd seen the head maid and her spindly little legs, Bryce had forced her to bring me clothes (I'd been naked) and keep watch outside of his room (I'd been his prisoner). Good times.

"Hey, Hazel. You scared me."

"I didn't mean to, Mrs. Windsor." She yanked the plate and cup from me as if they were her precious babies, and she'd caught me trying to steal them. "I'm just trying to do my job."

I nodded—Old Hazel took her position as Bryce's watchdog *very* freaking seriously. "How've things been around here?"

"Not well. It's been very hard on the elder Mr. Windsor and, of course, on *our* Mr. Windsor. He needs support." She eyed me, her heavily lined lids squinting in disapproval.

"I hope I can help." Despite my misgivings, I meant it. "How are *you* holding up?"

"So long as the family is intact, I'm fine." She straightened her skinny frame. "Good evening, Mrs. Windsor. Please don't forget the nine-o'clock curfew. Mr. Windsor—"

"Doesn't like to be kept waiting. I know, I know," I joked. But Hazel just scowled and clicked away. I wondered what she thought of all this. I wondered what she thought of me, if she approved in any small way, or if she wished that Bryce and Felicia Jones would officially reunite and finally make it down the aisle.

Ugh. My stomach twisted every time I thought of Bryce's beautiful ex-fiancé. Bryce may have been talking to her the whole time I'd been gone—or more—and there was little I could do. The fact that she'd been at the house yesterday, while I'd been hours away, made me feel sick. I still hoped she would go and die in a hole. Even though Bryce and I were just business now—if I caught that bitch texting my husband or coming around again... I was going to make her pay!

Ugh, ugh, ugh. Being back on the island was *so* not good for my mental health! There I was, already picturing bitch-slapping Felicia and thinking unkind thoughts about Hazel—not to mention Bryce.

Sighing, I went upstairs in search of my brother. I reminded myself that he was the bright spot, the reason I was there. It was no surprise that Noah was sprawled out on his bed, a plateful of homemade chocolate-chip cookies at his side as he cursed at whatever video game he was playing.

"Are you losing again?" I asked.

"Oh my *God*, Chloe, stop!" He threw down his controller and grabbed a cookie. From the number of crumbs on his comforter, it wasn't his first. "This game *sucks*. Bryce got me the version that hasn't even been released yet, and it's totally buggy. I keep getting knocked."

I also grabbed a cookie and sank down next to him. "At least Chef made your favorite dessert."

"Chef is the bomb. I'm so glad to be back." Noah grinned as he ate. Through a mouthful, he said, "Dale said he has a surprise for me. Something *alive*. It's coming tomorrow. Do you know anything about that?"

"Chew with your mouth closed, please! Ew." I grimaced as he dropped a bite onto his lap, picked it up, and shoved it back into his mouth.

"And yes," I continued, "I might know something about it. But like Dale said, it's a surprise." I hoped my brother loved having a puppy. I *also* hoped it was some sort of beast that would shed big globs of dog hair all over Bryce and his zillion-dollar suits. Not that I was holding a grudge or anything!

"Did you hear we have a curfew?" Noah picked up his controller again. "Nine o'clock. That totally sucks— no night fishing!"

"You shouldn't be out past nine anyway." I shrugged. "Better to get up early. But speaking of that, you need to check with Dale or one of the other staff members before you go anywhere or do anything— there's a ton of reporters hanging around. Midge said one of them camped out on the island overnight."

"Sick," Noah said. "Did Bryce fight him?"

"No—the guards found him. I think he got arrested for trespassing or something."

"Again, *sick*. Can you believe we live on a private island?" My brother started clicking the buttons on his controller crazy fast, already back into the game. "I can't believe there's reporters on boats watching us! How cool is that?!"

"Um, I don't think it's very cool. I feel bad for the family. They're under a lot of pressure."

He shrugged. "Do you think Bryce's dad is going to jail? I never talked to the guy, but I heard he's a jerk."

"Noah." I smacked his arm. "Don't talk like that! Mr. Windsor is perfectly...nice."

"That's not what I heard. *I* heard he's a douche."

"Noah Burke, do not use that word ever again!" I hopped up. "Where are you even hearing language like that?"

"Uh, first of all—you. Second of all, you *do* remember Dad and Lydia, right?"

"Ugh, right." My phone buzzed, and I glanced at it. As though Noah's mention had summoned her, there was a text from Lydia.

Don't hang up on me ever again, she wrote. *Just remember that you owe us. I expect a phone call soon!* Angry-face emoji.

I didn't bother to text her back. What was I

supposed to say? *You want another million dollars to blow at the blackjack table—and keep yourself in booze and Menthol cigarettes? No problem, Lydia! And please tell Dad that Noah and I are doing just fine!*

"Who was that?" Noah asked.

I sighed again. I had a feeling there was going to be a lot of sighing for the next few months. "No one," I said. It was the truth.

After I said goodnight to Noah, I headed for Bryce's primary suite. I hesitated outside the door. I felt sick, confused. Should I knock? Probably not—Bryce was likely still in a meeting. The curfew most certainly did not apply to His Highness!

I opened the door and stopped short. Bryce was already sprawled out on the bed, laptop at his side. He glanced at his watch. "You're late," he growled.

I checked the time on my phone. "It's eight-fifty-nine. I'm *early*."

Bryce scowled at me. "*Early* is on time. On time is late. And *late* is unacceptable."

"Well, I'm here now." I tried to keep my tone light. He'd changed into sweats and a tight-fitting white T-shirt, all the better to outline his enormous, muscled chest. *God help me!* It seemed rude, a slap in the face, to have him look relaxed and cozy—to be within reach—when emotionally, we were so removed from each other we might as well have been a million miles apart.

My eyes roamed over his face, his shoulders, his long legs. It was a strange sensation to be near him again—I felt oddly relieved. It was like I'd been in the desert, dying of thirst, and someone had finally offered me a glass of water. A glass of poisoned water. But *oh man*, would it feel good to drink it!

I couldn't take my eyes off of him. We'd been close once. It seemed impossible now that I'd ever been in a place where I could tell him the truth: I loved him. How had I ever been that brave? Or crazy?

Crazy. Crazy was definitely the right term.

"Your clothes are in that dresser." Bryce pointed to the far side of the room. "And Hazel moved all your toiletries into the bathroom. You should get ready for bed, Chloe. We have an early start tomorrow."

I jolted at the word *we.* "How come?"

He nodded, looking at his laptop and not at me. "My father met with his team this afternoon. We have a strategy meeting with them tomorrow."

"I'm part of your strategy meeting?"

He glanced up, his icy blue eyes raking over me. "You're part of my *strategy.*"

"What does that mean?"

He motioned toward the bathroom. "Your things are in there. Get changed, come to bed, and I'll tell you more."

Yes, Sir. With mixed emotions, I lifted my chin and did what I was told.

Inside the bathroom, I saw all my favorite luxury shower gels, shampoos, and conditioners, along with an enormous basket of skin care products and high-end makeup. Living in a billionaire's house did *not* suck, although living with a particular billionaire just might.

On a small table near the shower, I found my "things": a pair of lace g-string panties and a matching black tank. *Fuck.* He expected me to put this on and go out there to him. He was going to make good on our contract; I was going to die inside.

Cursing, I pulled on the lingerie. When I saw my reflection in the mirror, I winced. I looked sexy, all right. The lace tank was fitted, showing off my curves. And the g-string was...a g-string. Thank God I was young because my ass looked good even though I'd never attempted a squat in my life.

I washed my face. I brushed my teeth. I flossed. I brushed my teeth again. I was, most absolutely, stalling.

"Chloe!" Bryce called from the bedroom. "It's bedtime."

"Coming! I'm coming." The question was, would I be *coming* soon? Were we actually going to do this?

Please, God, don't let me cry. Don't let me have an orgasm, either. I won't give him the satisfaction!

Taking a deep breath, I went out to meet my torturer...also known as my husband.

tight

"It's about time," he growled.

With as much dignity as I could muster in the g-string, I lifted my chin and strutted to the bed. I *had* to strut—I had a massive wedgie!

Bryce didn't take his eyes off of me. He shifted on the bed, drawing my attention to the growing bulge of his crotch.

Holy hell, I'm in trouble.

I climbed in next to him, careful not to get too close. His erection looked as though it might reach out and grab me.

Bryce finally closed the laptop, put it on the night-stand, and then turned toward me. There was nothing between us now except for his hard length—which was gathering steam, getting bigger by the second. I couldn't face it. And yet, my eyes continued to be drawn *down there*, watching with fascination as his sweats tented. *Oh, girl. No matter what happens tonight, we are so fucked! Ha ha UGH.*

I took a deep, shuddery breath, then tried to stall some more. "You said you'd tell me about the meeting."

"I did." Bryce's gaze flicked down my body, and my nipples pebbled, the needy little traitors. He scratched his beard, his gaze lingering on my thighs, a funny expression on his face. Maybe he was wondering what his scruff would feel like down there, rubbing against my smooth skin...

Stop it, Chlo! But it was too late; a fire had already started deep in my belly. I fought the urge to squirm as heat and wetness built between my thighs. Damn him! I vowed right then and there to finish my contract and leave not only with the money but with some small shred of dignity intact. I just had to remember myself, remember what had happened.

He might be able to touch me on the outside. But on the inside—the places where he'd broken me? *Never again.*

"Chloe," Bryce was saying. "Are you even listening?"

"What? Of course." I nodded. "Go on."

A smirk tugged on the corner of his full, luscious lips. "I actually wasn't saying anything—that was a test. Your eyes looked glazed. What were you thinking about, huh?"

His dick twitched. When I glanced at it, his smirk deepened. The smug fucker!

"Nothing." I sighed. "Why don't you just tell me what I need to do tomorrow?"

"Fine." The teasing tone dropped from his voice. "We're meeting with my father's team—his lawyers, his marketing person, and a liaison from our board of directors. Daphne will be there, *our* family, and my brothers."

Our family. Did he mean him and...me? I swallowed hard. "I'm going to meet your brothers? Are they already here?"

"They flew in last night. They each have a house on Spruce Island, but they rarely come up. They like having their space from Dad, I guess. Lucky them." His brow furrowed. "But they'll be here first thing in the morning."

"Okay." I couldn't believe I was going to meet his brothers. I *really* couldn't believe that there was more than one of him. What were they like? Did they look like Bryce? Were they grumpy, too?

"What exactly are we meeting about?" I asked instead.

Bryce scrubbed a hand across his face. "Recommendations about how to move forward, based on the legal team's prognosis of the next steps."

"It sounds complicated."

Bryce looked grim. "It's an absolute cluster fuck. I was upbeat for that interview, but between you and me, I'm not."

"Do you think your father's going to be convicted?"

"I'm sure there's plenty of evidence. But we can spend with the best of them, including the government." He shrugged. "It'll be interesting to see what the lawyers say."

"Are you sure you want me to go?" I would be out of place with a bunch of fancy lawyers and other executives.

"Absolutely." He raised his gaze to meet mine. "I need you, Chloe. I need you to stay by my side through this."

"I will. That's why I'm here."

"I know we left things on bad terms." He rolled onto his back, and I noticed, with a twinge of regret, that his erection had wilted a little. "But it's essential that we act like a happy, committed couple. I can't have any rumors. It was bad enough that you were gone for two weeks; we can't risk anything like that again."

I nodded. "Just tell me what you want, and I'll do it." For millions of dollars, I would jump through all his hoops, no matter what it cost *me*. I had my brother to think about.

"It has to seem natural between us," he said. "That's part of the reason why I made it a contractual term that we share a bed. We got lucky with Kysa Reeves—she couldn't tell anything was wrong. But there's going to be a lot of scrutiny, Chloe. We have to act like newlyweds."

Bryce was quiet for a moment. "If my board gets suspicious about our relationship, my position with the company will be threatened. I can't let that happen —*especially* not now. This scandal with my father's terrible, but it's also an opportunity for me to show the board that I can run things on my own."

"Okay." I didn't consider myself much of an actress, but I would do my best to support him. I had no choice.

"Do you think that you can..." He blew out a deep breath and stared at the ceiling.

I stilled myself, bracing for it.

"Do you think you can come here?" He lifted his arm, making way for me to put my head on his chest.

I didn't say anything; I couldn't. I held my breath as I went to him. Tears pricked my eyes when I pressed my face against his massive chest. His scent, so familiar, engulfed me. *No, Chloe. Don't.* Bryce always felt so warm and clean...being held by him made me feel safe.

Not anymore. He told you to leave, remember? He fired you and sent you away. The pain, still fresh, tore through me.

He wrapped his huge arm around me. The tears threatened to spill over as he pulled me close. How could such a simple thing—a touch—undo me?

Hysteria bubbled inside my chest. *He* was about to tell me it was time to have sex. *I* was about to lose my mind.

The silence stretched out between us, almost unbearable. "Do you think you can sleep like this?" he finally whispered.

I peered up at him. He was staring straight at the ceiling. "Yes...?"

"Good." He closed his eyes. "Good night, Chloe."

I stared at his handsome face. Then I glanced down —his erection was massive again, raging. *What the hell?*

And yet, Bryce was saying goodnight.

"Good night," I said.

Without another word, my husband fell asleep, his arm still tight around me.

burn

I BARELY SLEPT. Why hadn't Bryce tried to make love to me? Wasn't that the whole point? If not, then why all the contractual terms, growling about getting into bed on time, and g-strings?

I wasn't sure if I wanted to laugh or cry. In any event, I didn't dare move all night—Bryce held me in a firm grip. Even in sleep, he was showing me who was in charge.

My thoughts circled, chasing each other. I refused to admit to myself just how good it felt to be back in his arms. It was heaven; it was also hell. It felt amazing, but how could I relax in his embrace when I knew that it was an act—his way of fighting for his company?

Just before dawn, exhaustion took over, and I fell asleep. When I awoke, Bryce was pressed against me. *All* of him was pressed against me—he was hard again. His erection throbbed against my thigh.

I opened my eyes to find his face one inch away. He was staring at me. "Hi," I said awkwardly.

Bryce didn't say a word. Instead, he leaned forward and brushed his lips against mine.

Electricity jolted through me. I fought to urge to reach for him, to cling to his massive chest. Instead, I held very still. I didn't know what to hope for. Part of me felt like I would die if this happened; another part felt like I'd die if it didn't.

Bryce pulled me closer, and his hands roamed my back. He buried his face in my neck—not kissing me, just breathing. How could he bear it? Tears pricked my eyes. To be back in his arms, but to be so *distant* from him, was torture unlike anything I'd ever experienced.

He pulled back. His pupils were huge as he gazed into my eyes. "We should get ready. Shower with me?"

I blinked at him. *He doesn't feel what I feel.* If he did, he could never be so casual about us being naked together. To me, this was The Biggest Deal Ever. To him, it seemed I was nothing more than a morning-shower fuck. "Sure." There was no way I could say more.

This is happening. I was under his spell, unable to stop time. In a daze, I followed him to the bathroom. He was so close, close enough to touch. But the distance between us seemed impenetrable. I was a transaction to him, an asset that he owned. He was going to do what he pleased with me.

But what was worse than even that? I *wanted* him. There was an undeniable ache between my legs. Having him inside me was what I craved—but like a cigarette or a hit of heroin, this shit was absolutely going to kill me.

Without a word, Bryce stripped out of his shirt and pulled down his sweats. His boxer briefs did little to conceal his bulging erection. I stared at it, at *him*, his well-defined muscles rippling as he reached into the luxurious shower to turn on the water. Without looking at me, he headed back to the bedroom. "I'll join you in a minute."

"Okay…?" As soon as he closed the door, I panicked. *Oh my God. This IS happening.* I only had a minute. I flew into action—brushing my teeth and flossing as though my life depended on it. Heart pounding, I jumped into the shower and washed my body and hair. I was going to be prepared, dammit! And I wasn't going to cry. *Please God, don't let me cry!*

After a moment, the shower door opened, and Bryce stalked in. The boxer briefs were long gone, of course. I tried not to stare at his erection and failed; it was pointing directly at me. Bryce's gaze was dark as it roamed my body, up and down. He took the shower gel from my hands. "Here," he said, his voice gruff. "Let me."

I braced myself as he squirted (even thinking of that word made me go all squishy inside) some gel into his hands and moved closer. We stared at each other. Time ground to a halt.

It was just my husband and me once again.

Bryce tentatively reached for me, then gripped my sides. Despite the hot water, I trembled beneath his touch. His big hands were just as firm and strong as I remembered; as he stroked my skin, lathering it, I turned to Jell-O inside. I remembered exactly what it felt like to be overpowered by him, to have him own me. I had loved every second of it, just like I'd loved *him*. Those feelings rose inside me once again. *Fucking inconvenient.*

His erection poked at me, but he ignored it. Instead, he seemed intent on stroking every inch of my skin. His hands worked up to my breasts, and his touch became more gentle, almost worshipful. But I had to be imagining that...

Still, Bryce slowed down, his movements rhythmic, as he cupped my breasts and circled my nipples with his big thumbs. *Unf.* Sparks flew through me as he increased the pressure and the sensitive buds. I couldn't help it; I moaned.

He moved closer, hands roaming my back, reaching down until he cupped my ass. He squeezed it, pulling me against him, as he buried his face in my neck once more. I moved to meet him as his cock slid between my thighs, and he began pulsing his hips. We weren't having sex, but the motion was *awfully* close.

I want you. Oh my God, I want this. Everything inside me cried out for more.

He kept it up, increasing the pace, pressing against me, his cock slick and insistent against my slit. The weight of his body engulfed me. Despite my best intentions, I got swept away in the moment. I got swept away by *him*. Desire tore through me, followed by a deep longing that once again brought tears to my eyes.

I loved him.

Fuck me, I was still absolutely in love with Bryce Windsor.

No. He thrust between my legs again, his lips brushing my neck.

No. He cupped my ass, pulling me close against him. *No.*

Bryce kissed my neck, groaning as he pulsed against me.

Yes. Oh fuck, YES.

Being back in his arms was heaven and hell all wrapped into one. It was *yes,* and it was *no.* It was love mixed with raw pain. He'd hurt me deeply; I *still* hurt. Desire and agony mixed as his lips roamed my neck, his big hands squeezing my ass. But I couldn't stop what was happening. Wild horses couldn't drag me away.

And then, caught up in the moment, I made the biggest rookie mistake of them all: I kissed him.

When his tongue connected with mine, my whole body buzzed.

Bryce met my kiss hungrily, devouring my mouth with his. He abandoned my ass, buried his hands into my wet hair, and pressed me against the wall. *Holy hell!* Our tongues lashed as he covered me with his body, taut muscles pinning me beneath him, the slick shower tiles pressed against my back. His cock was still squarely between my thighs, pressed against my sex. Having him so close—the promise of him entering me—made me crazy. I didn't want to do it, but I was absofuckinglutely going to do it. It was inevitable.

When this kind of fire started, there was only one thing to do: burn.

Bryce kissed my neck, moving down to my breasts. He greedily sucked the nipples. They pebbled, painfully erect. He trailed his hot kisses down my torso, devouring me. Before I knew it, he was on his knees before me, prying my thighs apart. The hot water rained down on us as he put his face between my legs and immediately found my clit with his mouth.

"What? Wait—"

I *wanted* his cock, but once again, he was showing me who the boss was. Bryce didn't answer, and he didn't wait. His expert tongue circled my clit as he suckled me, then spread my legs further apart and started lapping at my wet slit. Unexpected sensation exploded inside me. I wasn't ready! And he wasn't going slow, damn him—

He nibbled on my clit. Pure sensation exploded inside my core. All at once, my climax mounted, surrounding me. I couldn't think. I couldn't stop. My back arched, and my body moved in time with his mouth, meeting each stroke of his tongue. I scratched at his back as I held on for dear life. "Bryce! Oh *fuck*!"

No, no, no! I fought the orgasm. I didn't want to come for him so easily; I didn't want him to see first-hand just how my body responded to his touch. I didn't want to give him the satisfaction of seeing just how weak I was for him, how easy it was for him to make me scream his name.

But Bryce would take what he wanted. He knew exactly how to maintain control, to manipulate me into being *his*. He thrust two fingers inside me, almost roughly, and finger-fucked me as he clamped his mouth around my clit.

Oh, fuck. Game over! I couldn't resist him. He fucking owned me.

He thrust his fingers in and out as he sucked me hard. Time stopped. All I could do was feel. All I could do was give in to him, to the fact that he'd taken possession of me and that I was *his*.

The orgasm tore through me. *"Bryce!"* I didn't want his name on my lips. I didn't want my body clamped around him as I shook, coming blissfully undone as the pleasure overtook me. But what I wanted didn't matter. I cried out again, shockwave after shockwave of sensation ripping through me. There was no more *no*. There was only *yes*. Yes I was his, yes I still loved him, yes, he touched me in a way no one else ever could.

Tears streamed down my face as I finally came to, grateful we were in the shower, and he couldn't see me crying.

Bryce rose from his knees and cradled me against him, tenderly kissing my cheek and the top of my head. His erection still poked at me. I slid my hands around his shaft and started to milk him. What he'd just done to me with his mouth and his hand had been amazing, but it had done nothing to put out the fire. I still wanted him badly, and it went far beyond physical need. I stroked his hard length, and he grew bigger.

Maybe he didn't feel the way I felt.

Maybe he'd been happy when he'd sent me away.

Maybe I *was* only a transaction to him.

That didn't stop me. I moved my hand up and down, and he strained against me. If nothing else, I could make him come.

But suddenly, Bryce pulled away. He turned off the water, not looking at me.

"Where are you going?" I could hear the hurt in my voice, the surprise and rejection.

He shrugged, still not looking in my direction. He got out of the shower and started toweling off.

I chased him out. Apparently my dignity had left the building, along with my self-control. "Why won't you let me touch you?"

"Because." He concentrated on drying his legs, huge thigh muscles taunting me.

"Because *why*?"

Bryce wrapped the towel around his waist, his still-erect penis straining against it. "Because I said so. Now go get dressed—Midge should be waiting. She'll do your hair and makeup. We don't have much time."

With that, my husband stalked from the room, leaving me lost and alone once again.

blitz

MIDGE EYED ME WITH CONCERN. "What's the matter? Your complexion looks good, but your expression doesn't. Did everything go okay?"

I shrugged. "It was fine. I guess I just feel a little... off-balance." That was putting it mildly. Once again, Bryce had given me whiplash. He'd claimed my body and made me see stars; then, he'd refused to let me touch *him*. But I couldn't get into the details of our bathroom encounter with Midge.

I checked the time—I didn't have much. "We have a meeting with the lawyers." I fidgeted, my nerves beginning to thrum. "Can you help me? I don't know what to wear!"

"I've got you covered, hon." Midge went to the wardrobe and pulled out an expensive-looking black blazer and a pair of white trousers. "Billionaire-wife chic. Nobody's going to look better than you!"

"Thank you, Midge." I blew out a sigh of relief. "How's Daphne doing?" I asked as she ordered me into the bathroom and started detangling my hair.

"She's been kind of quiet, actually." Midge looked thoughtful. "Maybe she's worried she's not going to get any money if Mr. Windsor goes to jail or something."

"Right." I wondered how long it would be before the staff knew the truth.

"Of course," Midge said as she whipped out the blowdryer, "maybe she's been quiet because she's pregnant with Michael Jones's baby, and she doesn't want the whole world finding out. Ya know?"

I laughed. "You guys always know everything, don't you?"

"The help usually does." Midge waggled her eyebrows. "Except we didn't know where you went two weeks ago. *That* was driving everyone bonkers!" She started drying my hair, and when she was finished, she chattered at me good-naturedly while doing my makeup. By the time she'd gotten me into my outfit, I was feeling and looking much better.

"Thank you so much, Midge." I smoothed the blazer. She'd added a diamond-cross necklace and diamond stud earrings, sparkly but tasteful. "I look like an adult."

"You look like a *Windsor*." She winked at me. "And the best-looking Windsor of them all, if I do say so myself. Now go forth and meet with the lawyers—and then you and Mr. Windsor should sneak off someplace secluded and have make-up sex."

"Midge!"

She shooed me from the room. "Midge knows best! Make-up sex makes everything better. Just try it!"

I pondered her advice as I headed down the stairs. Since we'd already fooled around, maybe I could convince Bryce that a little make-up sex might be a good idea...

But he'd rejected me. *Again.* After giving me one of his signature mind-blowing orgasms. What the hell did he want from me, anyway?

And why was I still obsessing over having sex with him? Ugh, I needed to get a grip!

Bryce waited at the landing, handsome as ever in a dark-blue suit. He scowled as he read something on his phone.

"I'm ready," I lied. I'd love nothing better than to run, screaming, back to The Stratum.

He glanced up, his eyes widening as he took me in. "I like that outfit. You look great."

"Oh! Thanks." Once again, my husband had caught me off guard. I hadn't expected a compliment; I'd prepared myself for more of a grunt. "I don't think I've ever worn a jacket like this before."

"It suits you." His gaze trailed down me, and maybe I imagined it, but he looked like he was hungry. "We should get to my father's. I want to speak to him before everyone else arrives." He reached for my hand as though it was the most natural thing in the world. Once our fingers entwined, familiar, inconvenient electricity ran through me. I wondered if he felt it. Or was I alone in that, too?

Bryce led me down the hall, where the staff waited to greet us.

"Good morning, Mr. and Mrs. Windsor."

"It's nice to see you home, Mrs. Windsor."

"We're happy to have you back."

"You look lovely, Mrs. Windsor."

I smiled and thanked them but almost tripped when Hazel emerged from the shadows. Her lips turned down as she inspected us, her gaze traveling to our entwined hands. "Good morning, Mr. and Mrs. Windsor," she said stiffly.

Bryce smiled at her, and I followed suit. But Hazel looked anything but friendly as she watched us exit the house. I could still feel her eyes on us as we hopped into one of the golf carts and drove across the lush grounds, the grass still wet with morning dew.

"Your brother's dog is being delivered today." Bryce didn't sound happy about it. "The breeder's meeting Dale in Bar Harbor."

Noah was going to be *so* excited. "That's nice."

"It wasn't nice—it was a contractual term, remember?" He glanced at me. "Do you even *like* dogs?"

I shrugged. "I've never had one. What about you?"

"We had a Black Lab when I was a kid. Blitz. He was a good boy." Bryce looked thoughtful as we sped across the lawn. "He was my mother's dog, she loved him. He actually died the week after her."

"I'm sorry."

He didn't respond as Gene Windsor's enormous mansion came into view. Its gray-stone face was flocked by well-manicured shrubs. The home was regal in the morning light, the quintessential New England ocean-front mega-estate.

My stomach tied itself in a knot. I wasn't looking forward to seeing Gene. "So... How are things between your father and Daphne?"

Bryce snorted. "She's having his friend's baby. His assets are about to be frozen. They aren't exactly in a good place."

"But they're living together, I heard?"

"They have to. They're putting on a show for the board and the public, just like everyone else."

"You mean, just like us."

"They're nothing like us." Bryce frowned as he maneuvered the golf cart onto the motor court. It had never occurred to me before, but why the heck did they have motor courts and cars on the island? Everywhere we went, we took a boat. Or a golf cart.

Bryce still looked sour; for all the money he was paying me, I supposed I should help lighten things up before we went inside. "Hey, I've been meaning to ask... Why do you guys have driveways?"

He laughed. "For our trucks and other toys. Haven't I shown you my jeep?"

I arched an eyebrow. "*You* have a jeep?"

"Yes. I only take it out once a year, but I have it."

"For what? Are there even any roads on the island?"

"There's one." Bryce sounded a bit defensive. "And the jeep's for *off-roading*. So we don't even need a road."

"Hmm. I don't exactly see you as the off-roading type." I didn't see him as a dog person, either, but I kept that to myself.

"Well, I'll have to prove you wrong about that," he sniffed.

"Fine."

His brow furrowed. *"Fine."*

We were quibbling, but it felt so normal that it made me happy. He parked the golf cart, and before I knew it, Bryce was at my side, helping me down. "Don't want you to wrinkle that fancy outfit."

"Are you making fun of my blazer, now? You, who never takes off your suit? Are you going to wear it *off-roading*?" I teased.

For a brief moment, a smile crossed his face. "You'll have to wait and see."

"My money's on you staying in the suit," I chided.

"I'll take that bet," he growled, "*and* I'll show you I can off-road with the best of them." The way he said it made me go all squishy inside—as though he intended to show me something more than just how his jeep handled. Again, *fine by me!* But I didn't say it. He'd fooled me once already that morning, making me believe that he wanted to be close, at least physically. I had zero intentions of letting him fool me twice.

Still, when he grabbed my hand and tugged me toward the house, it tugged at my insides. *Damn him.* Why did my body have to respond to his every touch?

"Chloe! Oh, thank goodness!" Daphne sprung from the house and rushed us. She grabbed me in a hug and rocked me back and forth. "You can't *believe* what it's been like around here—a total cluster! Gene's under so much stress that I started eating carbs again."

She pulled back but didn't release me from her embrace, her slender arms surprisingly strong. Up close, I could see that Daphne looked good; her skin was clear and glowing, and the dark circles were gone from beneath her eyes. She wore a flowing dress that showed off her lithe frame.

"It's good to see you, Daphne. You look great."

"I know, right? I'm not showing yet. I'm only a few weeks." She rubbed her ultra-flat stomach.

"How are you feeling?"

"Great! I'm on these *insane* prenatal vitamins. I got them from a specialist in Dubai! Ooh, and of course, I've quit drinking. It's been amazing for my pores—my smoothie business is blowing up because everyone wants skin like this. It's a good thing because I need the money!" She rolled her eyes. "We could lose everything. I mean, *everything*."

Bryce cleared his throat. "Good morning, Daphne. Thank you so much for that thrilling synopsis."

She grimaced. "Whatever."

He nodded at me. "Chloe, I'm going in to talk to my father. I'll let you two catch up for a minute. See you inside?"

"Sure." As I watched him leave, Daphne watched me.

"Are you guys back on the love boat?" she asked.

"We never got off of it." I forced a smile.

She arched an eyebrow. "Then where the hell have you been? And why has Bryce been acting like even more of a douche?"

"I needed to take Noah back to Boston." That was sort of the truth. "But enough about me! What about you? Is everything okay? I mean, I know it's not *okay*—"

"Oh my God, it's been *hell*. I can't believe you didn't even call me!" Daphne pouted for precisely one second, but she couldn't bear to stop talking for long. "Michael Jones has completely ghosted me since he found out about the charges. He's only out for himself!"

If anyone was only out for themselves, it was Daphne. She'd gotten pregnant with a married man's baby while *she* was married to another man, and she'd done it in order to secure her position as a one-percenter. But I didn't say a word. I'd learned that getting along with my young mother-in-law was much better than being on her bad side.

Daphne scowled. "The Joneses turned out to be just what I thought: awful. Gene reached out to their family before the scandal hit, but Mimi Jones has been throwing a fit about my pregnancy. She refuses to take his calls or support Gene, even though they've been friends forever. And Michael wants nothing to do with him—or me."

"I'm sorry."

Her nostrils flared. "Oh, it's okay. We'll show *them*."

"What about Felicia?" I hated even saying her name. More than that, I hated the fact that she and Gene were close and that he wished Bryce had married her instead of me.

Daphne sighed. "I'm not saying anything nice about her—you know how I feel about that bitch—but Felicia's the only one of them to keep in touch with *my* poor husband."

I wanted to ask more but got sidetracked by Daphne's tone. "Wait—are you and Gene back together?"

"He wants to be." She lifted her chin. "And I guess I can't divorce him right now—he offered me a *very* generous stipend if I stay. There's even more if I sign an affidavit that the baby's his! He thinks it will look good to his shareholders if he gives off a 'family first' vibe. Plus, it'll make him look virile."

She rubbed her stomach again and shrugged. "Which he's not. But it's all for show, isn't it?"

Daphne's constant scheming was too much for me to keep up with. When we'd last spoken, she'd been ready to file for divorce and run to Michael Jones. "So... you're going to stay?"

"I am for now." Her eyes sparkled mischievously. "It depends on if Gene's assets are frozen and what happens with Michael Jones. If Michael's smart, he'll come around. If not, I have some ideas about how to handle him."

She linked her arm through mine and started up the steps toward the house. "Are you ready to meet the other boys—Jake and Colby? I'm surprised they're coming. They like their name and their money, but their actual family? Not so much."

"Are they here yet?" I was nervous but also super-curious to meet Bryce's brothers.

"They're always late." She rolled her eyes. "But it's good that you're here early—we have a lot to do."

"We do?"

"Of course." Daphne blinked at me. "Haven't you heard?"

"Heard what?"

"Ha!" Daphne dragged me into the house. "There's going to be a media blitz! We both have a starring role. Bryce is going to owe you for this—you should think about what you want as a reward. Think *big*. Like, owning your own private island big. Hedge-fund big."

Starring role? Reward? Think big?

I almost laughed—all I could think of as a "big" reward was Bryce's big...body...the very one he'd withheld from me that morning!

But as Daphne maneuvered me into Gene Windsor's mansion, I had a sinking feeling this was no laughing matter.

strategy

I'D NEVER BEEN inside Gene's home before. It reminded me of him—cold, formal, and a little scary. Breakable-looking antiques filled the entryway. An oil painting of a robed man preaching in what looked like Ancient Greece adorned the wall. Daphne caught me staring at it, and her eyes widened. "That's an original. It's valued at fifty *million*."

I couldn't believe anyone owned a painting worth that much money. "Woah."

Daphne nodded. "If the government tries to freeze our assets, you can bet I'm hiding *that*!"

"Ha," I said, but I had a feeling she wasn't kidding.

I followed her through the cavernous house into an enormous study. It was filled with more antiques, a massive floor-to-ceiling stone fireplace, and Oriental rugs. Daphne chose an armchair, and I sank down next to her, nerves thrumming.

Before I had the chance to ask her about the media blitz, several staff members bustled in with trays of coffee and baked goods. They glanced nervously at Daphne; she was notorious for being rude to the hired help. "We didn't realize you were already in here, Mrs. Windsor. Sorry to interrupt."

"No worries." Daphne sounded uncharacteristically kind. Maybe remembering the fifty-million dollar painting had cheered her? The staff set up the provisions on a long table and then hustled out, returning a moment later with a group of men and women who had to be the lawyers—they wore dark suits and glasses and wielded large laptops that could rival Akira Zhang's. They shook our hands and introduced themselves, whispering their names. It felt solemn, like we were at a funeral, waiting for Gene Windsor's fortune to be interred.

I waited nervously. I hoped Bryce would appear soon. Instead, two large, attractive men in suits ambled. With their tousled hair and achingly good looks, they had to be Colby and Jake Windsor. Before introducing themselves, they scanned the room, talking in low tones to one another.

Daphne shook her head. "They are *so* rude. Jake,

Colby, get over here! Come and meet your new sister-in-law."

"Aw, I guess our favorite step-mother needs some attention," the taller of the two joked as they headed toward us. "Hey, Daphne. Heard you're expecting...a lot of new TikTok followers."

"Ha ha." Daphne narrowed her eyes at him, then pointed to me. "This is Bryce's wife—Chloe. You'll be answering to her someday soon, so be polite."

He held out his large hand for me to shake. "I'm Jake Windsor. And I'd be thrilled if I was answering to you instead of my boss-hole of a brother."

"Nice to meet you." Up close, I could see that although Jake looked a lot like Bryce, he had a more narrow face, hazel eyes, and his hair was lighter.

"Enough about him—I'm Colby." He elbowed Jake out of the way and leaned down, surprising me with a hug. "I'm the baby of the family, but don't let that fool you. I'm also the smartest, the best looking, and the most accomplished." Colby Windsor was shorter than Bryce and Jake but was still six feet tall. He had one lone dimple, blue eyes, and enormous shoulders.

"He also has the biggest ego." Jake rolled his eyes. "But enough about him—I heard you were young, Chloe, but jeez. Did my brother ask to borrow your lunch money right before he asked you to marry him?"

"Good one." Colby laughed and punched Jake on the shoulder.

"Ha." I shifted uncomfortably in my chair. And here I'd thought my blazer made me look sophisticated!

"Back off, Jake," a familiar voice rumbled. I breathed a sigh of relief as Bryce maneuvered through his brothers and came to my rescue. He bent down and kissed my cheek, very clearly marking his territory. "Chloe's young, but she's very mature. Unlike you two bozos."

"Nice to see you, too." But Jake grinned as he shook Bryce's hand.

"Who're you calling a bozo, Bozo?" Colby hugged Bryce and clapped him on the back. He eyed him up and down. "Damn, Bryce, you look good. Have you been lifting?"

Bryce's nostrils flared. "I never stopped."

"Then it can't be that—there's something different." Colby's merry gaze traveled over to me. "Maybe being a newlywed suits you!"

Bryce tugged at his collar. Was I imagining it, or was his face turning red? "Being a newlywed is great," he said through gritted teeth. "Maybe someday when you're mature enough to stop dating strippers, you'll see what I mean."

Colby shrugged. "What if I marry one of the strippers? That still counts, right?"

Bryce scowled. "I guess it depends on the stripper."

"Right?" Colby laughed. "We'll have to wait and see!"

Jake groaned. "As long as you didn't marry the last one, you'll be fine. I hope."

"Briar? Aw c'mon, she was fine—"

"Enough about the strippers, boys," Gene Windsor's sour voice interrupted. "If I go to jail, there won't be any more funds to make it rain. Whatever will you do?"

"Go visit my old man in jail?" Colby smiled at his father. "Hey, Dad."

Gene surprised me by smiling back. "Hi, Son. Nice to see you."

Colby hugged him. Both Bryce and Jake looked away.

Once Colby stepped back, Jake extended his hand. "Hey Dad. Sorry there's been so much trouble."

"Eh, it comes with the territory. Good to see you, Jake." Gene turned to the rest of us. "These lawyers charge through the nose. Since my assets are about to be frozen, I suggest we get on with the meeting."

Everyone took a seat. I was relieved that Bryce was right next to me; I was surprised when he put his hand firmly on my thigh. Once again, inconvenient heat spread through me. I shifted in my seat, and he moved closer, putting his mouth next to my ear. "Don't make any plans for the rest of the day. We'll need to discuss strategy."

I nodded, but I was quivering inside. The whole day with my husband? Even though he was also my torturer, I had only one thought: *yes, please!*

The lawyers had set up their workstations and were about to begin when two women entered the room. One was short and voluptuous, with red hair and a fair complexion; the other was tall and lithe, with caramel-colored skin and dark hair pulled back into a high pony-tail. They introduced themselves to the attorneys, nodded at Gene, and sat next to each other at the table.

Bryce put his mouth next to my ear once more, making me shiver. He gestured to the redhead. "That's Olivia Jensen, our media strategist. The other woman is Romina Hernandez, our board liaison."

There was no time to ask questions—the lead lawyer stood and cleared his throat. "Thank you all for joining us this morning. I know it was short notice."

"They love short notice," Gene whispered dryly, "because then they can bill me at the emergency rate."

The lawyer smiled patiently. "That's true, but our goal here today is to protect and preserve your assets during this difficult time. My assistant is coming around with a non-disclosure agreement. Everyone present needs to sign."

Regina Hernandez raised her hand. "What about my duty to report to the board? What am I able to disclose?"

"Great question." The lawyer nodded at her. "Your fiduciary duty to the board requires you to be honest with them about the direction of our strategy, but exact details are non-disclosable. You're fully protected under this agreement. If the board has questions, have their counsel reach out to us."

He turned to face us. "As for the rest of you, you are not allowed to give any statements to third parties, including the press, without running it by Ms. Jensen first. She will be in charge of the family's public face moving forward. She's running everything by both the board and legal first. So there's to be no social media posts, no talking to friends, *nothing*."

Daphne raised her hand. "But I run my business from my social media accounts. You don't mean I have to stop—right? *Gene?*" She gave her husband a death glare, and he shrugged.

"I'm afraid your business will have to go on hiatus for the next few months as we prepare for a possible trial." The lawyer noted Daphne's reddening face. "I believe our client has an additional offer to make you, which should soften the blow."

Daphne sat back a little, slightly mollified. "It better be generous. My business is doing very well."

Gene patted her hand. "It will be, Dear. It will be."

Bryce, Jake, and Colby looked disgusted. Luckily, the lawyer moved on. "We've done the research and talked to our sources within the Justice Department, and we're fairly certain that this will be classified as a formal investigation within the next few weeks. That makes the time we have absolutely crucial for garnering public support. It's imperative that the world sees the Windsor family as people to root for. Which means you need to be accessible. Ms. Jensen will carefully control the family image, but everyone here has a part to play. Your family's known to be reclusive. That has to change over the next few weeks. The American public needs to understand who you are as people. They need to be able to find a reason to *like* you. With that, I'll turn this over to Olivia."

He sat down, and the redheaded media strategist stood up and cleared her throat. Despite her small stature, her energy commanded the room. She paced in front of us, calves straining in her high heels. "I've been working with Gene for a few months, and let me tell you, he's a pain in the ass." She laughed.

"Thanks a lot, Liv." Gene scowled, but he didn't

actually look angry. "For the record, you're a pain in the ass, too."

"That's why we work so well together." She grinned at him. "The board has hired me to strategize an aggressive public-relations campaign. We've agreed that what your family needs is a united front. The public doesn't perceive you well. They see Gene as a rich, entitled crook who's married to an insufferable, gold-digging TikTokker."

Daphne started to protest, but Olivia raised her hand. "My turn to talk. You might not like what I have to say, but in the end, you'll thank me. And I'll thank *you* when I drive off into the sunset in my Lexus SUV with my gigantic bonus."

Gene grimaced, but the media strategist ignored him. "Jake and Colby, no one knows who you are. That's not a bad thing. I'm going to spring you on them and position you both as America's most eligible bachelors. *And* you're both going to have to get married soon. It's imperative for your company's future."

"What?" Jake sat forward. "No way in hell! I'm not getting married because my father got greedy—"

"Can I marry anyone I want?" Colby interrupted, a mischievous sparkle in his eye.

"To answer you both: yes, you are, and no, you may not," Olivia said firmly. "For now, neither one of you is to go on a date, go to a strip club"—she eyed Colby—"or have relations with a lady-friend. *Nothing*. Consider yourselves celibate and dateless for the near future. I want the public foaming at the mouth to get you two married off. I want their interest vested."

When both Colby and Jake started objecting, she put her hands on her ample hips. "I said *no*. And when Olivia Jensen says no, I mean it. You know why? Because Daddy's gonna cut you off if you don't play along. Isn't that right, Gene?"

Gene nodded. "What Olivia said."

Jake cursed under his breath. Colby shook his head, looking like he didn't know what had just hit him.

"As for *you*." She nodded at Bryce and me. "You've missed an incredible opportunity here. A young, handsome billionaire falls in love with a gorgeous girl from the wrong side of the tracks. It's so intense he just *has* to marry her. Even though his heiress ex-girlfriend wants him back."

I stiffened, and Bryce gripped my thigh.

"That's a hot storyline," Olivia continued. "I saw Kysa Reeve's tape—you two do well on camera. I am going to position you as the flagship couple for this family. I'm arranging 'paparazzi' pictures of you to start with. I want the whole world to see that you're madly in love. I want the public obsessed with you."

Bryce looked sour; I felt dazed. Neither one of us said a word.

"Lucky for us, there's a wedding coming soon. Caroline Vale's circus of a society wedding is *exactly* what we need this summer. I couldn't have planned it better myself." Olivia rubbed her hands together. "We need to work quickly. By the time your cousin recites her wedding vows, the Windsor family will be front and center in the American psyche. This is an opportunity for greatness, people. I know that you will rise to the occasion."

Olivia Jensen smiled at us one final time. "Everything goes through me. I mean, *everything*. My client has given me full authority to kick ass and take names if anyone here goes off-script. Is that clear?"

I nodded; we all nodded.

There was a new sheriff in town, and her name was Olivia Jensen.

ELEVEN

coping mechanism

THERE WAS MORE talk from the lawyers about the investigation. Regina Hernandez spoke at some length about the Board's expectations. None of it registered with me. I was too dazed, thinking about what Olivia Jensen had said.

Flagship couple.

His heiress ex-girlfriend wants him back.

Hot storyline.

Public obsessed with you.

What on earth did all of this mean?

Bryce led me from the meeting while the others were still talking to the lawyers. We didn't speak as he helped me onto the golf cart and then sped toward the house. Dale was waiting outside. "Bryce, can I grab you for a minute? We need to talk logistics."

"Don't go anywhere," Bryce growled at me. "We have a lot to discuss."

I nodded as he climbed out and headed for Dale.

My phone buzzed with a text. *I told you we need cash,* Lydia wrote. *Keep ignoring me and you'll be sorry.*

I wanted to text her back, tell her to go die in a hole, and then throw my phone in the ocean. But I knew Lydia. She was loud. She was a pest. If I didn't do something, she was absolutely going to be a relentless pain in my ass.

I'll see what I can do, I wrote back.

You better, she responded. *Or Mr. Billions is going to be sorry he ever met you.*

A sick feeling gripped my stomach. I couldn't deal with Lydia on top of everything else right now. While Dale and Bryce were still deep in conversation, I quickly called Akira Zhang.

She picked up after one ring. "What's wrong? Do you need me to come get you? Do you need me to kick some billionaire ass?"

"Hi Akira. No, it's nothing like that." I watched Bryce with Dale. My husband was a problem, but he was *my* problem; I felt strangely protective of him. "It's my stepmother. She and my dad already ran through the money—she wants more and she wants it now. She keeps threatening me."

"They went through a million dollars *already*?" Akira sounded incredulous. "How?"

"Foxwoods." That was the name of the casino where they'd lost. "She said if I don't do something, I'm going to be sorry."

"We can't have her blowing things up right now. Does Bryce know about this?"

I sighed. "No, I haven't told him. He has enough on his plate. Is there any way you can wire her money for me? I don't even know if I *have* any money..."

"Of course you do. Do you really think I'd let you go back up there without some sort of guarantee? Your funds are being held in a private account. I'm authorized to distribute sums for your well-being and maintenance." She sighed. "I suppose I can do something. How much do you want to give her?"

"Nothing. But do you think we could do thirty thousand?" I swallowed hard. "That would cover their living expenses for a year. She might not be happy with it, but it's more than fair on top of what Bryce already gave them."

"Send me her number and consider it done. I'll take care of it." Akira paused for a beat. "Are you doing okay?"

"I'm fine," I lied. I was still watching Bryce. "I'm just fine."

Bryce had to take a quick phone call. He'd ordered me to change into something "athletic" but had declined to elaborate. Midge was nowhere to be found as I tore through the wardrobe looking for something to wear. I found leggings and a sports bra with the price tags still on. The leggings were *seven-hundred and ninety dollars.* I gaped at the tag. Who the hell wore workout clothes that cost that much?

I slid them on, wondering if they were somehow magic. They *were* buttery soft and made my ass look good, but for eight-hundred bucks, I was expecting some sort of miracle. I threw on the sports bra, impressed by how it lifted my breasts, and pulled my hair up into a ponytail. I was not an athlete, but at least I looked the part!

What kind of athletic activity does my husband want to engage in, anyway?

I shook off the thought. I'd do well to remember that only hours before, he'd rejected me yet *again.* He'd told me our marriage was a mistake and sent me away. Then once he had me back in his clutches, he'd pushed me over the physical edge, making me ache for him. But when I'd tried to get close, he'd fled.

And now we had to pretend to be the happiest couple on earth, or else. *The keyword is pretend, Chlo.*

I sighed as I laced up a pair of pristine white sneakers and headed out to find Bryce. Why was I nervous and excited to spend the day with him? How many times could I be a fool? I vowed that I was finished with that role once and for all.

Instead of Bryce waiting at the landing, there was Hazel. I cringed—the spindly-legged maid had never been a fan of mine, and she'd seemed even more sour since I'd returned to the island.

"Mrs. Windsor." Her lips puckered as she took in my outfit. "Mr. Windsor asked me to bring you outside to him. Is that what you're wearing?"

"He told me to dress like this." Cheeks heating, I glanced down at my sports bra. "We're doing something...athletic."

"Apparently," she responded dryly.

I nervously twisted my wedding band as I followed her down the hall. "I met Bryce's brothers this morning," I blurted out, just for something to say. "They seemed nice."

She arched a penciled-in eyebrow. "Both of them are quite special, I agree. I wish they'd come back and stay, but they're grown now and prefer their own estates.

They'd discussed building here on Somes Island, but then they made other plans."

She stopped before we reached the door. "Speaking of other plans..." Her gaze flicked over me.

I shivered. "Yes, Hazel?"

"Are you planning on staying this time? Or will you leave when it suits you again?"

I took a step back. "I didn't want to leave. Mr. Windsor asked me to."

Hazel pursed her lips as she opened the door. "As a child, Mr. Windsor used to cry for his mother. His father punished him for it. He said no boy should act like that."

I winced. Gene Windsor really was a douche.

"After that," Hazel continued, "when he would get upset, he told everyone to go away and leave him alone. It was a coping mechanism, you see."

I blinked at her. "I'm not sure of what you're getting at."

She glanced out the door. "He's waiting for you. And you know that Mr. Windsor doesn't like to wait."

"Right. Thanks, Hazel."

She disappeared without another peep.

Pondering her words, I made my way around the corner and almost ran smack-dab into Bryce and a mammoth, spotless black jeep. It had wide, giant tires, a roof rack with a row of spotlights, and some sort of tow rope attached to the front. Bryce himself was wearing a pair of shorts that showed off his muscular legs and a tight-fitting T-shirt, the kind that showcased his enormous shoulders and made my mouth water.

Not that my mouth was watering or anything.

"Wow. You were serious about the jeep—it looks like it eats other jeeps for breakfast." I walked around it, fascinated.

"Have you ridden in one before?" From behind his sunglasses, Bryce appeared to be staring at my sports bra.

"No, but one of the popular girls in my class had a red one. I was always jealous." I'd watch her drive by, hair blowing in the breeze, music blasting, seeming like she didn't have a care in the world.

"Well, now you have a jeep, too. So you don't have to be jealous."

"Does that mean you're going to let me drive?"

"Absolutely not." Bryce lifted me inside, his hand firmly and strategically on my ass, then stepped back and watched as I buckled in. "I like that outfit, too."

"There's not much to it." My boobs were on full display.

"I know." He sounded pleased. "You owe me, by the way."

For the handjob you wouldn't let me finish this morning? "For what?"

He fingered the sleeve of his T-shirt, all the better to let his colossal bicep peek out. "I'm not wearing the suit. What did we bet, again? I can't remember."

"We didn't actually bet on anything. You just said that you could off-road with the best of them." I slid my sunglasses down. "So let's see it, Boss. And maybe you can tell me more about what the heck Olivia Jensen wants from us?"

He frowned as he turned the jeep on, and it rumbled to life. "She's asking for a lot. Unfortunately, I think we have to give it to her."

We rolled out down the road, Bryce's gorgeous home fading into the distance behind us. We passed the guesthouse on our left, a fairytale "cottage" where Daphne had briefly stayed. It appeared empty now, but maybe the lawyers and Olivia Jensen were staying there.

We came to the end of the pavement, and the road turned to dirt. Bryce picked up speed, and I enjoyed the feel of the wind whipping my ponytail, the sun on my face, and the sound of the ocean crashing in the distance.

"They're going to start following us and taking pictures," Bryce said, raising his voice over the wind.

"We have to be very hands-on. Are you okay with that?"

"I guess so." I nodded. I craved it, even though I didn't want to admit it to myself.

He reached over and squeezed my thigh. "Good."

"Do you know when they'll start?"

He shrugged. "Soon."

He didn't take his hand off my leg, and slowly, a fire spread through me. *Holy hell.* No matter what I thought or what I *should* think, Bryce's touch undid me every time. I wanted him in a way that made me ache. It was a want beyond reason, beyond common sense, beyond what I considered "safe." I was not safe with this kind of need.

I'd vowed to fight it. And yet, as he gently stroked my thigh, all reason went out through the top of the open-air jeep.

"Are you ready to go off-road?" Bryce grinned at me.

"Sure!" Any distraction from the growing throb between my legs would be welcome.

Bryce veered off the dirt road into the forest, following a grassy trail. He released my thigh, wisely using both his hands to maneuver the jeep over the bumpy terrain.

"See? I told you." He was still smiling. "I know how to drive this thing."

"Of course you do." It seemed Bryce was good at everything. It was both handy and downright annoying.

We continued to cruise through the dense forest. A mixture of birch, pine, and fir trees, dead and alive, flew by in a blur. Bryce eventually slowed down as the trees thickened along the trail. The large jeep rumbled over the bumps, handling them with ease, as we came to a small clearing. Bryce slowed to a stop and turned off the motor. "You can usually see deer here."

"Cool." I'd never seen a deer in real life.

Bryce unbuckled himself, then me, his hands lingering on my skin. When he pulled away, I shivered.

He leaned back against his seat, settling in as we watched the small clearing. "Thank you for being a good sport at the meeting this morning. I know it's a lot."

"It was nice to meet your brothers," I offered.

He snorted. "I can't believe Olivia told them they have to get married soon. They're going to mutiny."

"Why don't they want to get married?"

He pulled his sunglasses down and stared at me. "My brothers? Jake's allergic to commitment. He has a new girlfriend every six months, then he breaks up with her. And so on and so on."

"What about Colby?"

"Ha! Colby only 'dates' strippers and bad girls. And

he doesn't actually date them if you know what I mean. There's no way he's ever going to settle down. He's twenty-seven, but he acts like he's still in his fraternity." He scrubbed a hand across his face. "My father is behind this, I know that for sure. It'll be interesting to see if they give in to him."

I wanted to ask, *Like you did?* But our arranged marriage seemed like a bad subject to broach at the moment.

"As for the rest of what was said..." Bryce's voice trailed off as he looked away. "I know it's going to be a lot on you. On us. But we can do it, can't we?"

He reached for my hand. In spite of my best intentions, I was eager to take it. "Yes, we can."

"Good." Bryce turned his gaze back on me. "Then... Can you please come here? We have some unfinished business."

We stared at each other for a beat, the silence of the forest heavy between us.

"Yes." *Yes, Sir.* My self-control had fled, along with all my good intentions. I moved out of my seat and slid onto his lap.

"There you are," he whispered in my ear. "Right where you belong." With that, he trailed his fingers down my exposed skin. I didn't know whether to laugh or cry.

"I have something for you, Chloe." His voice was hoarse. "Do you want it?"

I felt him pressed against my backside. Hard, throbbing, insistent. *God, give me strength.*

Was there any way I could resist him?

"Chloe?" He was waiting for my answer.

There was only one thing to say. "Yes."

TWELVE

bad

Yes. Bryce wanted to give me something, and I wanted him to give it to me. Badly. On his lap, there was no way to avoid what was between us: a growing heat and his screaming erection.

Oh boy. Once again, Bryce was giving me whiplash: rushing away from me, then pulling me close. But being close was what I wanted.

And like I said, I wanted it bad.

It was broad daylight, but we were alone deep in the forest. He kissed my neck, his scruffy beard drawing goosebumps all over my flesh. I wanted to ask him why he was kissing me, but I was too afraid that he'd stop, so I stuffed the question deep inside.

That was a bad idea; I'd pay for it later. But as he

trailed his lips down my neck onto my back, I decided it was absofuckinglutely worth it.

Bryce ran his hands down my arms and rested them on my hips. He pulled me back against his hard length, trailing hot kisses down my neck and upper back the whole time. I was already under his spell, completely lost in the moment.

He pulled me against him, grinding his cock into my ass. "Fuck, Chloe. How am I supposed to keep my hands off of you?"

"You managed it earlier."

"No, I didn't." He nipped at my ear. "I had my hands all *over* you if I remember correctly."

He reached down, his hand skimming my breasts. Then he reached straight between my legs. He started to rub me through the insanely expensive athletic tights, and it felt *awesome*. Maybe they were actually worth the seven-hundred dollars?

"Mmm, you feel so good." He rubbed my sex through the tights, pinching, palming, and exploring as his cock pressed against my ass. The onslaught of sensations overwhelmed me; I writhed against him. "I swore I wouldn't touch you again, but here I am..."

I froze on top of him. "Why did you swear that?"

Bryce didn't stop rubbing. "Because you make me

crazy, Chloe. Because you make me lose control. And I don't ever want to lose control again."

"It's just sex," I lied. I was lying to him, lying to myself. "We can do whatever we want."

"Can we?" He kissed my neck again as my clit throbbed against his palm.

"Yes. I w-want to. I want to so bad."

"So do I." He slid his hand underneath the tights and chuckled darkly when he felt my wetness. "Ah. My virgin needs me."

"I'm not a virgin anymore," I said archly. "You saw to that."

"Yes I fucking did." He rubbed my clit and pinched it between his fingers. I cried out and bucked against him, involuntarily grinding myself against his hand and cock. He laughed again, the smug fucker, as he rolled my clit between his fingers and made me see stars.

"No, *no*—" I didn't want to come already!

"There's more where this came from, Mrs. Windsor." Bryce kept up the relentless pace, rubbing my clit over and over. I ground myself against him, my hips bucking, his cock rubbing against my ass. *OMFG*. He was surrounding me, invading me. He was everywhere.

He pinched my clit hard, and that was all it took: I came undone.

"Bryce! *Bryce!*" Why did I have to scream his name every time I came? But I was powerless to stop myself as the orgasm crashed through me. He chuckled into my neck as I rocked against his lap, the spasms rolling to my core.

When I came to, he whispered in my ear. "Climb down from the car. *Now.*"

"Yes, *Sir.*" My legs were wobbly as I did what I was told. Bryce hopped down, too, pulling me in for a deep, penetrating kiss that did nothing for the weakness in my knees.

Before I knew what was happening, he whipped me around, so I was facing the jeep. "Hold on tight," Bryce panted.

I bent down and gripped the edge of the car where the door would have been. Bryce wrenched down my tights and thong, exposing my bare ass to the forest.

"Yes. *Fuck* yes." He gave it a smack, then bent and kissed each cheek. "Spread your legs for me, babe."

There was an urgency to his voice that I couldn't ignore. I wriggled my legs apart, and he didn't hesitate. Bryce slid his hands inside my thighs, his fingers dipping into the creamy wetness he'd created, swirling his fingers around my sore clit once again. I quivered for him. "That's right. You want me, Virgin. You want me and only me. *Say it.*"

When I hesitated, he slid two fingers inside me and

started pulsing. As soon as I moaned and bucked against him, he took them out. "Say it, Chloe. Say you want me and only me."

I looked back over my shoulder. He was behind me, erection raging, ready to give me the pleasure I'd been dying for. But the price I would pay was enormous: I'd have to tell him the truth.

But what was it I'd said to him only a few minutes ago? *It's just sex. We can do whatever we want.*

"I want you and only you." It didn't matter if it was the truth. He didn't ever have to know what was in my heart. The only thing that mattered was right now, what was happening between us in this forest. The truth was for later. The truth was just for me.

"I know you do." He pulled down his shorts, and finally, his gloriously erect penis was in between my legs. "That's why I'm going to give you what you want."

"What do *you* want?" My voice was hoarse, and I looked away.

"This." He noticed the head of his cock inside me, and I almost cried out in relief. "This." He thrust into me deeply, all at once, then stilled.

He leaned down and put his face against my back. "I don't *want* to do this, but I'm not going to stop."

"Why don't you want me?" Tears pricked my eyes.

"Oh, I want you." He laughed darkly, then started to

thrust. He stood up and gripped my sides as he pene-trated me over and over again. "But you left me, Chloe. You went away."

"You told me to go—"

"No. You left. You left *me*." Bryce clapped a hand over my mouth and fucked me from behind. I fought against him, but the tenor somehow changed, and my "fighting" became part of our sex. He thrust into me savagely, hand tight over my mouth, his heavy balls slapping against me as he drove deep.

Fuck! It felt so good. He owned me. I met him thrust for thrust, my sex throbbing around him, greedily sucking him in. His huge cock pumped into me, and for some reason, his big hand over my mouth turned me on. He yanked me back against him as he buried himself, and the sensation threatened to overwhelm me.

He released my mouth and grabbed for my breast, squeezing and kneading it as he picked up the pace.

Stars. All I could see were stars. Bryce was so huge that he overtook me; when he was inside me, I was possessed, owned by him. He could do whatever he wanted, and he knew it. With one hand on my hip and the other on my breast, he pulled me back against him as he rammed into me. He was so strong, so much bigger than me. The combination of sensations was too intense, pushing me to the edge, pushing away all reason. His hand trailed lower, and he found my clit again. It was all over, but I didn't want it to stop. I didn't ever want it to end—I wanted him inside me like this always, owning me, driving hard, ready to spill his seed into me and make me his, our bodies fused as one.

"Bryce, Bryce—oh my God!" Everything went white. The orgasm hit hard, pulling me under. I shattered beneath him, body convulsing. He thrust harder, fucking me through my orgasm, but his thrusts got slower, deeper, more insistent.

He gripped my hips hard, his rhythm insistent, inevitable. "Oh fuck, Chloe. What're you doing to me?" His balls slapped against me, and he moaned, a strangled sound, as his orgasm chased mine. Bryce unloaded inside me, cursing as he spent himself. *Unf.* I loved this part. I clenched around him, taking it, sucking him dry.

Bryce pressed his face against me as he climaxed, holding me tight, possessively wrapping his arms around me. In that moment, it felt like nothing could ever separate us again; we were one.

I love you, I thought. But I refused to say it.

Even as I clung to him, after the most glorious sex known to humanity, I would never tell him the truth. He would never know what was in my heart ever again.

Bryce kissed and nipped at my back, still inside me,

still holding me close. We were quiet, still entwined, as we caught our breath. What was he thinking?

"We should get going," he said after a minute.

I blew out a deep breath. Those weren't the words I'd been dying to hear. "Okay." I didn't look at him as I pulled up my pants.

"Chloe."

I raised my gaze to meet his. "What?"

"Come here." Bryce pulled me against his chest, cradling me, then kissed the top of my head. "I'm glad you're back."

I lowered my gaze.

"Me too," I lied.

boss

WE CLIMBED BACK into the jeep. I was sore from our lovemaking; at the same time, I wanted more.

At the same time, I wanted nothing to do with Bryce ever again.

Why had I done it? He'd said he didn't want to have sex with me but that he couldn't stop himself. So why had *I* done it? But of course, I already knew the truth. I wanted him, but that wasn't the reason.

It was because I was still in love with him.

What we'd done in the clearing wasn't love. That was sex. It had been *great* sex, but it was still just sex. And sex wasn't love: I'd do well to remember that.

Head on straight, Chloe. And keep your legs together!

We drove the jeep along the grassy trail to the other edge of the forest. It opened onto a rocky beach. Bryce maneuvered over the stones as the salty ocean air whipped my ponytail. He parked away from the crashing surf, then turned to me. "Do you know how to skim rocks?"

"What? No." I couldn't begin to keep up with him and his moods. *Push Chloe away. Have sex with Chloe. Push Chloe away again. Skim rocks with Chloe.* WTF?

"I bet you're a natural." Bryce helped me down from the jeep. My legs were still wobbly from our encounter in the clearing. For a moment, I hung onto him.

He surprised me by wrapping his arm around me and rubbing my back. "I enjoyed the hell out of that," he said.

"Yeah. Me too," I mumbled. When I tried to pull away, he caught me.

"What's the matter?"

I blinked up at him. *Game face, Chloe.* But I was too raw to pretend. "You seriously need to ask me that?"

His brow furrowed. "I'm asking, yes. What's the matter? I don't understand."

I hesitated for a second, but my emotions were climbing, getting the better of me. "Why did you say that to me?"

"What?" He looked confused. "That I enjoyed it?"

"Yes." I yanked free. *I should just let it go.* "No." *But it's too late.*

"Well, which one is it?"

I straightened my shoulders. "Back in the clearing—why did you say you didn't want to have sex with me?"

Bryce scowled and ran a hand through his hair. "I don't know."

"Yes you do," I challenged. "And I want to know why."

"I already told you." He turned and faced the water.

"Tell me again." My voice was hoarse.

He stared out at the incoming tide. "It's because I lose control. Every time I'm with you, I lose control."

"That's not how it seemed to me. You seemed like you knew exactly what you were doing."

Bryce sighed and held out a hand for me. "Can you come here?"

I crossed my arms against my chest and didn't budge.

"Fine." Bryce watched the water. "It's safer this way."

"What does that even *mean*?"

"It doesn't matter." He shook his head. "I need you here. I need you with me. We've already agreed, and it's already done. So are you going to fight me every step of the way?"

I threw up my hands. "You're the one who keeps pushing me away."

He didn't look at me when he said, "You only came back because I made you an offer you couldn't refuse. I need to remember that."

"You only asked me back because you need me to save your company. I need to remember *that*." I was surprised by the bitterness in my voice. Maybe I hadn't even let myself feel how deeply Bryce had cut me.

"I do need you to save my company. But..."

"But what?"

"Nothing. We're not getting anywhere with this conversation." Bryce bent down and picked up a rock. "Let me show you how to skim this. This beach has the best stones. I don't get out here enough."

I bent down and grabbed a rock. I didn't care about stupid skimming, but it was better than just standing there being pissed.

I threw it at the water, and it landed with a splash.

"What are you, pitching?"

"I told you I didn't know how to do it." I grabbed another rock, larger this time, and hurled it at the waves. It landed with a satisfying *thunk* and a big splash.

"You're mad," Bryce observed.

I might throw him in the ocean next.

"I'm not mad." I watched as he picked up a flat, thin stone and angled it between his fingers, holding it like a frisbee. He flicked it at the water, and it hit, bouncing nine times until it sank below the surface.

He was good at everything, it was true. It was also very fucking annoying.

When I picked up a huge rock, Bryce stopped me. "Put the boulder down and come here. *Please.*"

I considered dropping it on his foot, but I decided to act like an adult. I put it down and went to him, and he handed me a thin stone. "Put it in your hand like this." He inserted it between my pointer finger and my thumb, then angled my hand so the front of it was facing the water. "Then you move it like this." He slowly moved my hand in a flicking motion, aiming toward the ocean. "Then you just release it. You ever play frisbee?"

"No."

He arched an eyebrow. "Seriously?"

"I'm a city kid, remember? We swam in the public pool and played chicken on the T tracks for fun. There wasn't a lot of frisbees or rock skimming. Or off-roading, or tennis, or riding around in a yacht."

Bryce nodded. "Lucky for you, you're young. There's plenty of time for all that. And I happen to know a guy with a yacht."

I didn't want to hear the promise behind his words. There was no future for me here, with him; there was only now. "Just show me how to throw the stupid rock."

Bryce wisely shut his mouth and showed me the flicking motion again. Then I stomped away, down toward the water, and took aim. I flicked my wrist and released the rock. It bounced four times.

"Nice." He sounded impressed.

"It's not nine bounces, but it's a start." I started searching for another good rock.

"Four's pretty good."

"Stop being nice to me. Just be yourself."

Bryce laughed, and I found a good stone.

It was going to take some time, but I was determined. For once, I was going to beat my husband at his own game.

Bryce was quiet during the ride back. He appeared to be lost in his thoughts. He frowned as he parked the jeep in front of the house. "I can't believe you beat me."

I arched an eyebrow. "I didn't beat you—I *tied* you for most skips."

"A tie is a loss, in my book." He was taking it hard.

"Just wait until next time, when you *really* lose." I shrugged. "Then a tie won't seem so bad."

He pushed his sunglasses up on his head and looked at me. "Remind me not to get on your bad side."

"Too late." I hopped down from the jeep, feeling strangely calm. It was good to let myself be grumpy. Not walking a tightrope around Bryce, trying to guess his mood, was freeing. *And* I was pretty good at skipping rocks. I was absofuckinglutely going to beat him next time.

"Oh my God," Bryce said suddenly. "That thing's a beast!"

"Huh?" I whipped my head to see what Bryce was looking at. Dale was being dragged across the lawn by an enormous black ball of fur. It tugged on its leash as it bounded for us, big black paws flailing.

"Is that the *puppy*?"

Bryce scrubbed a hand across his face. "It's supposed to be. But it's at least fifty pounds. Maybe they gave us the wrong dog?"

Dale reached us quickly. He was breathing hard. He bent over and caught his breath while the huge dog flopped onto the grass and rolled onto its back, scratching itself while its tongue lolled out.

"He's so cute. Can I pet him?"

Dale groaned. "You can pet him, you can walk him, you can *have* him. He dragged me down Main Street in

Bar Harbor. He tried to jump off the boat to catch a duck. You try wrestling that thing!"

"I thought we bought a puppy." Bryce eyed the dog as it rolled onto its stomach and panted. "Isn't this one fully grown?

"Oh, it's a puppy." Dale straightened himself. "Three months old, already forty pounds. They said he's the biggest one they've ever seen. They made me sign an affidavit about how many acres we have here—he needs space to run."

"It looks like it needs a stable to live in. Not a house." Bryce glanced back at his pristine mansion. "He's like a fur hurricane. Maybe we can commission a dog house."

"Dale!" Noah shot out from the front door. "Is that the surprise? A *dog*? I've always wanted a dog!"

My brother threw himself down in front of the black beast. It promptly rolled onto its back for a belly rub. "That's a good boy." Noah was very gentle as he scratched him. The dog was loving it, paws up in the air, tongue out, looking as though it was in heaven.

The corner of Bryce's lip turned up. "He likes you."

"You think so?" Noah asked.

"Oh, I know so." Bryce squatted down next to my brother and scratched the dog's ears. "Dogs are very sensitive. And smart. They know good people."

Noah glanced up at him. "Really?"

"Really. They're excellent judges of character."

Noah kept petting; I could tell that within the one minute he'd met the ball of fur, he'd already fallen in love. "Is the dog going to stay?" He sounded like it was too good to be true.

"If you want him to." Bryce shrugged. "But he needs a name."

Noah stopped petting him for a second, and the dog gently swatted him with its paw, urging him to continue. "Ha, he's bossy," Noah laughed. "Hey, what if we named him Boss?"

Bryce reached over and ruffled Noah's hair, and although I would never admit it to myself, I died inside a little. "That's a good name, kid. Welcome to the family, Boss."

After a few minutes of explaining puppy antics to Noah, hanging out with Boss, and letting Dale recover his breath, Bryce and I left the three of them in the yard. I glanced back at my brother, who was still worshipfully petting the dog. Emotion overtook me. "That was really nice of you."

"It's nothing. I think every boy should have a dog. Plus, it's a contractual term you negotiated. Remember?"

"I remember." I nodded. "It's *still* really nice of you."

"I actually missed him—Noah." Bryce sounded surprised. "He has a way of making everything seem more normal around here. A kid, his video games and fishing aspirations, you know? Reminds me of a simpler time."

I nodded. "He's a good boy."

He opened the door for me, and we went inside the cool, dark house. "He's lucky he's got a great big sister looking out for him."

I melted a little. "Thank you." I *still* sort of hoped that Boss would shed on Bryce's suits. But it was hard to be vindictive when he was being so kind to my brother.

"You two!" A blur of red hair and porcelain skin jumped out at us from the kitchen. Olivia Jensen held a giant iced coffee in one hand, her cell phone in the other. "I already *love* what I'm seeing! I need more!"

Bryce looked confused. "What exactly are you seeing, Ms. Jensen?"

"The candid shots from this morning." She held up her phone. "Sexy. *Very* sexy."

His expression turned from confused to wary. "You've already taken pictures of us?"

Olivia smiled, not looking the slightest bit sorry. "Yes. You *have* to see these." She hustled toward the study, and we followed her.

Bryce looked tense. It occurred to me that I'd never

seen him following orders before; he was always the one giving them.

"Here." Olivia put her drink down on the desk and started tapping on her phone. "Look at these—like I said, hot."

There were a string of photos from earlier that day. Bryce and I in the jeep, turning off onto the trail. Bryce and I in the clearing, me on his lap. Us in a heated embrace. His arms wrapped around me, biceps bulging. I almost fanned myself—indeed, we looked like a hot couple. It was clear from the photos that, at least physically, we were into each other.

How had they followed us? The island was tiny, quiet. And if they'd taken pictures of us in the clearing, did that mean the hidden cameraman was watching us...the whole time? *Yikes.*

Bryce's fingers curled around the phone, looking as though he might crush it. "You followed us? Without my permission?" A vein bulged on the side of his forehead. *Uh oh.*

"I don't need your permission," Olivia said. There was no malice in her voice; she was matter of fact. "The board's paying me a not-so-small fortune to do this job. They've given me free rein to produce the story as I see fit. And Bryce, we already talked about this. You've agreed it's for the best. I'm selling the story of America's hottest young couple to the public."

Bryce held up the phone. There was a picture of us on the beach, deep in discussion. "Chloe and I didn't know we were being followed. We thought we were alone. It's not okay for you to have the hired help spying on us during a private, intimate moment."

Olivia crossed her arms against her chest. "I told the team they were not allowed to film *or* observe if things between you two got...involved. They've signed contracts. They want their jobs—trust me, they aren't going to breach their agreements."

"*They?*" His vein bulged out dangerously.

"Bryce, it's okay." I grabbed his hand. "These pictures look great. As long as we know they're following us now, we'll be more careful." I squeezed his hand. "Right?"

He grunted, still staring at Olivia.

"Now that *that's* settled," she said sweetly as she held her hand out for her phone, "we need more content. A *lot* more content. I have a romantic dinner staged for you at the restaurant tonight. You'll take the boat over, sit out on the dock, and have a lovely sunset meal. The public will go *bananas* over it!"

She checked her watch. "You have a few hours to rest, or whatever it is you want to do. You might want to get your *involvements* for the day attended to, you know what I mean?" With a chuckle, she grabbed her iced coffee and sashayed out.

Bryce gripped my hand. His face was twisted in anger.

"Bryce? Don't lose it. You look like you're going to lose it."

His nostrils flared. "I. Don't. Want. To be a fucking puppet," he spat out. "This is my father's problem. I don't want us to get dragged into it."

"But it's *your* company—your future." I sighed. He was on my Bad List, but for three million dollars, I should still try to help him calm down. "Anyway, it's not so bad." I smoothed his shirt. "All we have to do is go to dinner."

"There were multiple cameramen, and they saw your ass—not to mention every other thing I was holding onto in that clearing," he growled.

"They didn't watch us." I smoothed his shirt again, but what I was really doing was feeling his big pectoral muscles. "They signed a contract, Bryce. Everything's okay." I didn't know if that was true, but I also didn't want him losing his mind and beating up the photographers.

I needed to distract him. "Why don't we go upstairs

and relax, huh?" An unmistakable, inconvenient pang issued between my legs.

I shrugged. "Unless you have to work, I mean."

Bryce seemed to perk up a little. "I can work from bed." The way he said *work* made it seem like he didn't mean...work.

He grabbed my hand and hastily led us from the room. "Let's go, Mrs. Windsor."

FOURTEEN

involvements

From our bedroom window, I could see that Noah was still outside with the dog. Two of the female staff were out there with him; the puppy was taking turns running after a tennis ball and rolling on his back. I wondered if Lilly, one of the maids, would bring *her* puppy over to play with Boss or if the new dog was too big...

"Hey." Bryce emerged from the bathroom, towel-drying his hair. "I took another shower. I do that when I'm mad."

"No wonder you're so clean," I teased.

"Ha." He eyed me, then climbed onto the bed. He wore only sweats, his glorious chest on full display. "Join me?"

"Okay." I'd changed, too, into shorts and a tank top. I wasn't sure what I was supposed to dress for.

Watching Bryce as he glared at his laptop while he worked? Or having him rip my clothes off while he told me it was all a bad idea?

I climbed cautiously onto the bed, and Bryce rolled toward me. "I have an idea while I was in the shower."

Oh boy. "What's that?"

"No more talking. I mean, no more talking for *me*. You can talk as much as you like."

"Why don't you want to talk?"

He shrugged against the pillow. "It occurred to me that I always seem to say the wrong thing."

I sighed. "No... If you're telling the truth, you're not saying the wrong thing."

He brushed the hair back from my face, and for a moment, with his gentle touch, my hurt fell away. "I'm just going to take a vow of silence. But before I do, I have to ask..." He came closer, his face above mine. "We can't have sex on our date tonight. The photography team will be following us."

My stomach did a flip. "Were you *planning* on having sex?" I hadn't even known we were planning on having dinner!

"I've got lots of plans."

When I shivered, he ran his fingers up and down my arm. "If we were alone, we could do it on the boat. Or in the woods, if we snuck off from the restaurant..." His gray-blue eyes sparkled; it seemed as though he'd given this some thought.

"But I won't put you in that position. That being said, what we did earlier?" His gaze burned into mine. "It wasn't enough. I haven't had you in weeks. I need more. How do you feel about that?"

My stomach twisted with desire. This was exactly what I wanted to hear from him, at least in part. But I should be mindful of everything else that had happened. Before I threw all my cards on the table, I needed to play it cool. "Remember our contract? I agreed to have sex with you whenever you wanted."

"What about what you want, Chloe?"

I tried to keep my poise. "I'm here, aren't I? That should tell you everything you need to know. I'm here because I want to be here."

"You're here because of your contract." He watched me carefully. "Because you want to fulfill the terms."

"Bryce." I held very still. "Why are you doing this? You're the one who hired me to be your wife. You fired me, then you hired me back. I'm not the one who hired a bride so that I could inherit my trust. I'm just the virgin Elena found for you."

"You make it sound so formal," he sighed.

"I'm just telling the truth." Part of it. I'd left out the

part where I'd fallen in love with him, and then he'd wrecked me.

"Speaking of being a virgin..." He rolled over onto his back and stared up at the ceiling. "I know I should stop talking, but fuck it. I have to ask you something."

He was quiet for so long, I didn't think he'd continue. "Were you with anyone else back in Boston?" His voice was carefully controlled.

"*What*? No." I shook my head.

"Security kept a close watch on your room, and I had cameras installed, of course. But I wanted to ask." He didn't look at me.

"You really think I'm like that? That I'd just hop into bed with someone else?" I felt as though he'd slapped me.

"No, but I worried that someone would try. You're a beautiful girl, Chloe. A desirable one. And I wanted to know if anyone had tried anything, so that I could kill them."

"*Bryce.*"

He had the decency to shrug and look a little sheepish. "I'm just kidding. Kind of."

"I don't understand you. Like I said, you're the one who sent me away. I don't know why you'd even care if I was with someone else."

"I care because you're my wife. You're still my wife."

I took a deep breath. I needed to ask *him* something, but the last time we'd discussed the topic, it had ended badly. "What about you? Were you...with anyone...while I was gone?"

"Of course not." He said it as though it were ridiculous.

"It's a fair question." I knew that Felicia Jones had been to the house—what if she'd taken advantage of my absence? "I know that what's-her-face is still hanging around."

What's-her-face. Like I didn't know her name. Like I hadn't fantasized about scratching her eyeballs out!

Bryce grunted. "I don't care." His tone indicated the subject was closed for discussion. He turned back to me. "So you haven't been with anyone, and I haven't been with anyone."

I prayed he was telling the truth; he seemed to be. I sure was. "Right."

"And you're contractually obligated to sleep with me whenever I want."

I nodded.

"And like you said earlier, it's *just* sex." He turned toward me, his gaze hungry. "We can do whatever we want, here in our bed. Alone, without the photographers. Can't we, Chloe?"

I nodded again. I felt like he was hypnotizing me.

He trailed his fingers down my bare arm again, causing sparks to fly. "So I'm going to ask you again. What do you want?"

"I want to know..." The room was suddenly very, very hot. "I want to know what *you* want."

He flashed me the lopsided grin that I loved. "I *wanted* to have sex with you in the clearing today. And on the beach. And on the boat tonight. And in the woods. And I want to take you right now."

He lowered his face to mine and kissed me.

When our tongues connected, I felt an electric shock down to my core. Bryce was confusing the hell out of me, leaving me dizzy and breathless, but when he touched me, when he told me he wanted me, nothing else mattered. Not even the emotional whiplash he kept leaving me with.

His erection poked at me. In spite of my best intentions, I almost died of happiness.

"Since we can't have sex in the woods or on the boat tonight, we'll have to take action. I can't go that long without having you—I'd end up bending you over the table at the restaurant. And we can't have that, can we?"

"No...?" But was it really the worst idea?

Bryce rolled on top of me, his hard length pressed in between my legs. "We have this afternoon. So I want to know...do you want me to touch you?"

He thrust against me, his erection rubbing me through his sweats, and I whimpered. "I know that I can, Chloe. Per our contract, I own you."

He kissed me again, our tongues lashing. He thrust some more, and I moved against him, arching my back, desperate for more contact. *He owned me.* Fuck yes, then take me!

I knew it was bad that I felt that way. I knew it was wrong and that I'd pay for it dearly. But I was already burning for him. There was no way to stop it.

"I want to know if that's what you *want.* I want to know if you feel what I'm feeling." He thrust against me again, harder, making sure that I felt every inch of his raw power.

"Yes." I was having a hard time catching my breath. Pure, unadulterated need emanated through me, a deep ache. "Yes, I do."

"Good." He kissed me deeply, thrusting his cock in between my legs. I moaned, writhing beneath him. "Good." He trailed hot kisses down my neck, making me cry out.

"I want you to know that I *own* you. Literally. You left me, but that's not ever going to happen again. You're back and you're mine. You will do what I say—in bed and everywhere else. Say it." His kisses trailed lower.

"Yes. Yes...Sir." He'd loved it when I'd called him *Sir* before, back when we'd been happy.

"Good girl." Bryce was everywhere—taking off my tank, removing my bra in one swift motion, pulling down my shorts and thong. Before I even knew what had happened, he buried his face between my legs.

"Bryce!"

"Shhh." He pulled back and blew against my clit. "Let Daddy take care of you." He put his mouth back on me, and *holy hell.* He hummed, making my whole body vibrate as he devoured me. I writhed, wholly lost in the sensation, as he nibbled and sucked. His tongue, bold and sure, stroked the length of my slit over and over again until I reached the edge. His touch was a riptide, threatening to take me under, to take me away.

I was helpless against the onslaught; I was drowning. I didn't want to let him have this power over me. I didn't want him to own me. But he did. He fucking did.

And it felt so good to just let go.

Bryce relentlessly stroked me with his tongue, and I met him thrust for thrust, throwing any remaining restraint to the wind. A sensation was building deep inside my core, big and powerful. It was an undercurrent, dangerous, inevitable. I was right there: I'd already been swept away.

"Bryce! *Bryce!*" Tears pricked my eyes, and I sank my

hands into his thick hair, the orgasm crashing through me. The sensation dragged me under and then lifted me high: I felt like I was flying. He reached up and grabbed my hands as I soared, holding onto me, letting me know he was there through the whole thing.

I was out of my mind, still floating, when he pulled his pants down, then maneuvered both my legs to one side. He notched the head of his cock inside me, and I moaned. *Yes.* There was nothing I craved more than his raw power. I was still riding the waves of my orgasm, but it was Bryce's turn. He inched inside me, slowly, my pussy gripping him with wet heat.

"Oh *fuck*, you're tight." His enormous cock *was* a snug fit; strong, long and oh-so-thick. My body stretched to accommodate him. He grunted once he was all the way in. Our bodies fit perfectly together, as though we'd been made for each other. He owned me now—the power radiating from him spread through me. He began to thrust in time with my still-spasming body, fucking me through the aftershocks of my orgasm.

Holy hell. "You're in so deep like this."

"Mmm, I love it." He was above me, kissing me and inside me, thrusting deep. He covered me with his big body. A warmth spread inside me, a light. I was with him again. He was inside me. We were together, our bodies completely entwined.

It was heaven.

Bryce's thrusts started to get more urgent. He broke the kiss and leaned up on his forearms. His biceps and chest muscles strained as he thrust savagely, stroking the spot deep inside that only he could ever reach. His heavy balls slapped against me. Pleasure exploded inside me, but there was an even more powerful feeling chasing it, something emanating from deep inside my core.

"*Fuck.* What are you fucking doing to me." The cords in Bryce's neck stood out as he pounded deep. "Fuck!" He was out of his mind. He picked up speed, hips thrusting, and then it was like he was vibrating inside me. Fucking me so deep and so hard. We were fused at our root. We were one.

I went under. Pleasure exploded from my core, and I heard myself scream his name. My mind went blank. I saw stars; I saw white. Bryce was laughing or cursing, or both, I wasn't sure. He cried out as he exploded inside of me. I felt every ounce of him as he came, emptying himself, finding his release inside me.

Moments or minutes passed, I wasn't sure. Bryce slowly pulled out and gently lowered himself down next to me. Then, careful not to crush me, he pulled me against his chest. He seemed winded.

"That was fucking incredible," he said. Then he promptly fell asleep, his arms wrapped tightly around me.

"It was." But he didn't hear me.

I still fucking love you, I thought.

Even though my husband was asleep, it was too dangerous to say the words out loud.

worth it

WE HAD sex again when we woke up. We had sex again in the shower. By the time we had to get ready for dinner, I could barely walk.

Bryce looked concerned when he saw how slow I was moving. "Babe. Are you okay?"

"I'm good." I was shaking. My legs were jelly. In between my legs was sore, throbbing. It was absofuck-inglutely worth it.

"You *look* good." Bryce eyed me up and down.

"My hair's soaking wet and I'm wrapped in a towel!"

"Mmm, I know." He took a step closer, and I took a step back.

"We have to get ready! We have dinner reservations in an hour. I don't even have enough time to do my hair." Still, when he reached for me and pulled me against him—and kissed me—I didn't resist. It felt so good to be back in his arms.

"Mmm." He deepened the kiss, and I felt him stiffen against me.

"You're unbelievable." I laughed and ducked out of his embrace, even though he'd begun to stir something within me *again*. "But we have to go! Olivia Jensen has on a group chat. She's already texted four times to make sure we're going to be ready."

"Fine." Bryce pouted. "But if you don't let me take you right now, there's no guarantee that I won't try to on the boat. And, you know. We're not supposed to do that."

"Bryce!"

His erection grew bigger, stretching out his boxer briefs. His gaze was dark, smoldering. "Daddy will make it quick. And *deep*. Just the way you like it."

"You're crazy—"

But before I could finish the sentence, he had me in his grasp. His lips were on mine, devouring me. Our tongues connected, and I moaned as zips of electricity shot to my core. I was already wet again, so wet and aching.

He snatched the towel and tossed it, leaving my skin bare. "That's what I'm talking about," he growled. He whipped me around so I faced the bed, then gently bent me over so my chest was pressed against the mattress, my ass up in the air. "Fuck, Chloe—you're gorgeous. How am I supposed to keep my dick out of you, huh?"

He spread my legs a little and immediately slid his rock-hard length inside me, filling me. I was sore, but the pain only added to the onslaught of incredible sensations. Bryce immediately started pounding into me—his strokes were urgent, as though he couldn't get enough, and I fucking loved it. I felt the same way. I wanted him hard, fast, deep. He was out of his mind, and it meant something to me. *I* did this to him. He wanted *me*. He couldn't stay away from me. We'd made love so many times it hurt, and yet, we both wanted more.

Take me. Own me. Possess me. I'm yours.

I was sore, but the pleasure overrode it. He was responsible for the pleasure and the pain. As a result, I loved them both.

He drove hard; in this position, he stroked me so deep it was insane. Bryce was huge, filling every inch of me. I couldn't think. All I could do was hold on for dear life as he pounded me, and another orgasm built deep inside. My eyes rolled back in my head. He reached around and pinched my swollen, sore clit. "I'm not going to last long like this, babe. Come for me. *Now.*"

My only answer was to cry out again as everything inside me shattered.

"Yes. Fuck yes." He put his hands on my hips and rode me hard, slamming into me as I unraveled, my pussy gripping him, greedy for more. His orgasm chased mine —he exploded inside me, making me see stars.

"What're you doing to me, babe?" He rested his forehead against my back.

I couldn't respond, I couldn't speak; he'd literally fucked me senseless. We collapsed on the bed together, and he wrapped me in his arms. Just as we started drifting off, our phones started beeping.

Bryce squinted at his phone. "Fuck you, Olivia Jensen. My wife and I need time alone."

I couldn't help it—I laughed. "We have to get going. If there are pictures of us going all over the internet, we can't look like this." I motioned to our sweaty heap of entangled limbs. My hair was wet and matted; Midge was going to have a fit. "Must. Get. Dressed."

He captured my hand with his. "Thank you for a nice afternoon."

A wave of emotion passed through me; I pushed it down. "Thank *you*. And you did well—you barely talked." I winked at him.

"I think I mostly said the word' fuck.'" He laughed. "Sorry about that."

"Don't be." I squeezed his hand and then got up from the bed. I had twenty minutes to look like a decent human being. Wasn't the restaurant where all of Bryce's circle dined? If there was any chance in hell we might see Felicia Jones while we were out, I needed to look semi-decent. With that in mind, I threw on a bathrobe and hustled to my old bedroom to get dressed.

Did I imagine it, or did Bryce look a little forlorn when I left?

A glimmer of hope bloomed in my chest. *Stop it, Chlo.* What was the extensive discussion I'd had with myself earlier? Sex isn't love. We'd had sex all afternoon —hell, we'd been going at it all day—but that didn't mean Bryce was in love with me. It meant he owned my ass. Hell, he'd paid millions of dollars for it!

"What on earth happened to you?" Midge eyed me up and down. "You're a mess! Oh!" She clapped a hand over her mouth. "You look like you've had *all the make-up sex known to humankind.* Was it amazing? Are you two all better? Do we seriously only have fifteen frickin' minutes to do your hair?" She dragged me into the bath-room and shoved me into the makeup chair.

"Gah, you have got to be kidding me with this rat's nest!" She started detangling the snarls with a big brush. "Talk while I work. Seriously Chloe, spill it!"

"Well, I took your advice…" I winced as she yanked

on my hair. "We made up. With our bodies. We did lots of making up." I felt myself turning red.

"Girl, by the number of knots in your hair, I'm guessing you had more orgasms today than I've had in the past three months!"

"I don't know," I mumbled, "I lost count."

She threw back her head and laughed. "Chloe Windsor, you are something. Good for you! I *knew* it! Mr. Windsor was so grumpy these past few weeks because you were gone, and he is *addicted* to you. I bet when I see him next, he's going to be in a much better mood. Thank *God* you came back. Everything was going to hell, but I have a good feeling about all this. I think you're a lucky charm for this family, I really do."

"That's nice, Midge. But I don't think I've ever been exactly lucky."

"That's the good thing about luck—it can change." She waggled her eyebrows. "Hold still. I'm going to whip your hair into shape, do your makeup in three minutes flat, and put you in a dress that shows off that 'freshly fucked' vibe."

"Midge!"

"Sorry." But she grinned wickedly as she turned the blowdryer on. Midge was quick, running her fingers through my damp hair. She finished in record time and then went at me with a pouffy brush. A little concealer, blush, eyeliner, and several swipes of mascara later, I was finished. "It's good to be young and gorgeous. Voila!" She turned me around to face the mirror.

My hair was revived with big, beachy waves, and my makeup looked *amazing*. "I didn't even think you put that much on my face, but wow! It looks great. Thank you so much!"

"Ha! Honey, that wasn't me—that was Mr. Windsor. You look like you just had a thousand-dollar facial because he showered you with orgasms all afternoon." She shivered. "Ah, to be young and be in love!"

She dragged me back into the bedroom and started tearing through the wardrobe. My phone was blowing up with text messages from Olivia Jensen. *T-5!* She wrote. *Get a move on!*

"Ugh, I have to go. What should I wear?"

"Let me find it, I had the perfect thing—aha!" Midge pulled out a flowing back maxi dress with spaghetti straps. "This will look great on you, and it's totally in this season. Here, wear it with these sandals. You'll be so happy that they're flat." She pulled out a pair of simple black flip-flops, and I sighed in relief.

"Thanks, Midge. You're the best."

"Oh wait—you need these." She tossed a strapless black bra at me and a thong so delicate, I could floss my teeth with it.

Bryce would *love* it. I ran into the bathroom and changed.

When I came back, Midge clapped her hands together. "Perfect!" She pulled me in front of the full-length mirror, then arranged my hair over one shoulder. "You look beautiful, Chloe. It's so nice to have you back." She dabbed at her eyes.

"Midge, are you *crying*?"

"No." She shooed me out the door. "Go on, you're going to be late. I'm just happy, that's all. I really like working for this family. I feel bad that they're having so much trouble. The older Mr. Windsor's a pain in the ass, but your husband is a good guy. It's nice to see you back together."

My heart twisted. "Thanks, Midge." I didn't have the heart to tell her that what was happening was for show. I didn't want to admit it to myself, either, but it was safer to keep it in mind. "I'll see you later, okay?"

I hustled down the hall, eager to be reunited with Bryce. He was waiting in his customary spot in the landing, glaring at his cellphone. He'd changed into a white linen button-down shirt, a pair of khakis, and flip-flops. The outfit was casual, but he still looked impossibly rich and handsome.

The glare slid from his face when he saw me. "Don't you look pretty."

He sounded happy, normal...human. My heart leaped.

"Thank you. You look nice, too."

"Save it for the cameras, you two." A blur of red hair, Olivia Jensen crashed our party. She grinned at us. "Just kidding! But could you actually fawn all over each other outside and on the boat? The camera operators can't take pictures of you in the house. And we need content, so let's go!"

She shooed us down the hall. By the time we got outside, Bryce practically had smoke coming out of his ears. "Olivia." He stopped and turned to her. "I appreciate that you are taking my family's situation seriously —but you're overstepping."

Olivia nodded. "*I* appreciate that you feel that way. But the SEC had another meeting with your father's defense team this afternoon. Things are progressing quickly. This could become a formal investigation with subpoenas soon—we need to get ahead of it. We can't influence the outcome with the government, but winning over the public *will* help your company. You know that."

Bryce nodded. He seemed incapable of verbalizing that she was right.

"Okay, then." She smiled at him. "Now you two get

back to making goo-goo eyes at each other. The public's going to eat this up, I'm telling you!"

She motioned toward the bushes. "The photographers are hiding in there. Guys, wave!"

Three hands stuck out of the shrubs and waved.

"I told them to stay hidden and to stay away from you. These shots have to appear authentic—if there's any appearance of staging, it'll come back to bite us. So you don't talk to the guys, and the guys don't talk to you."

"And the guys don't look at my wife," Bryce growled. He turned toward the shrubs. "And if my wife and I are getting *personal*, the guys will leave immediately. Is that understood?"

There were three thumbs up from the bushes.

"Excellent." Bryce took my hand. "Then it appears we're going to dinner, and the paparazzi are following us."

The fact that my husband seemed all right with the photographers, the staging, Olivia Jensen, all of it was evidence of something... Perhaps hell was freezing over?

I followed him to the boat, intent on finding out.

SIXTEEN

date night

WE SAT OUTSIDE on the yacht's built-in couch. The camera crew had taken a skiff and were following us, as were two other boats filled with paparazzi. *Hmm.* There would be pictures of us, all right. We needed to keep our game faces on.

Bryce pulled me onto his lap and kept his arms around me the entire ride. It reminded me of when I'd first come up to MDI, and he'd made a big show of being all over me in public. Back then, I'd been petrified of him. I remembered how strange it had felt, how foreign, to be in his embrace. So much had changed. He'd taken me since then, made me *his*. And after being together all afternoon, our embrace seemed natural, familiar...necessary.

Dangerously necessary.

Still, I was being paid to do a job, and I was going to do it, dammit. I was kidding myself, of course. Kidding myself that the money was the reason, I ran my hands over his shoulders, smiling down at him from my perch atop his lap. Kidding myself that the butterflies in my stomach were somehow related to cold hard cash, not in response to the fact that his hands were possessively holding my hips.

"Are you hungry?" I asked.

"Yes." He kissed me, lips firm against mine. "But not for lobster."

"Ha ha." I squirmed as he tightened his grip on my waist. "I think you've had enough for one day!"

"You're kidding, right?" He pulled me closer, and I felt yet *another* colossal erection.

"You've *got* to be kidding." I raised my eyebrows. "You're a machine."

He looked smug. "Apparently."

"Ha!" I threw my arms around his neck. "None of that right now. These pictures need to be internet-friendly."

"Fine. But I reserve the right to take you below-deck on the way home."

"Fine," I said, blushing with pleasure. Bryce wanted me *again*. It had to be a world record!

We reached Spruce Island, and Johnny, our captain,

navigated expertly into the one free parking spot on the dock. He quickly tied the boat up. Captain Johnny was older, tall and trim, with thick white hair beneath his cap. Bryce had lured him out of retirement after Joren, the previous captain, had dared to talk to me one-on-one while Bryce wasn't onboard. He'd been fired immediately. I still felt guilty about that. I also felt guilty about the waiter I'd gotten fired, the one from the benefit dinner Daphne and I had organized... *Ugh.* Per the terms of the new contract, I wasn't allowed to speak to any males unless Bryce was there. Maybe it was for the best, I mused. The young men of MDI would be safer that way!

Bryce helped me from the boat while Captain Johnny watched the harbor. "I can't believe you've got boats following you. I've never seen that in all my years."

Bryce scowled out at the water. "Our" photographers were in a small skiff, their zoom lenses trained on us. The three other boats were filled to the brim with paparazzi eagerly taking pictures of us, the restaurant, and the dock.

A maritime police boat appeared from the channel and cruised over. Bryce and Johnny watched with interest. "Those boys are going to get in trouble up here," the captain noted. "We don't take kindly to outsiders messing with our locals."

Bryce sighed. "I'm sorry to be causing such a circus."

Johnny straightened his shoulders. "Absolutely not, Mr. Windsor. You've done nothing wrong. Our society's the thing that's gone all haywire—everybody lookin' at their cell phones instead of each other's faces. People want to read about your story instead of living their own lives. It's a shame you're being bothered if you ask me."

"Thank you, Johnny." Bryce seemed touched. "I sure am glad your wife let you out of retirement."

"Just don't tell her I'm sticking around!" The captain grinned. "Like I said, that woman had me canning tomatoes. This is much more dignified." With a nod— and a glare in the direction of the photographers—he hopped back on the boat.

Bryce put his arm around my waist and led me toward the ramp from the dock. "Captain Johnny seems like good people," I said.

"He is." Bryce glanced out at the water. The police craft was next to the largest of the paparazzi boats; a uniformed officer was talking to their captain. "I wonder if they're going to get a ticket for loitering or disturbing the peace." He whipped out his phone. "I'm texting Olivia so she knows this is going to be an issue.

We'll have to inform the authorities that our team's authorized."

"I've never seen a police boat before."

He nodded. "They have a very active presence up here. Usually they enforce fishing rights, but I guess these guys are under their jurisdiction, too, as long as they're on the water."

"It's nice to know they're looking out for us."

Bryce palmed my hip. "It *is* nice to know."

We walked up the ramp to the landing. The restaurant was a long structure that jutted out into the harbor. More than a dozen well-dressed people were waiting for tables outside, but I didn't recognize anyone. Children threw rocks into the water, people were laughing and taking pictures, and one older couple had drinks from the bar and were toasting each other. It was a happy, relaxed vibe. Everyone seemed grateful to be on the island on such a gorgeous night.

I squeezed Bryce's hand. I knew I was lucky to be here, too.

The hostess came outside and scanned the crowd. When she spotted Bryce, she waved. "Mr. Windsor! Your table's ready."

The other customers eyed us, maybe wondering who Bryce was. A young couple whispered to each other as we passed. I straightened my shoulders, wondering if the photographers were already taking pictures of us or if the police were still questioning them. The hostess led us through the restaurant, which was packed.

"Bryce! Chloe!" Kelli and Kenji Nguyen waved to us from their table, and we waved back.

"Hey there, Bryce!" boomed another voice. It was Donald, the gentleman who had lost fifty-thousand dollars on a bet that Bryce would never get married.

Bryce pulled me closer, grinning, as he waved back. As we made our way to the restaurant's deck, we said hello to several other diners. "You literally know everyone here," I joked.

"Like I told you, there's only one restaurant."

The hostess sat us at a secluded table outside with a spectacular view of the water. "This is perfect," Bryce said as he pulled out my chair. "Thank you."

She beamed at him. "Of course, Mr. Windsor. Our pleasure. Your server will be right with you."

Bryce sat down next to me and for a moment, we were both speechless as we stared at the view. The moon was rising, three-quarters full, a bright shiny white. One side of the sky was dark, nighttime just beginning; the other, where the sun had just set, was streaked with pink. The mountains rose majestically in the distance. The ocean stretched out before us, dark, mysterious, yet somehow still peaceful.

"I love it up here. It's the most beautiful place I've ever been."

Bryce nodded. "I've traveled the world, but these islands have my heart."

"It even smells good." I inhaled deeply, enjoying the pure scent of unspoiled nature. "I noticed that when we came up the first time. It's no East Boston, but I'll take it."

"I"m glad. Once I moved up here full-time, I couldn't imagine going back to live in the city. I like to visit, but this is home."

"I liked the Bahamas, too." Bryce's family had a gorgeous home there. I shivered, remembering the sexy vacation we'd spent on the island. That trip held a lot of firsts for me. It was the first time I'd ever been out of the country, ever been anywhere tropical—and most importantly, the first time Bryce and I had made love. It had been incredible. I would never forget it. "But this is my favorite view ever."

"Me too." But Bryce wasn't looking out at the ocean and the majestic mountains—he was looking at me. "I'm so glad we're here."

I melted a little. In spite of my better judgment, I reached for his hand. "Me too."

The server came. We hastily looked at the menu and ordered crab cakes, a lobster roll, and at Bryce's insistence, lobster fried rice. "You'll love it," he declared. He also ordered us two Maine Wild Blueberry sodas.

I blinked at him once the server left. "You're drinking a blueberry *soda*? Whatever happened to bourbon, huh?"

He shrugged, a smile tugging at the corner of his lips. "I guess hanging with my underage wife has me in more of a soft-drink frame of mind."

"Ha." But the sodas, and the rest of dinner, were no laughing matter. We feasted on the crab cakes, and I tried aioli dipping sauce for the first time—it was insanely good. Our blueberry drinks tasted like the berries had been hand-picked moments before. The lobster roll was excellent. Despite being intimidated by its kimchi and shallots, I even enjoyed the fried rice. Whatever they were, they tasted great. Our server returned and lit the candles at our table; their glimmers echoed the winking stars appearing above.

Throughout our meal, which was excellent, Bryce kept his hand either on mine, around my shoulder, or on my thigh. We never lost contact. He gleefully ate with one hand. With the moon reflecting on the ocean, the excellent food, and the attention from my husband, I was high as a kite. I leaned over and kissed him automatically, without thinking it through.

"Ah." Bryce nuzzled his face against my neck. "I'm so glad you're back. I missed you, Chloe."

"I missed you too." I held my breath, hoping I wasn't making a mistake by admitting it.

"Oh, shit. Seriously?"

I winced. "Um..."

"Nice timing." Bryce pulled back, and I realized he wasn't talking about me. I followed his glare: Michael, Mimi, and Felicia Jones were being seated at the table right next to ours.

Motherfucker! If it wasn't Bitchface herself!

And she was staring at my husband as though he were the only man left on earth.

below deck

MIMI AND MICHAEL didn't look in our direction, but Felicia did.

First, her gaze lingered lovingly over *my* husband.

Then, her eyeballs almost popped out of her head when she saw me.

Finally, she narrowed them into a glare as she took in James's arm wrapped protectively around my shoulder.

Despite her sour expression, Felicia looked great. Her long, dark hair cascaded in waves around her shoulders. Her complexion was perfect, fair, and sparkling, and her blue eyes shone underneath her insanely thick lashes. The smattering of freckles across her nose was unexpected, making her that much more striking.

"Hi Bryce." She tossed her hair and didn't acknowledge me.

"Felicia. Mr. and Mrs. Jones." Bryce's voice was cold.

"Bryce." Mr. Jones's lips were set in a grim line. Probably seeing Bryce reminded him that Bryce's stepmother, who was less than half his age, was pregnant with his baby. More precisely, it probably reminded his wife. Mrs. Jones looked sour indeed as she gulped the martini she'd brought from the bar. She stared at the table, her face ashen, and I felt sorry for her.

An awkward silence descended over our tables. Bryce motioned for the check, and the server brought it blessedly quick. As we stood to go, Felicia only had eyes for Bryce. "I didn't expect to see you here."

"There's not exactly a lot of options." He pulled me close against his side. "Have a good night."

"You, too." She still didn't look at me. It was like I didn't even exist.

I was shaking by the time we got outside. "Don't let her get to you." Bryce squeezed my hand. "She's the ultimate mean girl, Chloe. She's always been the most popular, the richest, the best at everything. She doesn't know how to handle not getting her way."

"And what does she want, huh?" I glanced back at the restaurant. Michael Jones angrily gestured at the water, where the paparazzi boats floated, their zoom lenses still angled at the restaurant.

Bryce shrugged. "Who cares?"

I wished I could be so cavalier about Felicia Jones. The way she acted like I wasn't standing right there was disorienting, unnerving, and totally fucking rude. She made me feel like I was nothing, no one. Which was probably exactly what she wanted, but still...

Bryce kept his arm around me until we reached the dock, then he kissed me briefly before we boarded the boat. "Thank you for dinner. I enjoyed it." Again, things seemed so normal between us—in spite of the paparazzi floating in the water and Felicia Jones and her family glaring at us from the deck—that I melted a little.

"Thank you."

"We didn't get dessert, though." Despite the lobster fried rice, Bryce still looked a little...hungry. "Below deck, Mrs. Windsor," he growled as he helped me on board. "We're going to take care of that right now."

He tugged my hand and pulled me inside the cool interior of the yacht. And I, as usual, was helpless to resist my handsome husband.

We headed straight for the living room, where there was an oversized sectional couch. Bryce hit the intercom. "We're ready, Johnny. Mrs. Windsor and I will be downstairs until we dock at the house. Is everything clear?"

"Crystal, Sir," the captain replied. "I'll take the long way around the island and use the new dock. Is that acceptable?"

"Perfect." Bryce hung up and grinned at me. "We have a little longer. Perfect for what I have in mind."

"What's that?"

In answer, Bryce grabbed my wrist and yanked me onto his lap. I straddled him. He was already thick and hard against me as he kissed my neck, delving his hands deep into my hair. The familiar, almost insane, heat kicked on between us. How could I want him again? I rubbed myself against his erection, delicious soreness mingling with pure, aching need once again.

Bryce's hands were all over me as he devoured my neck. He wrenched my dress over my head, his hands greedily rubbing my breasts, snaking down around my waist and finding the thin straps of the g-string. "I love it," he growled. He tugged it tight against my sex, and I cried out. Wrapping his hand around the strap, he continued to increase the pressure, pulling it taut against me as he rubbed his cock against my clit.

Oh my God. Yes. I wanted him so badly, I was shaking.

"I need you." What was I, crazy? *Yes.* "Now, Bryce!"

I shifted, fumbling with his zipper and finally freeing him. His hard length sprang out, proud, huge and perfect, and he didn't hesitate. He wrenched the thong to the side, lifted me by the hips, and slowly lowered me onto the head. My sore body stretched to accommodate him. Bryce had pushed me to the edge, to the limit of what I could handle.

And yet, I wanted more. I wanted to take him and to be taken by him. I wanted him inside me, to *own* me, to make me see stars as we became one yet again.

Bryce threw his head back as he lowered me inch by inch until he was all the way in. We both cried out. The cords in his neck strained as he gripped my hips, guiding me up, then slamming me back down. I was so full of him like this—he was *so* deep. My eyes rolled back in my head as he slammed me down, over and over, totally owning me.

But I wanted to play, too. I *loved* being on top. I tucked my feet under his thighs, propped him up a little, and then took control. I bounced up and down, loving the feeling of taking his shaft deep inside. I relished how his balls slapped against my ass, how he threw his head back, his features contorted in pleasure as I rode him. *Yes.* He might own me, but I owned him, too. I bounced harder, riding him for all I was worth. He started to shatter. "Fuck Chloe. *Yes!*" Our sex became frantic, rough, as we both picked up the pace, chasing our release.

Oh my God, oh my God, oh my GOD!

I shattered, screaming his name as he exploded inside me. I saw white, I saw stars, everything stopped. I was one with the moment, with the absolute pleasure of my body, the pleasure of having my husband in me, of being one with him, the true pleasure of being alive. The experience of loving and being loved. Nothing else mattered. Nothing else existed.

Bryce wrapped his arms around me and buried his face against my chest. "I can't. No words," he panted.

"Same." I was glad we weren't talking because I absolutely would have spoken the words I'd vowed never to say again: *I love you.*

Instead, I hung onto my husband for dear life, grateful to keep my secret.

EIGHTEEN

necessary

BECAUSE BELOW DECK had been so *ah*-mazing, I was practically floating by the time we got docked. Bryce kept his palm on the small of my back as we drove the golf cart from the new dock, then went inside the house. "Let's stop by the kitchen."

Chef was inside, slicing vegetables. Apparently, he never left the kitchen. "Good evening, Mr. and Mrs. Windsor."

"Hi Chef. Would you happen to have any of that blueberry crisp left over? Chloe and I didn't get dessert at the restaurant." Bryce turned and winked at me.

"Of course, of course." Chef abandoned his chopping and headed for the row of massive refrigerators that commanded one entire wall of the working kitchen. He rummaged around inside, humming to himself until he found what he was looking for. When he returned to the kitchen island, he set down two bowls of delicious-looking blueberry crisp, the plump berries practically bursting out of the bowl.

"No touch. Not yet!" He grinned as he returned to the fridge, retrieved some fresh whipped cream, and then grabbed some sugar and a mini blowtorch on his way back.

When Chef saw the way I was looking at the blow-torch, he laughed. "Let me show you." He spooned the cream onto the desserts and then sprinkled the top with sugar. Then he fired up the blowtorch and browned the sugar, caramelizing it until it was brown and crispy. Appearing quite pleased with himself, he handed us each a spoon.

"Oh my God." I felt like my mouth had an orgasm! The crunch of the caramelized sugar, the fluffy texture of the cool, lightly whipped cream, and the taste of fresh blueberries was *insane*. "This is the most delicious thing ever."

Bryce nodded. "It's excellent, Chef. Thank you so much."

"My pleasure." Chef went back to humming and chopping.

We finished our desserts and then crept up the stairs. "Dale texted me earlier, I forgot to tell you," Bryce whispered as we reached the second floor. "Boss the puppy is apparently a very good boy. He's sleeping in the servants' wing tonight—the staff has already fallen in love with him. There's going to be an instructor here in the morning. Noah's going to meet with him for puppy training."

"Aw, that's nice." I glanced down the hall in the direction of my brother's room. It was close to midnight; he was probably asleep. "I'll go down and meet the instructor, too. Noah's never had a dog before, I should help him."

"We can all go," Bryce offered.

"That's nice." It was also unusual. Bryce was always in meetings, and especially with everything happening with the company, I was surprised that he was spending so much time with me. It must be to keep Olivia Jensen and his shareholders happy...

"Here we are." Bryce ushered me inside the room. He went into the bathroom, leaving me alone to change. I put on yet another pair of sexy underwear and a tank top. We'd literally had All The Sex that day, but that hadn't stopped us yet. I still needed to be prepared!

Bryce eyed me appreciatively when he came back

and climbed into bed. *Hmm.* I hustled into the bathroom, brushing my teeth and scrubbing the makeup from my face, wondering whether Bryce would want to make love yet again.

But when I returned to the bedroom, he was already fast asleep. I almost laughed as I climbed in next to him. I snuggled up to his broad chest, and he sighed, sounding happy. He wrapped his arm around me. Then, with my face pressed against my husband, surrounded by his warmth, muscles and scent, I fell into a deep sleep.

Eight hours later, I woke up in his arms.

Bryce was, of all things, still asleep. I stared at his handsome face. He was relaxed, completely adrift. I glanced at the clock: eight a.m. Had he ever slept this late in his whole life?

He opened one eye and stared at me. "What?"

"It's eight. What time was the dog trainer coming?"

Bryce grimaced as he glared at the clock. Even with only one eye open, he was an expert glare-r. "Eight-thirty. Ugh, I can't remember the last time I slept this late. You ruined me yesterday." He sat up, wincing a little. "I'm *sore*. What the hell did you do to me, Chloe?"

I laughed, but it hurt—which only made me laugh more. "I'm sore, too."

"Stay on your side of the bed tonight, dammit." He leaned over and kissed me. "I don't mean that, by the way."

"Ha." I pulled back. "Stay on your side for now—and I do mean that. We need coffee, not more sex."

He waggled his eyebrows. "We *always* need more sex—"

Both of our phones beeped, and he cursed. "Two guesses who that is. The first is Olivia Jensen, and the second is a pain in my ass. Oh wait, they're exactly the same."

I stared at him.

"Is there something on my face?" He scrubbed a hand across it.

"No. It's just that... You made a *joke*."

"I do that from time to time."

I arched an eyebrow. "Really?"

"Really." Bryce snatched his phone and glared at it. "She wants us in the kitchen ASAP. I think maybe my father's paying her extra to be demanding and difficult. Come on, let's get this over with."

He threw on sweats and a T-shirt, so I did the same. We walked down to the kitchen hand in hand. Something had changed between us; probably it was just all the sex, but the idea of walking next to him and not touching him seemed nearly impossible. Bryce must have felt the same way. As a maid prepared our coffee in the kitchen, he tucked me beside him, his hand around my waist.

Unf. We'd said no more sex, but as he palmed my hip, I lit up inside...

"There you are!" Olivia Jensen hustled in, holding an extra-large, half-empty iced coffee. She wore a teal dress that hugged her curves, her red hair was pulled back into a sleek ponytail, and she was already in full makeup. Unlike Bryce and I—un-showered and in our sweats—she appeared fully caffeinated and accomplished, as though she'd already checked several items off her to-do list.

"Well, well, well." She eyed us as the maid slid two enormous lattes across the counter. "Aren't you two looking all...reunited."

Bryce cleared his throat. "What did you want to see us about, Olivia? We have an appointment."

"Then I'll get right to it." She took out her phone and rapid-clicked through several screens, her fingertips flying. "Here we are—the shots from last night. Fab. You. Less. I can't even tell you how happy I am with these! Look at them in order, so you see the progression."

We took the phone and scrolled through the

pictures. The first was Bryce and I climbing onto the boat, hand in hand. Then there were shots of us onboard—me on his lap, smiling down at him. Bryce's arms were around me, and the way he was looking at me? Hoo boy, it was like he was going to have *me* for dinner!

There was more. Us disembarking at the dock, his arm around my waist. The maritime policeman interrogating the other group of photographers. When we reached those shots, Olivia jabbed a finger toward her phone. "I talked to the police this morning. They know that *our* team is authorized to follow you but that these other guys are pests. I wouldn't be surprised if they ended up getting arrested. They had too many people on that boat last night—they got a ticket."

"I hope they give up and go home, but I doubt it." Bryce frowned until he reached the next set of pictures. They were of us having dinner at the restaurant. In each shot, we were either laughing, kissing, or smiling. It was weird to see myself captured in the photographs. Even though I'd known we were being watched, I'd forgotten about it. To see myself laughing and smiling —not to mention looking at Bryce like I was head over heels in love with him—was strange. If I didn't know myself, I'd guess that the Chloe Windsor in these pictures was secure, happy, and in love. But none of those things were actually true. Well, almost none of them.

Olivia beamed at us. "The ones from the restaurant are the Crown Jewels. I cannot *wait* to release them. Who doesn't want to be young and in love, huh? Who doesn't want to have a romantic, candlelit dinner overlooking the ocean? Especially with a hot billionaire?"

At that, Bryce smirked a little. I couldn't help but laugh.

But once we kept scrolling, my cheerful mood dissipated. Felicia Jones had entered the picture, and how she looked at my husband made me downright *pissed*. Of course, she looked gorgeous in the photos. I hadn't even noticed what she'd been wearing last night, but it was a short white dress that showed off her toned body and light tan. The photographers had taken a burst of photos of her—one right after the other. They formed a mini-movie of her expressions. Felicia looking shocked and hurt to see her ex and his new wife. Felicia, staring at Bryce with longing. Felicia, completely ignoring me. Felicia, only having eyes for Bryce.

The last few pictures were of her staring at his retreating back. She appeared sullen, lost, and forlorn once we'd left.

The thing I hated the most about these pictures? She wasn't pretending. She wasn't putting on a show the same way that we were. It was clear from the photographs that she still had feelings for my husband, and they didn't appear to be diminishing over time.

Bryce started deleting them, and Olivia cleared her throat. "That won't do anything, silly. The team has the originals. Besides, you don't have the authority to delete them."

"My ass, I don't." Bryce kept clicking.

Olivia sighed. "Leave it alone, Bryce. If Felicia Jones helps garner interest for your family, so what?"

He palmed my hip. "My past is just that—the past."

"No one needs to know what happened—all they need to see is Felicia's face. It's not like she looks good in these pictures. I mean, she looks *good*, but she also looks like a jealous cow. That sells internet ad space. That's what we want, remember? We want addictive drama. That's what our partners want."

"We have partners, now?" Bryce threw the phone down.

"Yes. Wait, you didn't see the rest of them." Olivia opened the pictures back up. "Check *these* out. They're hot!"

Somehow, the photographers had managed to take pictures of us *inside* the boat, below deck. *Oh boy.* Me, straddling Bryce. Bryce, kissing my neck. Me, with a look of ecstasy on my face...

"No fucking way." That vein throbbed in Bryce's temple again. "I told you, nothing private—"

"Babe, they're not that bad. See?" I scrolled through the end of the photos. They stopped discreetly, right before he'd ripped my dress off and we'd had super-hot, deep, penetrating sex. "No harm in it. We look good. These are clicky." In fact, I hoped Felicia Jones herself clicked on them. Then she could see how happy we were together, even after seeing her sorry, rich, snobby, perfectly round ass.

I hoped she clicked on them and then went and died in a hole!

I smiled at Bryce, masking my vengeful thoughts, and he seemed to calm down. "Fine. If Chloe says they're okay, they're okay. But if my wife changes her mind, they're out."

"Fine." Olivia looked pleased. "Now, what is this appointment we have?"

"We? No, *Chloe* and I have an appointment."

"For what?" Olivia wasn't going to let it go.

"For... Training." Bryce did not so much as speak as spit the words. "Puppy training."

She looked positively gleeful as she drained her iced coffee. "You guys are making this too easy. Let's go, Bryce. Watching the grumpy billionaire and his hot, barely legal wife play with a puppy is gonna sell a ton of ad space. I might buy a whole *fleet* of Lexus SUVs after this job. Woo hoo!"

She clearly wasn't taking *no* for an answer. It was as if the word *no* didn't exist for her.

So with that, we followed Olivia Jensen out to see the other Boss.

NINETEEN

so much more

Noah was already out on the lawn with the instructor. Boss the puppy was wagging his tail, blithely ignoring the patient commands to sit and stay.

"Who's that adorable little boy?" Olivia asked.

"That's my brother—Noah." I licked my lips. "He's not really a part of all this, you know what I mean? He's just visiting."

"He's so cute! I'll definitely have them take some pictures of him. It's a great angle." Olivia's fingers were already flying across her phone. "Is he here for the summer?"

I glanced at Bryce. He looked wary. "Yep. He's just visiting." I refused to get into the particulars of the custody arrangement. I didn't want Olivia Jensen using my brother's situation as an angle to sell ad space. The fact that Bryce had rescued him from my deadbeat dad and derelict stepmother *was* newsworthy, but my brother's life wasn't for public consumption.

"Keep the pictures of him to a minimum." Bryce's tone was final. "He's a minor. His image doesn't need to be splashed all over the internet."

"I agree." Olivia looked up from her phone and smiled. "Ah. There they are! I took the liberty of making plans for your family for the rest of the day."

A golf cart appeared, flying across the lawn. Jake Windsor was driving; Colby Windsor was holding on for dear life.

"You did *what*?" Bryce glared at her.

"Hey Bryce. *Hey* Chloe. Olivia." Jake parked right next to us and jumped out. Colby followed suit.

Olivia Jensen gave them a big grin. "Boys. Glad to see you made it on time."

Colby scrubbed a hand across his face. "I could use some coffee."

"I'll get it for you." Olivia hustled off immediately. "Cream?"

"And sugar!" Colby called. "Two sugars. Please ask Chef to make it extra-large. Thank you."

He turned to us and scrubbed a hand across his face.

"I'm hungover. Jake here beat me at cards last night, and the only way he could do it was by feeding me whiskey. He won from a drunk man. So cheap, bro. You should pay me back!"

"Nah." Jake smiled. "Your body, your choice. You chose to get hammered. Not my responsibility to save you from the card gods."

Both of Bryce's brothers were tan and looked rested; they were dressed for a day at the beach in swim trunks and baseball hats. Both Jake and Colby looked more like fraternity brothers than actual adult billionaires.

As he watched Noah, Boss, and the trainer, Colby scratched his head. "No way that's a puppy. Who's the kid?"

"My brother, Noah," I answered. "And Boss is a puppy—he's only three months old."

"He's cute—your brother, I mean. The dog's a beast." Colby looked like a man dying from thirst in the desert as Olivia returned with his coffee. "God bless you, Olivia Jensen. I cannot cope with the world without caffeine."

"I'll drink to that." She raised her refreshed iced coffee in a toast. "Now then, let's get to business. Bryce and Chloe, I'd *love* to get some pictures of you with Noah and the puppy. And then the five of you have a cabana reserved at your club. You need to go hang by the pool and get lunch. See and be seen. Get your picture taken. Get *all* the pictures taken."

"I have to work." Bryce said it as though it was so obvious, it was annoying to have to say it out loud. "I don't have time to 'hang by the pool.'"

"Your father's still your boss, right?" Olivia's voice was firm. "This is his directive. He said you'd complain. He *also* said you can work at the club."

She took a step closer, softening her expression. "Think of it this way—this is crucial for the survival and, more importantly, the *success* of your company. The public needs to see the next generation of Windsors as a family, as real people, even if your lifestyle's completely out of reach. We actually *want* them to see the lifestyle —it's unattainable for most people, but it sure is fun to watch."

"I don't see the point of us frolicking at the pool club on a Tuesday when most people are hard at work. I don't think it sends the right message," Bryce said.

Olivia nodded. "I understand your point, but showing images of you with your family—with your adoring wife at your side—makes you relatable. That's what we need, the human element. People don't connect with your father. He's out of touch. The public doesn't love him."

"I think it makes *me* look out of touch to be flaunting my wealth."

"That's not what you're doing." She put a hand on his arm. "I've seen the pool club, and it's not lavish. It's old money. You were born into this lifestyle, just like a Kennedy. And you still work hard. We want everyday people to see you with your family because *everyone* can relate to family. We need to give them something to root for. We need them to fall in love with you and your brothers and get obsessed. I need them foaming at the mouth to see pictures of all of you at your cousin's wedding. Please work with me, Bryce. I promise you won't be sorry."

She checked her phone. "Okay, I have a meeting with legal. The photographers are here onsite—they're discreet, of course—and they've requested that Bryce and Chloe play with the puppy. They'll be at the club, too, so keep that in mind. Also, Bryce and Chloe, you have exactly five minutes to change into your suits after this photo opportunity. Chloe, wear something tiny. That'll keep Bryce at least somewhat happy."

He glared at her, but she ignored it. She turned to Jake and Colby. "No ladies, you two. I mean it! Oh, here comes Daphne. You guys should be all set."

"Daphne?" Jake, Bryce, and Colby looked at her in horror.

"I said the *five* of you were booked for the club. Weren't you listening?" Olivia sashayed away before the men could object. "Don't forget—both the authorized and the unauthorized photographers will be following you. *And* the security team. It's going to be a production. Anyway, have fun and be good!"

Daphne power-walked toward us. She wore a long, white caftan, and her hair was up in a bun. The straps of her black bathing suit peeked through the top. Once again, I was struck by how pretty she looked— pregnancy agreed with her. "Hey guys." She perched her enormous designer sunglasses atop her head. "Thank you *so* much for the invite. I'm bored to death since they shut down my social media. And Gene doesn't want to leave the house, so." She shrugged.

"How is the old man, anyway?" Colby asked.

"He's preparing for the fight of his life," she sighed. "The lawyers are telling him to expect a formal investigation and an indictment. The negotiations aren't going well, and that's in part because my husband is stubborn." Daphne eyed Bryce. "You need to talk some sense into him."

"I've been trying." Bryce reached for my hand. "He doesn't want to listen to me, which isn't anything new."

"Try harder." Daphne scowled.

"Yes, Your Highness." Bryce arched an eyebrow.

I checked in with Noah; he was thrilled to be reunited with the puppy. He said he was glad he didn't sleep in his room, though—the staff had to take him out to pee in the middle of the night. Bryce and I played with Boss, as instructed. The dog was adorable; after five minutes, I was baby-talking to him just like my brother. Even Bryce cracked a smile as he scratched him behind the ears.

Hadn't I asked for a puppy because I'd been trying to spite my husband? Hmm, none of what I'd been planning had turned out like I'd expected...

It was time to head to the club. Bryce and I went and quickly changed; he complained the whole time, a string of colorfully strung together curse words. We headed back outside, and I hugged Noah goodbye—he didn't want to come because he didn't want to leave Boss. He planned to play with the dog and later, to fish off the private dock. My brother seemed genuinely happy and in good spirits. Accepting Bryce's offer had been the right thing to do. Noah was happier than he'd been since our mother died.

As we rode our boat over to the club, the sun was warm on my face. I ignored the boats that trailed us, the photographers, and a team of Bryce's security guards who were frowning at them. I focused on the gorgeous scenery. The water was calm, a magnificent blue; the green mountains of Acadia rose in the distance, and the clean, salty air whipped my hair.

I said a prayer that my mother could see us from heaven. I prayed that she knew that I was doing my best to care for Noah, that he was happy and thriving. And that he had a puppy—my mother would love that! *I know this is all crazy,* I thought, *but I'm doing my best. Noah's happy. That's all that matters, right?*

I prayed she agreed.

Jake, Colby, and Daphne chatted about her pregnancy. She seemed completely comfortable, as though it was the most normal thing in the world that she was pregnant with Michael Jones's baby. Bryce was on his phone, working. I sat next to him, remembering the first time we'd visited Bryce's club. It had been our first full day together, and we'd "paraded" around the bay in his yacht, waving to people he knew, before going to the club. Once we'd gotten there, Bryce had been very... hands-on. That day had been my introduction to his commanding touch. We'd sat on the dais by the pool, hanging all over each other while the other members watched us...

"We're here." Bryce's voice woke me from my reverie. "Are you ready?" He reached for my hand and gently helped me onto the dock, and I marveled at the difference in our relationship. The first time we'd been to the club, he'd been an icy stranger. One that I was insanely attracted to, but still. Now he was so much more than that. Now he was my everything...

Contract, contract, contract, said the voice in my head.

Love, love, love, argued my heart.

I sighed, praying they'd both be quiet and vowed to enjoy the day.

the club

THE SECURITY TEAM parked their boat, and several be-suited guards climbed out. They kept a respectful distance but were close enough to protect us. I didn't want to imagine from what.

We headed up the ramp to the club, a chic, upscale pool area sprawled beneath an elegant outdoor dining room. It was exactly as I remembered—the pale-gray stone pool deck, the crystalline, aqua water. The affluent guests who lounged poolside were dressed like Daphne in flowing caftans and designer sunglasses. The restaurant patrons dressed up for each other, the women in elegant dresses and the men in suits. The martinis and flutes of champagne were already flowing.

A hush fell over the club as the five of us reached the entrance, followed by the guards. Did I imagine it, or were the other guests staring and whispering? I noticed the Mayweathers, Bryce's friends, but they didn't make eye contact with us. Unlike the restaurant the night before, there were no warm welcomes, no friendly waves.

"What's the deal?" Daphne smiled at a few people she knew, but no one returned her overtures. Her expression became pinched. "We better not get kicked out of here—and they better not cancel our freaking membership. There isn't even a waiting list. You can't get back in, even if you're reincarnated as royalty!"

"They're not going to cancel us, Daphne," Colby assured her. "Dad's been a member here for years. He paid for the tennis courts, for Christ's sake! We have a membership into perpetuity."

Serge, the head server, immediately joined us. He wore an impeccable tan linen suit and an intense expression on his face. "Mr. Windsor, we're honored that you've joined us again so soon."

"It's always a pleasure, Serge." Bryce nodded to him. "I see that our spot's available. Thank you for always accommodating us."

"I'm happy to be of service, Sir." But Serge grimaced and wrung his hands. He looked past Bryce to the guards, who had fanned out and were inspecting the premises. "Your assistant *did* book you on the pool dais, but is it possible your party would be more comfortable in one of our *private* outdoor spaces? They're away from the hustle and bustle of the over guests."

Bryce peered past him at the other members who were pretending not to watch us. "Are you asking us to stay segregated from the general population?"

"Not at all, Sir," Serge said quickly. "Management thought you might be comfortable with more...privacy... given recent events." There was a thin bead of sweat on Serge's upper lip. He didn't appear happy to be delivering Management's news.

"Please tell *Management* that I'd like to speak with them immediately, as in *now*. I'll wait." Bryce crossed his arms against his massive chest.

"Of course, Mr. Windsor. Just one moment." Serge fled.

"What's going on?" Jake asked Bryce, careful to keep his voice quiet. "I feel like we're pool pariahs. Why is everyone staring at us like that?"

Bryce shrugged. "They probably don't want the press sniffing around this place. There's a no cellphone rule at the club, remember? These old dogs want to keep their names and faces out of the news."

At that moment, Michael and Mimi Jones emerged from inside the restaurant. Upon seeing us, Michael Jones's shoulders slumped. He looked anywhere but at

Daphne, who pouted and stuck her chest out in his direction. Mimi Jones, however, stared directly at our party. She looked like she wanted to claw Daphne's eyes out and then spit in the sockets.

Oh boy.

"I think there might be other factors at play, too." Bryce watched the Joneses, looking amused. "I'll handle it. Mom loved this place, remember? We're not leaving quietly." He started rapid-texting on his phone while the rest of us stood there awkwardly, weathering Mimi Jones's hateful gaze.

A moment later, an attractive woman with caramel-colored skin, who wore a linen suit like Serge's and a sour expression, strode toward us. Serge followed her, looking miserable.

"I'm Angela, the Club's Manager." She stiffly shook Bryce's hand. "It's nice to meet you, Mr. Windsor. I'm sorry if our offer of an enclosed room isn't appealing to you, but out of privacy concerns for our other members, we feel it's appropriate to have your party accommodated this way."

"Thank you, Angela." Bryce smiled at her. "I'm happy to say that we'll take our usual spot—at the dais overlooking the pool."

"I'm sorry, but that's not possible—"

"It's absolutely possible." Bryce held up his phone

so she could see the screen. "Because I just bought the club. I overpaid, of course. By a *lot*. But it was worth it."

Angela blinked at the screen. Serge read it over her shoulder, looking impressed. The other club members pretended not to watch the showdown.

After a moment, Angela stepped back. "Then by all means, right this way, Mr. Windsor."

"Thank you, Angela," Bryce said smoothly.

She cleared her throat. "I hope you're a better boss than the last guy."

"I'm not." Bryce didn't wipe the smile from his face. He threw his arm around me and started for our seats. "And it's nothing personal, but I'm demoting you. Serge, you're the manager now. Will you please let the other guests know that, as of today, the Windsors own the club? And I'm increasing the prices. If anyone has a problem with that, throw them off the dock."

Serge blinked at him. "Seriously?"

Bryce laughed. "No. But you are the new manager. So can you have someone get my brothers drinks? They look like they need them." He sauntered over to the pool dais, blithely ignoring the other member's stares.

And I just followed the club's new owner, shaking my head.

∽

The paparazzi was out in the water, hidden from our view. I forgot all about them—if they were ensconced somewhere in the bushes, taking pictures, we were blissfully unaware. Same thing with the Windsors' security team. Bryce's men were positioned around the club, but they somehow faded into the scenery. I felt safe but not smothered by their presence.

Owning the club, Daphne declared, did not suck. Michael and Mimi Jones had abruptly left. They looked as though they were arguing. Then the Mayweathers came over and offered their congratulations to Bryce for buying the club and to Daphne for her pregnancy. The staff attended to our every need, and the other guests were much friendlier once they realized Bryce could, and would, happily revoke their legacy memberships.

"Remind me to tell them to order that new alcohol-free champagne everyone's been telling me about," Daphne said as she laid back in her lounger. She wore a black bikini, and her stomach remained super flat. "And can we revoke the Jones's membership?"

Bryce didn't answer her. He'd declared our party exempt from the club's no-cell-phone rule and had been texting with legal for the better part of an hour. He seemed distracted. Still, he'd managed to position me right next to him on our double-wide lounger and had kept at least one hand on me the entire time. The man could multi-task!

Jake was drinking a beer and reading on his phone. Colby was the only one in the crystalline aqua pool beside an older woman with gray hair who'd been swimming laps for what seemed like hours. He'd borrowed a float and didn't appear to be in any rush to get out. When he floated into the lady's path, she scolded him.

Colby smiled at her good-naturedly. "Sorry, but I own this pool. Maybe you could swim around me?"

When she looked horrified, he started to laugh. "I'm just kidding! I'll stay on my side, I swear. Nice form, by the way. Do you swim professionally?"

It seemed as though he'd made a new friend. She took a break and started chatting with him. He waved a server over and ordered another beer for himself and an iced tea for her.

"Well, now I know why everyone was staring at us." Jake looked up from his phone. "You guys are all over the news. All over each other *and* all over the news."

Bryce stopped trailing his fingers down my arm long enough to glare at his brother's phone. "What's that?"

"That's the announcement about the Kysa Reeves interview, which airs tonight." Jake scrolled down.

"And *these* are pictures from yesterday. You have to give it to Olivia Jensen. She works fast."

He handed Bryce the phone. The first image was of Kysa Reeves interviewing us; the news program was airing that evening. I'd almost forgotten that I was going to be on cable news—thank goodness I hadn't said much!

The following images were all intimate ones of Bryce and I—embracing in the jeep, staring at each other on the rocky beach, kissing and holding hands at the restaurant. There were pictures of his gorgeous house. The headline read:

Despite Mounting Woes, Billionaire Bryce Windsor's Still Honeymooning

Even I had to admit the pictures were clicky. The headline was irresistible. Who was the billionaire who dared to enjoy his honeymoon while his company's woes mounted? It wasn't the spin I'd expected, but the article was kinder to Bryce than the title suggested. It stated that he was making his new marriage a priority in the midst of the scandal because he'd waited so long to find the right woman and settle down.

That's when the pictures of Felicia began. There were only two of them—her staring at Bryce, then her looking upset when we'd left the restaurant. The caption read: *The honeymoon's over for ex-flame.*

Ugh, the past wasn't in the past now. Instead, it was all over the internet. But the article only stated that Bryce and Felicia had been previously "linked as a couple" and then went on to say the heiress was rumored to be dating a guitar player for some famous band. *Please God, let that be true.* It was the first I'd heard of it.

I watched Bryce's expression when he scrolled to the section about Felicia, but he seemed indifferent. However, his brow did arch when he clicked on the next batch of pictures, which were of us in a heated embrace below deck on his yacht. *They Just Can't Keep Their Hands Off Each Other*, read the caption.

Jake watched his big brother, a bemused expression on his face. "I never thought I'd see the day. Not only are you in the tabloids, but you look *happy*." He turned to me. "Nice work, Chloe."

"Ha." I didn't know what to say.

"How did you two meet, anyway?" Jake got a sparkle in his eye. "I didn't even know Bryce was seeing anyone. Next thing I heard, he was married."

"It was love at first sight, silly." Daphne came to our rescue by inserting herself into the conversation. "She was working at a Dunkin' Donuts, of all things, and

Bryce kept going in to get coffee while he was onsite down in Boston. The rest is history."

"Interesting." Jake looked skeptically at his brother. "I can't picture you in a Dunkin's, let alone chatting up one of the workers."

"Chloe was irresistible." Bryce kept his hand clamped on me.

"I can see that." When Bryce scowled, Jake grinned. "I mean, I can see that *you* find her irresistible. I'm really happy for you two."

"Thanks, Jake." Bryce relaxed. "If Dad has his way, it sounds like you're next."

"Not going to happen. I don't know why the old man's so intent on marriage, anyway. What's he on, number four now? Or is it five?"

Daphne slid her sunglasses down her nose and glared at him. "I'm sitting right here. You know that, right?"

"Sorry." Jake waved her off. "It's nothing personal, Daphne. I just mean, in general—why is Dad so fixated on us getting married?"

"He thinks it makes us look more stable to the shareholders. I think he might be right about that. It sends a message that you've grown up, put away your toys, and are ready for real commitments." Bryce snaked his arm protectively around my shoulders and pulled me closer. "I personally think being married is...great. It *does* make your life more stable. I enjoy it."

Jake and Daphne openly gaped at him. I couldn't see my own face, but I probably was, too.

"I'll keep that in mind." Jake looked impressed. "On to other pressing matters. How the hell are we going to break the news to Dad that you paid ten million for this place?"

Daphne spit out her water.

Bryce shrugged. "Mom would've wanted me to. I'll tell him that."

Jake nodded, then rolled onto his back to face the sun. "That's a good reason."

"I know," Bryce said.

TWENTY-ONE

happiness

THE REST of the afternoon passed in a similar fashion. It was surprisingly pleasant spending time with Daphne and Bryce's brothers. By the end of the day, I felt more comfortable with all three of them. My mother was an only child, so we didn't have cousins; I didn't grow up with a lot of family around. But as Captain Johnny drove us home and we all made plans for dinner that evening, a tiny, funny feeling settled into my stomach.

I felt...happy.

Bryce kept his arm around me all day, and I probably had a contact high from that. But it was also nice to have his brothers visiting the island. Jake was sweet, observant, and a little introspective. Colby made friends with everyone and was generous with his laughter and attention. Even Daphne, who was so often scheming and insufferable, wasn't all bad. She'd shown me pictures of how she was decorating the nursery. She shared the designer brand of baby clothes she'd started ordering. She hinted that she wanted me to throw her a baby shower before her husband ended up in jail.

When we got back to the house, and Colby started throwing a football to my brother, it all felt a bit surreal. Not that long ago, I'd only had Noah. I'd lost my mother, who had been my heart, the person I'd been closest to in the world.

Not long ago, my step-monster Lydia had thrown us out on the streets, and my father hadn't stood up for us because he never stood up for us. I'd felt so alone. Not to mention desperate—which had gotten me onto the *Sugar Finder* app and introduced me to Elena the Madam in the first place. Now I was married and living on Bryce Windsor's private island. It was the opposite of my life before, not just because of the wealth surrounding me. I wasn't alone anymore. I didn't have to do it all myself. I had...

I had love in my life. I still didn't want to admit it to myself, but it was true. I was in love with Bryce. The thought of being separated from him ever again was terrifying.

So don't think about it. As we stood outside on the lawn, I reached for his hand and squeezed it. My heart stopped when he looked up from his phone and smiled at me.

When his look turned smoldering, my legs turned to jelly.

He didn't say a word, and he didn't have to. We left our brothers, Daphne, Dale, and Boss to the beautiful, sunny afternoon and crept upstairs to be alone.

As soon as he closed the door behind us, he was on me. And I couldn't get enough of my husband. I could never get enough.

He stripped me out of my coverup, and my bikini was off before I knew what had happened. I had faint tan lines; my breasts were a creamy, pale white in contrast. Bryce kissed my neck—his hands were everywhere, roaming. He took my nipple into his mouth, suckling me, and I sighed in pleasure and relief. All I ever needed, all I ever wanted, was to be with him like this. I slid his swim trunks down, and his stiff erection sprung out, pink, perfect, and huge. I spit onto my hand and started milking him, our bodies beginning to slide and writhe together in time. When he stiffened further beneath my hands, it emboldened me.

I sank down onto my knees and took the head of his cock into my mouth.

Bryce tried to hold still as I sucked his crown like a lollipop. "What're you doing? Oh *fuck*, Chloe."

When I took him deeper, he groaned. When I took him briefly all the way in, he cursed. He'd asked me what I was doing, so I was going to show him. I put my hand around his shaft and milked him into my mouth with one hand. With the other, I gently massaged and squeezed his balls. With his grunts and moans, along with the barely controlled pulsing of his hips, I could tell he was enjoying himself. So was I. Something about having control over him, of being the one to give him pleasure, was insanely satisfying.

I picked up the pace, chasing my mouth with my hand. When I squeezed his balls, he barked out a litany of curses—in a good way. He was close. I felt his ball tighten; I could taste the salty pre-cum in my mouth. Pure female satisfaction bloomed inside my chest. I was the one who'd brought him to the edge. It was *my* touch, my mouth, my hands that had him losing his mind.

"Get up," he said roughly. "Stand up and bend over the bed *now*." There was an unmistakable urgency to his tone. I did as I was told, climbing up, putting my palms on the bed, spreading my legs, and sticking my ass up in the air.

"Thank fuck." Without hesitation, Bryce notched himself inside me. When he felt how insanely wet I was, he laughed.

But when he started to thrust, there was no more laughing.

Oh, fuck! He was so deep like this, and he didn't hold back. His strokes were urgent. "Yes, Chloe. *Fuck yes.*" He punished me with his cock, driving all the way in, filling me, claiming me. My clit rubbed up against the bed, and I cried out.

"Yes!" He smacked my ass. When I cried out again, he drove harder. I was about to come when he pulled out. He spanked one ass cheek, then the other, and then slapped my sex with the open palm of his hand.

"Ow!" The pain was bright and unexpected, but I didn't have time to process it or complain—Bryce had already buried himself in me again and gripped my hips. He was driving for home. The stinging sensation across my ass and sex, coupled with the friction against my clit—not to mention his insanely deep penetration —pushed me over the edge. "Fuck...fuck... *BRYCE!*"

He grabbed my ponytail and yanked it, riding me as he fucked me through my orgasm, and then it was his turn. He groaned, he cursed, and finally, he laughed as he erupted inside me. His hips thrust cruelly as he spent himself, filling me once again, making me see stars. I cried out in pleasure as he emptied himself inside me, still gripping my hair and my hip as thrusts slowed. We stayed like that for a while, connected, sweaty, and spent, until he pulled out and collapsed on the bed next to me.

He glared at me with one eye open. "Mrs. Windsor," he declared, "I believe you're trying to kill me."

"Ha! You were the one spanking me. What's with that?"

"I don't know." He smirked as he pulled me closer. "Just trying to spice things up."

I laughed again. "You're obviously trying to kill *me*."

"I would never do that." His voice was no longer teasing. "I love you too much."

A heavy, unexpected silence fell between us. I didn't know what to say, what to do.

"I... I love you, too." Tears pricked my eyes. Damn him, why had he made me say it?

But I couldn't ask; my husband was already asleep, lightly snoring.

Maybe he hadn't heard me. Maybe. In any event, I snuggled into his arms and pressed my face against his chest. It was the truth; I *did* love him.

For better, or much more likely, for worse.

notifications

NEITHER ONE OF us mentioned the "l" word as we took our respective showers and got dressed. There was a lot of kissing, though. And hugging.

I could *feel* the love. But I'd be damned before I'd say it again—not unless he said it first!

Chef prepared a picnic dinner that we ate outside on the patio. There was corn on the cob, steak tips, grilled salmon, and Caesar salad. Jake and Colby took turns throwing the football to Noah and tossing a ball for Boss. Daphne still seemed high as a kite from our day at the club, regardless that Michael Jones had blown her off. She actually ate an entire plate of food. Dale sat with us, talking in low tones to Bryce about the upcoming schedule. Gene Windsor didn't join us for dinner. Daphne explained that he was meeting with Olivia Jensen to review strategy and plan next steps.

I didn't think much of it when my phone pinged. I casually checked the screen, then almost fell out of my chair when I read the latest text from Lydia.

Who do you think you are, lowballing us like that?

Just remember who took you in when you had nothing!

I saw your pictures online. You're living in a mansion while we starve! I'm going to make you pay.

She'd ended with a devil emoji, followed by a stick of dynamite.

I pushed my food away, completely losing my appetite. I didn't think that giving my father and Lydia thirty thousand dollars—on top of the million Bryce had already paid—was "lowballing" them. But apparently, what I thought didn't matter. Lydia was greedy, that was for sure. Seeing the pictures of me online, living on Bryce's private island, obviously wasn't helping. I needed to do something to make her happy, but what?

I glanced nervously at Bryce. He wouldn't be happy that she was harassing me, and he would be angry about her threats. The last thing we needed was pressure from my step-monster right now. There was enough trouble to go around!

"Hey, your interview's coming on. Let's go watch it!"

Daphne hopped up and headed into the house uninvited.

"I guess we're following her." Jake and Colby followed Daphne, and Noah followed them.

"Hey Noah, wait up." I caught up to my brother. He had Boss on a leash; I was surprised that the puppy behaved for him. "Did you have a good session with the trainer this morning? Boss seems almost...obedient."

"He's really good. Aren't you, Boss?" Noah reached down and scratched him behind the ears. "The trainer said it's important to let him know I'm in charge. Be firm but gentle, you know?"

I ruffled his hair. "You're a good kid, you know that?"

"Ew Chloe, let *go*." He ducked out from under me. "I'm so glad to be back, though. I don't ever want to leave again, okay?"

"Okay." I glanced at Bryce, who was still deep in conversation with Dale. "I don't ever want to leave, either."

"Then let's stay." Boss tugged on the leash, and Noah started to run. "I'll see you in there!"

We gathered in the living room, and I sat on the couch, hugging a pillow to my chest. All of a sudden, I was nervous. It had been bad enough to see myself online earlier that day. But watching myself on television? I broke out into a sweat.

Even though he was still talking to Dale, Bryce sat beside me, his hand on my thigh. His constant presence, combined with his physical touch, made everything better. He was a source of strength and comfort for me. Only recently, I'd considered him my torturer. But somehow, everything had changed. If he'd sat away from me on the couch, if he hadn't put his hand on my skin, I would've cried.

What the hell, Chloe? It seemed I was breaking promises to myself. That was never a good idea, but as I settled in next to my husband, his hand on my thigh, warmth spread through me. Until the interview with Kysa Reeves came on, and then I was filled with terror.

Kysa looked fantastic, of course, in her charcoal dress, her hair pulled back in a sleek bun. "Good evening, and welcome to a *very* special, totally exclusive interview. You're going to hear from Bryce Windsor tonight. He's the son of Gene Windsor, the embattled founder and CEO of Windsor Enterprises. Bryce Windsor is the youngest billionaire in the world."

"I'm close," Jake said. He scowled at Bryce. "And after I vest, I'm taking that title."

"Then when I vest, I'm taking it from *you*." Colby grinned at Jake.

"Can you two be quiet?" Daphne asked. "If your father's convicted, no one's vesting anything. *Shh.* I want to hear this!"

An image of Bryce's island filled the screen. It was an aerial view of his estate, then of Gene's. "This is the Windsors' private getaway—a remote island off the coast of Maine. As you can see, no expense was spared at these amazing compounds. But everything is in jeopardy because of the insider trading allegations against Gene Windsor. At the time of this writing, both the SEC and the Department of Justice are investigating the Windsor Enterprises CEO. If convicted, Gene Windsor could be fined up to twenty-five million dollars and spend twenty years in prison. It's no surprise that Bryce Windsor is doing everything he can to protect his father's reputation, their family name, and their company."

The picture changed to one of Bryce and me from our wedding day. I cringed at the image. I looked so stressed, and my makeup was cakey from the humidity. Bryce looked handsome as ever in his suit, but his expression was all business. "In happier news, Bryce Windsor recently married a young woman from Boston, Chloe Windsor. I met with the newlyweds at Mr. Windsor's home in Mount Desert Island, Maine."

It flashed to the interview, and I hid behind the

pillow. "You look great, Chloe!" Daphne enthused. I squinted at the screen: Bryce looked ridiculously handsome in his dark suit. As for me, I appeared much more pulled together than I'd felt. My emerald-green dress looked simple, elegant, and chic. Thank God for Midge; she'd made my hair and makeup look flawless.

"You look weird," Noah said. I elbowed him.

Kysa started her questions, and the interview progressed. When it got to the part where Bryce discussed the plans for leading the company in his father's absence, it got very quiet.

"No one said he's stepping down," Bryce said as he faced the camera. *"But for now, he's going to concentrate on the investigation, and I'm going to concentrate on running our company. My family is committed to the success of our business. We aren't going anywhere. We intend to come out of this stronger than before."*

When it got to the part where I spoke—and declared that not only was my husband the youngest billionaire but also the most handsome—I completely shut my eyes. I wasn't meant to be on camera. I tried to block out the sound of my voice.

When it was over, Bryce rubbed my leg. "I don't know why you're hiding—you did great."

"Thanks." But I felt miserable. I'd never been

someone who wanted a lot of attention. Seeing myself on the news was basically a nightmare.

Jake turned back to Bryce. "You, on the other hand, are going to have some explaining to do. Dad's not going to like what you said."

"He'll be fine." Bryce shrugged.

"Uh, maybe not." Colby held up his phone. "He said he wants us to come over for a meeting. *Now*."

"Fine." Bryce sounded resigned.

We stood to go, but Noah stayed on the floor and played with the puppy. "I'm not included in that."

Colby nodded at him. "Good for you, kid. Good for you."

TWENTY-THREE

relatable

WE DROVE the golf carts over to Gene Windsor's estate in silence. "Are you nervous?" I asked Bryce when we parked.

"Not at all. I told him ahead of time what I'd be saying. Those answers were vetted and prepared—it's fine." He reached for my hand, and I followed him into Gene's cavernous house.

"Hi there." A maid greeted us at the door. "Mr. Windsor's just in the study with Ms. Jensen. I'll let him know you're here."

"Um, this is my house," Daphne called, but the maid had already disappeared.

After a moment, Olivia Jensen hustled out. "Gene's ready for you guys. Come on." She clicked down the hall, and I wondered how she still had so much spring in her step after almost twelve hours straight in spiked heels. "We watched the interview. You handled the questions well," she told Bryce and me. "Your father's coming to terms with it."

"Then why do I have an impending sense of doom?" Bryce looked grim, and for a good reason. The atmosphere turned heavy as soon as we entered his father's study.

Gene Windsor paced the room, clutching a colossal bourbon. "Nice of you to finally join us. You *do* remember who's writing the checks, don't you? Or did you all forget while you were out frolicking at the pool on my dime?"

His watery eyes flickered over us, coming to rest on Bryce. "Ah, my oldest son. The man who would be king. I saw your interview. Think you're taking the reins already, eh?"

He chugged his drink, and Daphne went to his side. "Easy, dear." She rubbed his back. "Bryce's answers were pre-screened. Even Olivia said he did well."

"Since when did you defend him? He's always been a thorn in your side. Or...wait a minute." Gene's tone turned nasty, and I could tell his half-empty drink wasn't his first. "Are you planning on sleeping with him next?"

Daphne straightened her shoulders. "Wasn't there

some stipulation in our new agreement that you wouldn't be a dickhead? No? Remind me to call my lawyers in the morning." She headed for the door. "Goodnight, everyone but my husband. I had a lovely day."

"Goodnight, dear." Gene raised his glass to where his wife had been standing, then turned to his sons. "Perhaps Daphne's done me a real favor by sticking around. She's making prison look good." He laughed, but when the rest of us just stood there, obviously uncomfortable, he scowled. "What's with the sour mood? I thought you'd all be celebrating yourselves, as usual."

"Why'd you call us over here, Dad?" Colby helped himself to the bourbon. "Did you just want to soft-launch your prison humor? Or were you looking for someone to drink with?"

"Both." Gene scrubbed a hand across his face. "You know Colby, if and when you get your life together, I'll give you the company. You're the only one who's nice to me."

"Aw, thanks, Dad." Colby patted him on the shoulder. "But you shouldn't take it personally. I'm nice to everyone."

Gene looked a little confused, so Olivia Jensen took the opportunity to speak. "Your father and I just watched the interview. Like I said, Bryce, you did well. You came across as strong but supportive."

Gene scowled, but she ignored him. "I think the interesting thing," Olivia continued, "was how Chloe came across in the piece."

She turned to me. "You looked great, of course. But I also thought you were very relatable. Initial polling indicates that you scored well with females in the lower economic echelon of viewers, which our partners really like. That segment is a hot target for ad space. So I'm thinking that we could use you more."

"I'm sorry?" I scooted a little behind Bryce as though he could shield me from whatever she was saying, along with the nasty stare Gene Windsor was shooting in my direction.

"Sorry—sometimes I lapse into PR-speak," Olivia said. "What I meant was, the audience liked you. Particularly young mothers and working-class women. You polled well with them."

"How do you know that?" I asked. "The interview only aired a half-hour ago."

"I work with some pretty sophisticated contractors. They're able to gather this information in real-time. With how fast the internet moves, it's necessary to strategize quickly. So I'd like you to do another interview—a lifestyle piece."

I gaped at her. Bryce shielded me. Gene poured himself another bourbon, and then I *knew* we were in trouble. He was really going for it if he wasn't waiting for the hired help to fetch his drinks. "I don't want her to do another interview—I already told you that," Gene said.

"I'm aware of your concerns." Olivia's voice was gentle but firm. "But you hired me to do a job, and this is when you need to take a step back and let me do it."

"She"—Gene jabbed a finger in my direction—"is not a Windsor. She's from the projects in East Boston. Her father's unemployed, her stepmother's a drunk—"

"Father." Bryce stepped forward, hands clenched. "That's enough."

"I had her file run, son, I know who she is. And this is not how I want my family represented!"

"Not. Another. Word." Bryce's fists were clenched so tight, his knuckles were white.

Gene was half-drunk and obviously agitated, but he was no dummy. Bryce was twice his size. "Fine, Son, fine. Forgive me. I'm just upset because I'm used to running things. Now it seems as though nothing's my choice." His gaze flicked over me, then away.

"Chloe," Bryce said without looking at me, "do you want to do another interview?"

"N-No." I shook my head.

"Father, Chloe won't be doing another interview. But not because you don't want her to— because *she* doesn't want to do it. Are we clear?"

"I'm not taking orders from you yet." Gene shook the ice in his glass. "If Olivia wants her to do it, she's doing it." He was changing his tune awfully fast; he sounded like a petulant child who was about to have a temper tantrum, fighting just to fight.

"Do you even hear yourself? You're so off-base right now that I don't even know what to say. Jesus!" Bryce ran his hands through his hair. "By the way you're whining, you'd think your biggest problem was your family. But go look in the mirror, Dad. You're your own worst enemy. Only you could piss on the thing you say you love the most, then cry when you might lose it." Bryce grabbed my hand and stormed out. "Olivia, if you ever let him call a meeting when he's been drinking again, I'll fire you myself."

"You don't have the authority to do that," Gene warned.

"Shut *up*, Father. Once you're in jail, you'll wish you'd stayed focused on what matters."

By the time we got out to the golf carts, Bryce was breathing hard. "I'm sorry about that. He doesn't want to give up control. I hope you don't take it personally. At least, not too personally."

"Well, he *was* insulting my person."

She's from the projects in East Boston.

Her father's unemployed.

Her stepmother's a drunk...

And of course, weeks ago, Gene had offered to pay me to get an annulment from Bryce and leave the family for good. It's not like he'd ever been my number-one fan. I shrugged. "I didn't have any real hope that he would turn around and welcome me to the family. But it could be a problem, couldn't it? Because he *doesn't* approve. He could discover the truth about our marriage if he starts digging."

Bryce shook his head. "First of all, we're legally married. It's legitimate, it's consummated, it's all the things. Our marriage is valid in the eyes of the law and by the terms of my trust—there's nothing he can do about it."

He patted my thigh. "Second, he won't find that I found you through AccommoDating. I have an airtight nondisclosure agreement. Elena cares about her business, and she has high-end, sometimes famous, clients all over the world. I'm not worried about the truth about our contract getting out. I'm more concerned that my father is spiraling and that he's going to blow our family up. And I'm not going down with the ship—neither is my company."

I nodded. "I know you won't let that happen."

Bryce was quiet as he navigated the golf cart across the lawn. "About what Olivia Jensen said. About you doing another interview, more press."

"Yes?"

He sighed. "If she thinks it will help, I guess you should do it. I hate to put you in that position, but we're doing all this for a reason. I have to throw everything I've got to keep my company healthy during this storm. My father isn't helping anything, so it's up to us."

I nodded, even though my heart was pounding in my chest. I didn't want to do any more interviews—in fact, if I never had to pose for a picture again, that would be fine with me. But the images on the internet didn't bother me as much as the taped interview. Hearing myself talk had been painful. I wasn't someone who had ever craved attention; presenting my science project in school had literally given me hives. Ugh. But as Bryce said, we were doing this for a reason. The whole point of us getting married in the first place had been to protect his stake in the company. His motive for asking me back was because of the scrutiny his family was under due to the investigation.

I was a tool. What he was asking me to do was part of my function. I just hated it and hated that he knew that and was still asking me to do it.

"Sure." I sounded calm, which masked the truth: I was hurt that he would put me in that position.

"Thank you for being so flexible." He squeezed my thigh. "I know I'm asking for a lot."

"It's fine," I said, even though I didn't feel fine.

When we went to bed, Bryce was still distracted. He pulled me against his chest, but he seemed far away as he stared at the ceiling.

"Are you okay?" I asked.

"I'm fine. I'm just thinking about the company and about my father."

"And?"

"I'm worried."

I snuggled against him. "I'm sorry."

"Thank you. You should get some rest, Chloe." He kissed the top of my head. "Big day tomorrow."

I didn't want to ask what that meant. It probably had something to do with an interview for another major news outlet, God help me. The whole idea—and the fact that Bryce had outright asked me to do it, even though he knew I was petrified—left a bad taste in my mouth.

I burrowed against his big muscles. "Good night."

"Good night."

There was no "l" word. There was no sex. Stress emanated from Bryce. As I lay there, I reminded myself to be understanding—he was in for the fight of his life. Because of the investigation, everything his family had worked for was vulnerable. Even if his father managed to avoid the charges, the company's forecast could suffer because of all the upheaval. The future of Windsor Enterprises hung in the balance, and the responsibility for that future lay largely with my husband.

Even as I was pressed against his chest, he felt far away from me, removed. No one would notice the shift except me, but I knew his focus had changed. Gone was the relaxed, happy Bryce who cracked terrible jokes and had a constant hard-on. Back was the focused, driven entrepreneur that let nothing interfere with his work. I loved them both—I loved *him*—but I vastly preferred relaxed and happy Bryce. Still, my job was supporting him in good times *and* bad. Wasn't that what our marriage vows said?

But I wondered as I drifted off toward sleep if Bryce could say he'd do the same for me.

TWENTY-FOUR
drama

WHEN I WOKE UP, I was alone. Bryce hadn't left a note, but I already knew where he was—down in the study, in his suit, up to his eyeballs in strategy. I'd slept fitfully, and every time I'd rolled over, I'd sensed that my husband was still awake. His mind must've been churning all night. No wonder he'd fled our bed for the office, and it wasn't yet six a.m. Bryce was a do-er; he wanted to make things happen. He wanted to save his world before it collapsed.

I sat in bed, letting my thoughts roam. Gene Windsor had been an absolute nightmare last night; no surprise there. The fact that he'd singled me out as a target for his wrath was awful. But there was nothing I could do about it. Bryce had been right to a certain extent: I shouldn't take it personally. Gene didn't even know me as a person. The fact that he hated me because of where I came from said way more about him than it did about me.

The thing that hurt—the thing I did *not* want to process—was that my husband said I should do more press. He knew how I felt about it. He knew I didn't want to put myself out there, to be under a microscope, to pretend I had something of genuine interest to say to the world. I was nineteen, about to turn twenty, and although that was young, it was also old enough to know better. Like Gene said, I wasn't truly a Windsor. I didn't have any right to speak for the family or to be showcased in any way. I was a fraud. I was a hired bride!

I couldn't help but wonder—and it made me hate myself for doing it—how Felicia Jones would handle the situation. With grace, most likely, and acumen. She was born to be in the public eye. She would be, as Gene Windsor might phrase it, an asset.

I was nothing of the sort. I was the opposite...a liability.

Groaning, I got up and grabbed my phone. *Oh, crap.* There were nine messages from Lydia, and three missed calls, all from the middle of the night. With shaking hands, I opened the messages.

We saw you on the tv. Who do u think you are?

Talking about your billionaire husband while your father and I live in this shit hole!

You outta be ashamed of yourself

I am going to fuck your shit up just like I told you

Watch your back you little bitch

Acting like u r something special

I know the truth about you

I am going to tell that husband that you're a no-good whore who turned her back on her family

Just like your mother. A fucking stuck-up bitch!

My blood was boiling by the time I put the phone down. Call me a bitch, tell me how I'm selfish, do what you like. But insult my *mother*? My dead mother, the only person in the world who ever looked out for Noah and me?

My father had been living with Lydia before my

parents were even divorced. Not that it was her job, but she *never* encouraged him to spend time with us or help out. When we'd occasionally stay with them, she treated us like we were a nuisance. And she was threatening to fuck *my* shit up? She was the one who needed to watch out, the leech-faced whore!

Boiling blood aside, and wondering whether it was technically possible to be leech-faced aside, I recognized that I had a problem. Lydia could and absolutely would come after me. She wanted money; she wanted all the money. I needed to deal with her before she got even more out of control.

I took a deep breath and dialed her number.

It went straight to voicemail. I didn't leave a message, I sent a text instead. *I'm sorry you're upset*, I wrote, even though that was a lie. I hoped Lydia would be so upset that she'd go die in a hole. *Please tell me how much more money you need. I'll see what I can do.* I hit "send," and the messages turned green, which I thought meant they hadn't been delivered yet. I still shut down my phone and sighed. She'd see them soon enough. And then she could ask for the sun and the moon, and I would have to give them to her.

I took a shower and trudged to my room to get dressed. I felt lost without Bryce by my side, disheartened by the texts from Lydia, and just generally down.

Maybe because yesterday had been such a high, I mused. All the sex, all the attention, the puppy, the pool, the fun dinner. Maybe I should remember next time not to fly so close to the sun. There was no good outcome: either I would get burned, or I would wilt as soon as the weather changed.

Midge wasn't in my room. She'd left me a note.

I'm helping out at the older Mr. Windsor's today, so I won't see you. I left an outfit on the bed. Please do Midge a favor and wear mascara like a good girl! Get breakfast, and then you have a meeting with Olivia Jensen at eight out on the patio.
See you tonight. I think you have another dinner?
Never fear—I'll find something sexy for you to wear!
xxoo
Midge

I eyed the outfit on the bed—linen shorts and a nice tank, nothing too fancy. I breathed a sigh of relief. It definitely wasn't a "going on national television" outfit. It appeared I was safe, at least for now. I took a shower, dressed, obediently put on mascara, and headed for the kitchen. After grabbing a yogurt parfait and an extra-large coffee from Chef, I headed to find Olivia Jensen.

Once again, Hazel sprung out at me from a shadowy

part of the hallway. "Gah!" I nearly spilled my coffee. "We've got to stop meeting like this!"

She didn't appear to get the joke. "Good morning, Mrs. Windsor." By the way she scowled, she didn't seem to think it was really all that good.

"G-Good morning. What's up? I was just on my way to meet Olivia Jensen."

"Yes, I heard." She pursed her lips. "Mr. Windsor wanted you to know that he'll be in meetings all day. He expects to see you this evening for dinner."

"Okay, thanks. Tell *him* I said thanks?" Why was he using his creepy maid as an intermediary? "Is there some reason he can't talk?"

"He's *very* busy. He wanted to make sure you got the message, so he asked me to find you." She straightened her shoulders and raised her chin. Being needed by her precious Mr. Windsor must make her feel proud. "And might I add something?"

"Sure, Hazel." I braced myself.

"He seemed under a lot of stress this morning. I would've expected that he'd be in a better mood, given the outing you had yesterday." Her tone sounded vaguely accusatory like I'd failed him in some way.

Did Hazel know that Bryce and I had literally had sex about a *thousand* times yesterday? And that I'd clung to him in our bed last night and fallen asleep in his arms? I hadn't failed him! I was absolutely doing my best. I was on my way to a meeting with stupid Olivia Jensen just to make him happy!

"We had a tough meeting with his father after the interview aired. I don't think he slept well," I explained.

Hazel hesitated. "May I...comment?"

I swallowed hard. "Sure...?"

"He needs your loyalty. Your support," she said. "Mr. Windsor has worked his entire life to grow his company. I can tell that his stress level's increasing. If whatever you're doing isn't helping enough, you might want to consider doing...more."

Give him a thousand-and-one orgasms instead of just a thousand? Go on national television and tell the world that not only is my husband the youngest and the best-looking billionaire in the world, but he's also the hottest in bed? And that he'd do a much better job running his company than his douche father?

I arched an eyebrow. "Like what?"

"Like whatever he asks of you. And everything that he doesn't. You need to read his mood, Mrs. Windsor. Help him when he cannot help himself." She bowed her head. "Good luck with your meeting." She clicked down the hall in her black maid's uniform, and I wanted to run in the opposite direction, screaming. What did Hazel want from me, anyway? She had more to say about my relationship with Bryce than anyone. Why did she make me feel like I *wasn't* giving him my best? Or maybe she thought my best wasn't good enough...

Sighing, I went out to the patio. Olivia Jensen looked impossibly pulled together for eight in the morning. She wore a form-fitting black jumpsuit, platform sandals, full makeup, and her hair was perfectly blown out. Maybe Midge was moonlighting and doing Olivia's hair and makeup instead of mine?

Her laptop was open, and she had yet another giant iced coffee in front of her. She smiled warmly as I joined her. "Boy am I glad to see you," she said. "I was worried you were going to run away after that scene last night!"

"Gene's tough, but I know that Bryce needs me right now. I'm here for him. I'll do whatever it takes to support him."

"I love it." Her smile widened. "And frankly, that's exactly what I was hoping you'd say."

"Oh." I nervously sipped my coffee. The run-in with Hazel had left me rattled; how Olivia looked at me wasn't helping. "What do you need?"

She turned her laptop around to face me. There was a picture of Mimi and Michael Jones on the screen, a shot from yesterday at the pool club. Mimi Jones looked down at us with disgust; Michael Jones looked pale as a ghost. Olivia clicked and showed me the following picture. It was of Felicia Jones in a bikini, basking in the sun on the deck of her boat.

My stomach twisted. "Why are you showing me this?"

"Because of this." She clicked to the picture published the day before—the one at the restaurant of Felicia Jones staring longingly at Bryce. "Guess which image and text got the most clicks in the past twenty-four hours? This one of Felicia. *'The honeymoon's over for ex-flame.'* People went bananas over it!"

"Okay." I licked my lips. "How is that helping Bryce save his company?"

"Because there's high engagement. Overall, the family is testing super well."

"The family's testing well because of the *family*—right? Not because of Felicia Jones." I hated even saying her name.

"It's not her per se," Olivia said. "It's because people love *drama*. Last night when the results came in after your interview, and *you* tested so well, I had an inkling this might be a hook. And when I got the report this morning about which link got the most hits? I *knew* we had a winning angle. People like you, Chloe."

Olivia looked straight into my eyes. "And they're already curious about Felicia. They're asking questions like, what does Chloe have that Felicia doesn't? How does an heiress feel about losing out to a girl from the wrong side of the tracks? Is Bryce still interested in his ex?"

I felt like I might throw up. Olivia must've sensed my discomfort because she patted my hand. "We both know that he's not. I can tell just by the way he looks at you! But that doesn't matter. What *matters* is getting the public invested in the Windsor family. Think about it like the royals—every article talks about their personal lives, their drama. But most of it's a lie."

"I don't like lying."

"And I'm not asking you to lie." Olivia squeezed my hand. "All I'm asking you to do is go along with my plan."

She looked like the cat who was about to swallow the canary.

I bit my lip, waiting—scratch that, *dreading*—to hear precisely what Olivia Jensen had in mind.

TWENTY-FIVE

extreme measures

I LICKED MY LIPS. "What's your plan, Olivia?"

"To work with what I've got." She looked thoughtful as she tapped her fingers against the table. "Like I said, I want the public foaming at the mouth for glimpses into your lives. I need to feed the machine. But in order to feed it, it's got to be hungry! And the Felecia-Jones angle will make it crave more. Is she really dating that guitar player? Is Chloe jealous of her? Is there some sort of revenge plot on either side?"

I swirled the remaining coffee in my cup. It had gone cold.

"This is low stakes, Chloe. Think about it. With celebrity love triangles, it's safe for the public to play judge *and* jury. The people clicking on these articles are in the cheap seats—they don't actually have any real stake in the outcome, so there's zero risk for them to be invested. In real life, being the other woman will get you a brick thrown through your window, or probably worse. On the internet, the bricks are nasty comments on social media. And anyone can throw them. People *love* this shit!"

"It doesn't have anything to do with the company, though." I frowned. Olivia wasn't convincing me that this was a good idea. "I don't think more drama looks good for the family."

"It doesn't matter if it looks good. It matters if it gets people *looking*. I need obsession, Chloe—Kardashian-level obsession. I promise that if I run these pictures of Mr. and Mrs. Jones looking angry, and then Felicia in her bikini, and I pitch some sort of copy, like...let me think..." Olivia drummed her fingers on the table for a moment. "Ooh, like this: *'Heiress ex-girlfriend wants him back bad'*—I guarantee the public will go bananas. *That* will drum up the interest I'm looking for. It will also get you invited onto the morning talk-show circuit. Everyone will tune in to see if you have something to say, some dirt to dish about Felicia Jones."

"No." I shook my head. This was literally my worst nightmare. *"No."*

"Chloe." Olivia Jensen closed her laptop. "What if I

told you that both Bryce and Gene Windsor approved this?"

I felt as though she'd slapped me. "Bryce wouldn't do that without talking to me first."

"Did he talk to you before you came here?"

"N-No."

She tilted her head. "Then he didn't talk to you first."

"I'm *not* saying yes to this until I talk to him."

"That's fair. But talk to him soon because I have work to do." Olivia pursed her plumped, glossy lips. "And Chloe, can I say something?"

I blinked at her. "It's not like you've been holding back so far."

"I'm actually a nice person, even though you'd never guess that." She sighed. "I'm also very good at my job—which is why an old grump like Gene Windsor would not only pay me an exorbitant fee but would also listen to me."

Her expression softened. "We aren't dealing with normal people. A *normal* husband wouldn't take his wife back—for show, mind you—after she slept with one of his friends, not to mention got pregnant doing it. And she's not even sorry. A normal guy wouldn't pay her to stay. Right? These aren't normal people in normal circumstances."

"Go on," I said, my voice gravelly.

"In *normal* life, in a *normal* situation, your husband wouldn't ask you to pose for pictures making out with him. He wouldn't be trying to garner public support, under the threat of federal charges, with the ultimate goal of saving his company. We aren't dealing with the familiar. This is the realm of the extreme. And you need to understand that the stakes are so high, these people are willing to take extreme measures to protect themselves. We might not agree with the methods, and some of what we have to do might make us uncomfortable, but at the end of the day, we all have roles to play. The question is, do you have the stomach for it—"

"No," I said immediately.

"You didn't let me finish my question, Chloe." Olivia took a deep breath. "Do you have the stomach for it *if* it means you're protecting the man you love?"

"I don't think selling a fake love triangle on the internet is protecting anybody."

"You're right—it's not." Olivia nodded. "But what it *is* doing is giving the public a chance to look into the lives of the rich and soon-to-be-famous. It's driving interest and obsession, which will only help you guys if Gene gets indicted and goes on trial. We don't want this to be a business story, Chloe, something only the financial outlets cover. They'll lose out if that's the case."

She sat back in her seat. "But if *you're* out there, and people like you—and so far, so good—that changes the narrative. It gives the Windsors a human, relatable element. People might choose to buy their stock just because they *like* the family. It's emotional, not rational. Think about it, and talk to your husband. I'll be in the guesthouse working today. Come and see me."

"Okay, Olivia." I didn't thank her for her time. I wasn't sure I *was* grateful for her time.

Olivia was obviously good at her job. Maybe she was also a nice person in her non-work life. But for me, this morning? She was a giant-sized pain in my ass.

At that moment, my phone pinged with a text from Akira Zhang. She complained that Lydia had texted her several times last night, sounding drunk and threatening. *Speaking of giant pains in the ass!* Karma had a sense of humor, I guess. At least someone did!

I'm dealing with it, I wrote back. *Talk soon.*

But I needed to deal with, and talk to, my husband first. I hustled to his office, nervous about disturbing him. But when I peered through his half-open door, I found him sitting at his desk, staring out the window.

"Bryce?"

He didn't seem surprised to see me. "Hey Chloe. Come on in. Did Hazel find you this morning?"

"Yes, I talked to her." It's not like she'd let her Mr. Windsor down!

"Sorry I sent her instead of touching base, but I had back-to-back calls."

"It's okay." I sat down across from him. It seemed strange, having his big desk between us. It made him seem foreign, like someone else—possibly a very hot principal who was about to give me a suspension or a boss who might fire me. But wait, technically, he *was* my boss...

"Did you just come from meeting with Olivia?" Again, he didn't sound surprised. He seemed as though he'd been expecting me.

"Yes. She wanted to talk to me about her proposed strategy."

He sat back in his chair. Bryce was handsome as ever in his zillion-dollar suit, his cufflinks winking in the morning sunlight. But he had dark circles under his eyes. I'd been correct—my husband hadn't slept much last night. "And what did you think?"

I blinked at him. "Do you know what she wants to do? The angle she wants to push?"

He frowned. "I'm pretty sure I do."

"About Felicia? She told you?" My voice rose. I didn't want to believe that Bryce had not only known about the proposed plan but that he'd sanctioned it.

"Don't get upset, Chloe. It's not like any of this is real. Olivia's run some tests, and she thinks this is a good hook."

I blinked at him again. "What, exactly, is a good hook?" I wanted to hear him say it.

He had the decency to look slightly uncomfortable. "The 'heiress wants him back' hook."

"And you're okay with that?"

"Of course not," he said quickly. "But they're moving forward with opening a formal investigation into my father's trades. If that happens—and it looks like it probably will—our stock could go into a free fall. I can't let that happen."

I scrunched my forehead. "None of this makes sense to me. Why would you think that pretending we're involved in some love triangle with Felicia Jones will help your company? It's a dumb idea! Why would we want to look like there's even more drama in our lives?"

He held up his hands. "I said the same thing to Olivia before she met with you. But she's done work like this before—she knows what she's doing, even if I hate it. She's convinced that because you tested so well with the public, this angle will drive support for you and, as an extension, for me."

"So you think this will help you. And *that* will help

your company." I didn't phrase it as a question because there was no point: I already knew the answer.

He blew out a deep breath. "I don't like it, Chloe, but I'm running out of time here. I think we have to try it."

"Even if I hate the idea?" I struggled to find my composure. Losing it wouldn't help me right now, and I needed all the help I could get.

"Even if you hate the idea," he said. "If it's any consolation, I hate it, too."

"I bet your father doesn't hate it."

He sighed. "It doesn't matter what he thinks. He's the one who got us into this mess. It's my job to get us out of it."

"I'm not happy that Felicia's involved."

Bryce nodded. "I'm not happy, either."

"I've been meaning to ask you something." My stomach tied itself into a knot. "I heard that she was here the day before I came back. Is that true?"

Bryce didn't hesitate. "Yes."

"Why? Why was she here?"

"Because I had to talk to her in person. I needed to tell her the deal my father asked her to consult on had fallen through," Bryce said.

"You couldn't do that in a phone call?"

"I could have. But it was business—the *end* of some business. She thought she'd be partnering with us on a venture, and it didn't work out. When something like that happens, and I have to tell someone news that's going to make them unhappy, I prefer to do it face-to-face. I think that's the decent way to handle it."

"Even though your wife wouldn't like it." I stuck out my chin. "You know I don't want her anywhere near you."

"You weren't on the island, and like I said, it was just business." Bryce looked straight at me: he didn't appear to be hiding anything. "I'm sorry I didn't tell you about it. I didn't even *think* of telling you—ever since you've been back, I've been...occupied."

"You should've told me. But...fine." A business meeting was a business meeting, right? Still, as I sat there, fidgeting, I started to feel a little sorry for myself.

"Now I need to ask *you* something. I'll be direct," Bryce said. "Will you help me do what Olivia's asking? Will you give this a try and help me to save my company?"

"Of course, I will." I didn't hesitate; my answer was automatic. How could I say no to him? Not only was he paying me millions, but I would do anything for him. Literally. Me saying yes to this was proof of that.

His shoulders relaxed. "Thank you. I'm sorry we have to do it, but it's not really a big deal. Right? It's just pictures on the internet. Olivia said she'll book you for some morning talk shows. It won't be that bad, right?"

"Right." I forced myself to smile at him, but inside, I was hurting. I didn't want to do this; he *knew* I didn't want to do it. And yet, he was still asking me to move forward in order to save Windsor Enterprises.

I knew how much my husband loved his company.

What I was no longer sure of was how much he loved *me*.

TWENTY-SIX

work with it

"WHAT IS this I hear about you going on a *talk show*?" Daphne called as she hustled across the lawn. Noah, Boss the puppy, and I were headed toward the private dock. My brother wanted to fish, and I wanted to get the heck away from everyone who wasn't my brother and his dog.

I was so upset about the conversation I'd had with Bryce that I couldn't even think about it. I hadn't begun to process what I'd agreed to and why. *Bryce says you should try it, and you'll do anything for Bryce,* the voice in my head reminded me. I wanted to tell her to shut up, but I was only talking to myself, which seemed crazy.

But I *felt* crazy. "I don't want to go on TV again," I told Daphne. "But I don't think I have a choice. Olivia wants the family to be more accessible or something. I have no idea what I'm supposed to talk about."

"They should've asked *me*." Although she hadn't been invited, Daphne joined us as we trekked to the dock. "I have *tons* of experience with interviews! If I'd known any of this would happen, I wouldn't have slept with stupid Michael Jones and gotten pregnant with his stupid baby!"

"*Daphne!*" I eyed my brother. "Can we talk about something else?"

"A talk show could *make* my smoothie empire." She absentmindedly rubbed her stomach. "I can't believe *you're* the one getting all the attention. It doesn't make any sense!"

Noah laughed, and I rolled my eyes. "Thanks a lot, Noah. And you too, Daphne. Jeez, tell me how you really feel!"

"Oh, it's nothing personal." She shrugged. "It's just that I know you don't want to do it, and I would *love* to do it. Life's funny that way sometimes, you know?"

"I guess." We headed out to the end of the pier. Noah insisted that Daphne and I sit with Boss in between us, so the puppy didn't try to jump in the water or otherwise get into trouble. We chatted about the baby and Daphne's plans for the nursery while Noah cast out. I glimpsed one of the paparazzi boats in the harbor, but it didn't come too close.

All in all, it was a pleasant way to pass a few hours. The sunlight dappled the water, and Boss's tongue lolled out as we scratched him behind his ears. Even Daphne thought he was cute. I was happy to be distracted by her self-centered chatter, which was something to focus on other than my conversations with both Olivia and Bryce. Oh yes, and the one I'd had with Hazel in the hallway. Of the three encounters, maybe the one with Hazel had been the best. Honestly, if that's what my life was coming to? *HELP!*

Noah measured each fish that he caught. He had to toss them all back. "It's a catch-and-release kind of day," he said, but he didn't seem disappointed as he packed up his things. With Boss's leash in one hand and his fishing pole in the other, my brother definitely seemed as though he was living his best life.

Eye on the ball, Chloe. The ball being my brother and the fact that I was here on this private island in order to help him. I sighed. It was working, wasn't it? It didn't matter if I had to do some things that made me uncomfortable. It didn't matter if I was about to be pitted in a tabloid battle against Felicia Fucking Jones. What mattered was *Noah.* What mattered was that he wouldn't ever have to eat a stale granola bar for dinner again. What mattered was that Lydia couldn't ever kick us out of her apartment again, leaving us scrambling to scrape up enough money to stay in a squalid motel room.

"Wow, these are great." Daphne stopped halfway across the lawn, suddenly engrossed in her phone. "I have to hand it to Olivia Jensen. She might be a pain in the ass, but she's a social-media genius."

"What're you looking at?" I peered over her shoulder as Noah went to put his fishing things away. "Oh my God!"

Daphne was on some gossip website. There was a picture of my brother tossing a ball to Boss. *Check out Chloe's adorable brother as he visits for vacation!*

"I *told* her my brother wasn't a storyline." I clenched my hands into fists. "I told her that!"

"Relax! He's not heavily featured, it's just that one pic."

"I know, but I don't want his picture online. *Ugh.* Like I said, I told her that."

"So tell her again." Daphne's brow furrowed as she scrolled through the pictures. "Ah, now they're getting good! Look at us at the club! Ooh, there's even a headline about Bryce buying the place!"

She showed me the images of us from the pool dais. Bryce had his arm possessively around me, even as he glared at his phone. I squinted, trying to avoid looking at myself in a bathing suit. Not that I thought I looked terrible, but it was just weird! I felt so exposed. Being on public display was sort of a nightmare.

Only a few months ago, I'd been Chloe Burke from East Boston—recently homeless, recently motherless, so desperate for money that I'd posted a listing on the skeevy *Sugar Finder* app. No one had known or cared who I was. And now I was all over the internet. In my bathing suit. In pictures where my husband was practically feeling me up.

My phone started buzzing. It was a 207-area code, which I didn't recognize. I sent it to voicemail. The phone immediately began ringing again, so I turned off the sound.

"I really don't even look pregnant yet, do I?" Daphne enlarged a picture of herself and intensely examined it. "But why is there only one picture of me?"

I squinted over her shoulder. "Maybe because there are so many of the boys." Indeed, Jake and Colby were heavily featured. It was no surprise—with their washboard abs and big smiles, revealing perfect, blinding-white teeth, they were definitely clickbait.

The headlines from the day were also quite clicky:

Bryce Buys Chloe Her Own Pool Club

Billionaire Brothers Live it Up

Colby Windsor Makes a New Friend—And it's So Cute

There was a picture of Colby talking to the older woman who'd been swimming laps in the pool. She was smiling from beneath her swim cap; he was laughing.

"I don't have a headline. I'm the only one who doesn't have a headline." Daphne frowned.

"But you look awesome in that picture," I offered. "And anyway, I'm pretty sure headlines are overrated."

"How would you know, huh? The press is already using just your first name. You're on a first-name basis with the public!" Daphne put her phone away. "Anyway, see you tonight? I heard we're going to a lobster bake at the Nguyen's."

"We are?" The last thing I wanted was to go out in public—or worse, a private party filled with Bryce's wealthy friends, possibly including the Jones family.

"We're doing whatever Olivia Jensen says, remember?" Daphne waved at me as she headed back across the vast lawn. "Anyway, I'm happy to go out. Gene won't leave the house, and I don't want to be stuck with him."

It was the one time she'd mentioned him, and although she didn't sound happy, she didn't sound mad. Maybe Daphne had made her peace with her unhappy marriage. Maybe all the money she was making made it worth it, I mused.

Maybe I should take a page from her playbook.

But that reminded me—I was supposed to go and see Olivia Jensen. I needed to be clear that I didn't want any more pictures of Noah going online. I also needed to tell her that I'd talked to Bryce and that he'd approved the Felicia-Jones angle. Hadn't she said she'd be working at the guesthouse? I headed in that direction, dreading telling her I'd go along with her plan. Because that meant I would have to go along with her plan...

It was quiet except for the crickets as I walked down the path to the guesthouse. I liked it out there, away from the main houses, away from the staff. It was peaceful. The guesthouse itself was a mini gray-stone mansion with ivy climbing its facade, a beautiful home in its own right. I knocked on the door and was surprised to see both Gene and Bryce inside, talking to Olivia. A staff member opened the door. "Mrs. Windsor."

"Hi there. I was here to see Olivia."

Hearing my voice, Bryce craned his neck in my direction. "I was just coming to find *you*."

"Oh. Is everything okay?"

"He's good. Just some business to catch you up on!"

Olivia smiled at me, then quickly maneuvered a particularly *unsmiling* Gene Windsor out the door. "I'll circle back with you later, okay, Chloe? Gene and I need to meet with legal ASAP. And I'm sure you saw the picture of Noah—I promise you, it's a one-and-done. We won't feature him again."

Gene looked as though he had something to say about all that, but Olivia dragged him away before he could comment.

I appreciated what she said and that she'd gotten Gene out of there, but I wondered what else was going on. I turned to Bryce. "What was that about?"

He scrubbed a hand over his face. "Our legal team talked to the SEC this morning. They plan to start issuing subpoenas. My father might be deposed as early as next week."

"I'm sorry. Are you worried?"

"I am." Bryce stalked through the room to the windows. He stared out, watching his father and Olivia cross the grounds to his house. "You know I'm not exactly my father's biggest fan."

I sighed and sank down onto the couch. "That doesn't mean you want him to suffer."

"No, it doesn't." Bryce turned to me, a funny expression on his face. "I'm surprised, though. I thought I'd be more relieved when his ego finally caught up to him. I didn't expect to feel sorry for him."

"He's still your father." I thought about my own dad. I didn't feel any warmth toward him, but I still wouldn't wish him any harm.

"Have you heard anything from yours?" Bryce asked.

"No." That was technically the truth. I didn't want to tell him about the messages from Lydia. Bryce had enough going on with *his* family—he didn't need to hear about mine. "And I'm not going to lie, I don't miss him."

"That's fair." Bryce came and sank down onto the couch.

"Are you okay?"

"I'm fine." He looked at his hands. "I'm feeling conflicted about everything that's going on. But I *also* feel like things have already been set in motion and that there's nothing more I can do now. I just have to move forward. Whatever's going to happen is going to happen."

I nodded. "It'll all work out in the end." I hoped.

Bryce leaned back against the couch, and despite my better judgment, I moved closer to him. I pressed my face against his chest and curled up beside him.

He trailed his hand down my back. "I'm sorry that I'm so stressed. We've been having fun, but now I feel like this is all spiraling, and it happened like that." He snapped his fingers.

"It's happening fast," I agreed.

"If my father's deposed, it could turn into a nightmare. I wouldn't be surprised if his counsel advises him to take the fifth amendment and not answer any questions."

"Why would he do that?"

"So that he doesn't implicate himself any further. But the problem is, it looks bad to plead the fifth. So our shareholders aren't going to love that approach." He pulled me closer. "*Fuck.* I just feel like this is going to spin out of control, get away from me. I can't let that happen."

"You won't." I ran my fingers across his chest. "You're giving this everything you've got. You've hired the best lawyers, the best PR person, and you're doing everything that the board's asked. Your brothers are here, too. Everyone is doing their part. It's going to be okay, okay?"

He kissed the top of my head. "When you say that, I almost believe you."

"You should." What was it Hazel had said? *If whatever you're doing isn't helping enough, you might want to consider doing...more.*

Probably listening to Old Hazel's advice wasn't the

best approach. Still, she'd worked for the Windsors since Bryce was a baby. She knew him well.

"Do you need to de-stress?" I asked.

He scoffed. "Of *course* I do." Then a knowing look settled over his features. "Why're you asking me that?"

I tossed my hair over my shoulder. "Maybe I can help." *Maybe when I see the upcoming headlines about Felicia Jones, I can look back on this moment and feel a tiny bit better.*

What I was doing was manipulative—to myself, and probably to Bryce—and I knew it. Sex wasn't love. But if my husband wanted me, if I could take him and make him forget about everything else for a little while, it was *something*. It was what I had to work with.

"Is there a bedroom in the guesthouse?" I asked innocently.

"Of course there is. Let me show you," Bryce growled.

He got up, and I followed him into the bedroom, knowing full well that my question had not been innocent at all.

TWENTY-SEVEN

the guesthouse

I'D NEVER BEEN in any of the bedrooms at the guesthouse before. The one Bryce had brought me to had to be the primary suite. It was sumptuous, with floor-to-ceiling windows with a private, unobstructed view of the water. The bed was enormous and simple, set in the middle of the room facing the ocean. A deep-maroon tapestry adorned the wall behind it, giving the room a luxurious, rich vibe.

Bryce locked the door behind us, and I raised my eyebrows. "There's staff in the kitchen. Olivia Jensen's been staying here in the guest room, which I'm none too happy about."

"Why do you care?" I asked, my curiosity rising.

Bryce started to undo his tie. "I've been wanting to ask you to come down here with me."

My heart rate kicked up. "Oh? Why's that?"

"Because I thought this could be a place where we could get away from everyone. The staff, my work, appointments..." He stalked over to the closet and hung up his jacket. "I actually began preparing this room after you left. I thought if I could ever get you back up here, this could be a place where we could...play."

My legs turned to jelly. "Play what?"

"Whatever we want." His voice was full of promise. The promise only my husband could fulfill of pure, unadulterated pleasure.

He slid his tie off, undid his cufflinks, and watched me. "I want you to get undressed, Chloe. Then get onto the bed, on your knees."

"Yes, Sir."

When I said his pet name, his eyes sparkled. "You haven't called me that in a while."

"I haven't had a chance to."

"Fair enough, Chloe. Now no more talking. Do as I say." He disappeared into the bathroom.

Heart pounding, I quickly stripped out of my clothes. Thank goodness Midge made me live in sexy g-strings every day! Today I wore a white, skimpy lace bra and matching thin-strapped underwear. I hadn't even really looked at it when I'd gotten dressed that morning, but as I glimpsed myself in the mirror, I was pleased to see that it was sexy. I shook my hair out, my loose waves tumbling over my shoulder, and then got into position on the bed.

Why did he want me on my knees? What did he want to play? What did Bryce mean when he'd said he'd been "preparing" the room?

I got wet, so wet, waiting for him. Wondering what he had planned.

When he came out of the bathroom, he was naked. His cock, enormous and proud, was completely erect. It jutted out at me, bobbing as he walked. I stared at it, transfixed. My gaze wandered over the rest of his glorious body, all hard, bulging muscle. By the time he reached the edge of the bed, I was a quivering mess. I wanted him, and I wanted him bad.

Bryce smiled at me, smug as fuck. "What're you looking at, Chloe?"

My gaze trailed back down to his cock. It had a bead of moisture at its tip. I licked my lips. "Nothing."

His grin widened. "Liar. You know what happens to liars, don't you, Chloe."

I nodded, eyes wide. He would probably spank me for lying. And then fuck me senseless.

Yes, please!

He stalked over to the nightstand and pulled out a pair of padded handcuffs. Then he eyed me possessively, making my nipples stand at attention. "I'd like to put these on your wrists and bind them tightly. And then I'd like to have my way with you. Do you agree?"

I nodded. Bryce couldn't control much in his life at the moment, but he could control what happened in our bed. He could control my pleasure; he could master my body and make me come as soon as he called. I longed to give myself over to him. He was the master. *My* master. And even though I'd just counseled myself against flying too close to the sun, I was powerless to resist him.

He'd bought me. I was already his on paper. But the truth was that he owned me in a way that had nothing to do with our contract, binding though it was. I was *his*. Of course I would give myself to him, give until there was nothing left to take.

Bryce came at me, his rock-hard cock pointing straight up in the air, then surprised me by climbing onto the bed behind me. He took my arms and drew them back, then placed the cuffs around my wrists. He fastened them tighter than the last time we'd used a pair; for some reason, that made my heart race. He meant business!

With my hands securely fastened behind me, I was powerless.

"Are you ready to begin?" Bryce asked, still behind me.

"Yes." My voice was hoarse.

He sidled up behind me, his thick erection pressing against my ass, brushing against my cuffed hands. I longed to touch him, but I was bound. Bryce moved my hair to one side and kissed my neck, his breath hot and urgent. He trailed his fingers down my sides, making my skin light up. His kisses became more insistent, and I moaned as I moved against him; my g-string rubbed against my wetness as I massaged my thighs together, trying to gather as much friction as possible. Time stopped, and the world slipped away as Bryce undid my bra and threw it to the side. He grabbed my breasts from behind, kneading them as he devoured my neck and rubbed his cock between my ass cheeks.

Unf. I was lost in him, following the rhythm of his lead, already delirious from his touch. The fact that I was restrained meant that I couldn't reach for him, touch him, or take control; I loved it. I was under his spell. Bryce was in charge. He was going to take what he wanted, and I was lucky enough to be able to give it to him.

He pushed on my shoulders, pressing my face and upper torso down toward the bed. My ass was up in the air; my hands were in the cuffs, bound behind my back. Bryce nudged my knees apart.

"I like this view." In one swift motion, Bryce tore my thong off. "I like it even better now."

I felt so exposed. My sex was already wet, ready for him. He positioned himself behind me, and then suddenly, I felt his mouth on me, tonguing my slit from end to end. "Bryce...?" I wasn't sure what I was asking. He started to lap me, relentlessly stroking me with his tongue. All the while, he was massaging my ass, spreading me open more, making me *his*. His hands came closer to the apex, fingers skimming the tight bud between my cheeks.

I stiffened beneath his touch, unsure of where he was going with this.

"Relax for me, babe," he said, his face still buried between my legs. "That's an order. I'm going to own your ass by the end of this."

I took a deep breath and exhaled. He gently stuck one finger inside me and began to lap at my sex again. *Oh my god.* Bryce had never touched me there before; it felt foreign and slightly uncomfortable. But the more I relaxed—not to mention the more he tongued my clit—the sensation started to shift to something more pleasurable. Mmm, the pressure began to feel amazing as he picked up the pace. His face in between my legs, his finger inside me, gently exploring the tight space with small, insistent thrusts. *Fuck.* What was he doing to me? My hips started to buck as he increased the pressure on my sex and inside me, making me wild. "Bryce...Bryce..."

Before I could find my release, he took his mouth away. "No!"

"Don't say no to me, Chloe. I told you—I'm in charge."

With his finger still stroking me, he notched an inch of his thick cock inside my pussy. The simultaneous pressure drove me wild. With my face pressed into the bed, my hands bound behind me, and Bryce penetrating me in two different ways, I was at his mercy.

He thrust into me, taking his time. I was so close, on edge. I heard myself begging, pleading. Bryce grunted, pulsing inch after thick inch inside me. "Oh fuck, Chloe. You're so fucking tight. And you're mine. I. Fucking. Own. You." He thrust all the way in, filling me, and I cried out.

He drove hard. Deep. He stuck another finger inside me, and in time with his thrusts, he stroked my ass. *Oh my God.* I was so full of him, I saw stars. The pressure built inside me. Bryce slammed into me, my hands bouncing against my back as I took him in, helpless to resist. My clit rubbed against the bed. All of the sensations overwhelmed me. Bryce was everywhere. Bryce was everything. I heard myself curse, scream, and laugh as I came.

"Oh fuck—I wasn't going to let you do that yet. I lost control again. Why do you do that to me, babe?" He picked up the pace, punishing me, savagely penetrating me, although he was still gentle with his fingers. It didn't matter. The pressure built inside me again, and I was flying, singing, the whole world going white. I made him lose control. He couldn't keep his hands off of or outside of me. *Me. Him.* We were together; we were part of each other. He was inside me every which way, and I fucking loved it. I loved him. His thrusts became ragged, and he came in a torrent, cursing while palming my hip, his face against my back, his laughter against my skin.

We collapsed against each other, and Bryce eventually took off the cuffs. I didn't care; I couldn't move.

Bryce Windsor not only owned my ass, he owned all of me.

And there was nothing I could do about it.

TWENTY-EIGHT

closing in

LATER—HOW much later, I wasn't sure—Bryce nudged me awake. "We have to get going. We're supposed to be at the Nguyen's for cocktails and dinner. We need to get ready."

"Huh? Hi." I peered up at him, a dopey smile on my face. "You're already dressed?"

"It's almost six o'clock, Chloe. Of course I'm dressed." His voice bordered on cold.

"Oh...okay." Gone was the playful Bryce of a few hours ago, the one who'd made me see stars.

"You should go online and see what Olivia released this afternoon. You need to be aware of the direction this is going." That was all he said, no further explanation, no emotion. Bryce tapped out a message on his phone, then read something. "I'll see you on the boat, okay? I need to take a call."

"Okay...?" My voice trailed off as he left the room, cellphone already glued to his ear. I quickly got dressed, wincing as I pulled my shorts up. Not only did I have to briefly go commando, courtesy of Bryce tearing off my underwear, but I was already sore. I shivered. What we'd done that afternoon had made my limbs loose; the soreness I felt was almost pleasant, a physical reminder of our encounter. I just wished that Bryce was still with me and that he wasn't stressed to the point of distraction, stressed to the point of being distant.

I needed to check in and see what Olivia had sent out. I picked up my phone and scrolled through some of the gossip sites.

Putting the "Ex" into "Sex"

Felicia Strikes Back

From Humble Beginnings, Chloe Fends Off Heiress

Um...what the *hell*? She'd told me the angle, but I wasn't really prepared to be jarred by the impact so soon. I knew it was "just the internet." But... It was also my life.

And Bryce had been so removed about it like it was just business as usual. What was it Olivia had said? *These people are willing to go to extreme measures to protect themselves. We might not agree with the methods, and some of what we have to do might make us uncomfortable, but at the end of the day, we all have roles to play.*

My role as Bryce's wife was one I desperately wanted. But this other function, this facade? I had a feeling it was going to break me.

I scrolled through the stories. The first was the worst, and the title said it all. There was picture after sexy picture of Felicia—in her bikini, lounging on her yacht, in a slinky dress at some sort of gala, walking on the beach with a guy loaded with tattoos. The caption said he was Finn Ryder, guitarist for a wildly popular band. The "article" was light on details, merely stating that Felicia Jones, American heiress, was in fabulous shape and had told a UK magazine four years ago that she worked out every day and greatly enjoyed the outdoors. It also said that she'd been linked to Finn a year ago but that they hadn't been seen in public together recently.

The "Felicia Strikes Back" piece showed another picture of her in her bikini; a shot of her from the restaurant the other night, staring at Bryce's retreating back; and a candid shot of Felicia smiling, talking away on her cellphone. The implication was, of course, that she was talking to Bryce. The article didn't come out and say it. All it *did* say was that Felicia Jones was summering in MDI with her family and that she'd crossed paths with Bryce and Chloe Windsor several times. A "local source" was quoted: "Everyone knows she wants him back." That was it. That was practically the whole story.

It still made me want to throw up.

The final article was centered around me. The first picture was of Constitution Beach in East Boston. Rather, it was of an overflowing trash can at Constitution Beach. The following image was of me, standing on the remote, pristine beach in front of Bryce's mansion. I didn't even know when it had been taken. The caption read: *What a difference a year makes!* The article went on to say that I'd grown up in a working-class area of Boston. It described my marriage to Bryce as a "Cinderella story" and then showed a picture of us embracing. Next, there was a picture of Felicia Jones scowling at who-knows-what. "Can Chloe compete?" asked the article.

Can Chloe compete, indeed? Maybe the better question was whether Chloe had the stomach for all of this. Or: was Chloe going to implode and run away, screaming?

Disgusted, I went to shut off my phone—or possibly

go throw it in the ocean—when I saw I had several missed calls and a couple of voicemails. I scrolled through the call list. They were all from the same number, the 207 area code I'd seen earlier. I listened to the messages.

"It's Lydia." She sounded as though she was blowing out cigarette smoke. "You better call me back, or you're gonna be *very* sorry."

The next one was even worse. "Me again. I guess you're blowing me off, huh? Your father and I saw Noah in those pictures. Shame on you for using your brother like that! We are going to file a claim to get him back. We never should've trusted you with him! You better call me back, Miss Thing. And use this number! My phone got shut off, thanks to you!"

With shaking hands, I googled the phone number. The search pulled up an image of a familiar-looking motel. *Northeast Nights Inn & Cabins.* It was a run-down establishment located in Northeast Harbor, near the dock.

No. No fucking way.

I sank down onto the bed, feeling the walls closing in on me.

⌁

I didn't call Lydia back right away. I didn't know *what* to do, so I went and got dressed. Bryce wouldn't be happy if I missed the boat to the Nguyen's. Bryce wasn't happy anyway, even though I'd followed Hazels' advice and given to him and then given him some more.

What did my husband want from me, anyway? Besides everything?

Midge was waiting for me in the bedroom. "Oh my God, you're late! And your *hair*! And the internet! I might need a glass of wine to deal with all of this!"

"Please have one." I threw myself into the makeup chair. "I don't drink, but I totally understand. I'm facing off against Felicia Jones online—heiress versus peasant. Please, have wine. Have all the wine."

"I can wait." She eyed my hair. "I need to be sober to straighten *that* out. What happened to you, anyway?" She started to detangle it.

"You know." I shrugged.

"Your husband?" She grinned.

"Yes. My husband." But I couldn't force a smile.

"What's the matter, hon? This hair didn't get *that* messed up from nothing. Did he hurt your feelings or something?"

I sighed. "I don't know. My feelings are definitely hurt, but I don't know if it's his fault. I think it might be my own fault."

"What do you mean?" She finished detangling and started flat-ironing.

"Well, you saw the stories online. I agreed to that—they're not true or anything."

"Of course they're not!" Midge snorted. "They weren't even articles. It's just a bunch of strung-together pictures, conjecture, and one stupid quote from an anonymous source—probably not even someone real. It's not even a story. There's no reporting. It's all BS."

"Thank you, that makes me feel better." Still, tears pricked my eyes. "But the thing is, Midge? I don't actually feel any better. I'm going along with this because I have to, but I hate it. I hate Felicia Jones, I hate having my picture on the internet, I hate that they're making me go on some stupid morning talk show. I'm going to look like an idiot. Felicia Jones would probably charm the pants off of everyone and look good doing it. B-But I'm not her, you know? It's true what they said about me. I'm from nothing. I'm no one."

"Aw honey. That's not true." Midge put the flat iron down and hugged me, careful not to muss my hair. "Just because you weren't born into money doesn't make you nothing. You're important. You matter. You matter to me, you matter to the rest of the staff, you matter to your brother. You matter to your husband."

"Do I?" I blinked back the tears. "He wants me to do this. He told Olivia it was o-okay."

Midge sighed and started doing my hair again. "I'm not saying it's okay, him asking you to do any of this. But he's under a *lot* of pressure. Their company's worth billions of dollars, Chloe. He's responsible for a lot of people, people with families. If the business goes under, it will hurt a lot of people, you know? I can't imagine what that's like, that kind of responsibility."

I nodded. "You're right. I didn't think about that, all the employees who work for them. I was just thinking about myself."

"And that's okay." Her voice was sympathetic, soothing. "Your job *is* to worry about yourself. You have to do that. But you know what I think?"

"What?"

"I think you should tell him how you feel. Give him a chance to hear you out, you know? I bet he doesn't want you to be uncomfortable. If you talk to him, he'll listen."

"I already did."

Midge nodded, smoothing the remaining locks of my hair. "Did you say no? Did you say all this crosses a line for you?"

"No, I didn't." I sighed. "I don't feel like 'no' is an option."

"Just talk to him, Chloe," she counseled. "People aren't usually as bad as we think."

Midge stuffed me into a *very* sexy, formfitting, spaghetti-strapped black dress and a pair of heels. "No argument on the heels," she ordered. "That ass needs to look good tonight."

"I thought the Nguyen's were having a lobster bake," I moaned. "Why do I need to look like I'm going to a club?"

"Olivia Jensen sent me a note—she said sex it up." Midge's brow furrowed as she adjusted the straps of the dress, ensuring that my chest was on perfect display. "There you go."

"Thanks." But I was worried about why Olivia wanted me to look so sexy. "Any idea who's on the guest list?"

"No, hon." Midge winked at me. "But I *do* know that nobody's going to look better than you. So try and have some fun, okay?"

"Okay. I will."

With one final smoothing of my hair, she sent me out the door. My phone buzzed—it was that 207-number again. *Fuck!* "Lydia?" I didn't wait for her to answer. "I can't talk to you right now. I know what you want. I promise I'll take care of you. But I have to go, all right? I'm late."

"Don't you dare hang up on me!"

I stopped and leaned up against the wall for support. "What do you want from me, huh?"

"I already told you. You didn't listen." Lydia coughed —a phlegmy, congested sound. "I want more money, and I want it *tonight*. If I don't get it, you're going to be one sorry little bitch. Do you hear me? We're stayin' at a motel near the dock. Find a way to get over here, or you'll be sorry. Call me at this number—our phones got cut off, thanks to you."

I wasn't sure how I was responsible for their phones being shut off. I *also* wasn't sure how they'd made the five-hour trip up to MDI; Lydia's vehicle was an old, rusted-out truck that leaked. "I don't think I can get over there until tomorrow, Lydia. I have to take a boat, and we're going to dinner tonight. I can't get out of it."

"Poor you, huh?" She exhaled deeply, and I pictured a cloud of smoke.

"I'm not complaining—I'm just saying I don't think I can come over there tonight. I have to get someone to take me over on the boat. I can't just drive over to you, okay? I'm not trying to be difficult."

"You don't have to try." Her voice was nasty.

"Can I talk to Dad?" I asked, my voice small. "Please?"

"Whatever." She sighed. "She wants to talk to you."

I heard my father mutter a curse, then he got on the line. "Hello, Chloe."

"Hey Dad." I wished, not for the first time, that we had a better relationship. "I know Lydia's mad—"

"I can't believe you'd put pictures of your brother on the internet like that." He actually sounded *upset*.

"I didn't. The photographers are taking pictures all the time without us even knowing about it! Then they're selling them. I would never do that to Noah—you know that."

"I don't know anything." He sounded a little baffled. "I don't know how you got mixed up with these people, and I don't know how you got your brother dragged into it."

"*Dad.* You're the one that took the money. You said you were fine with it—"

"I didn't know what was going to happen," he interrupted. "I feel misled. Like I agreed to something where I didn't understand... What was that again, Lydia? What didn't I understand?"

"The *material terms*," she hiss-whispered. "That's what the lawyer said!"

"I have to go, Dad. I'll get a ride over tomorrow and

give you some more money." My voice was flat. I felt dead inside. Lydia and my dad were consulting with lawyers, trying to fight me for Noah. Or more likely, trying to fight me for more money to let me keep Noah. "Bye, Dad."

"Bye."

Hands shaking, I hung up. *It's only money*, I told myself. It didn't mean anything.

But of course, that wasn't the reason I found myself blinking back tears once again.

TWENTY-NINE

belief system

BRYCE DIDN'T SAY much on the boat ride to Spruce Island, where the Nguyen's had a gorgeous estate. He kept firing off emails, scowling at his phone. Daphne filled the silence with her endless chatter, talking about the jumpsuit she was wearing, wondering whether she could ever wear it again or if she'd be too pregnant and have to donate it. Jake and Colby were meeting us at the party. The paparazzi, both authorized and unauthorized, followed us by boat, but we'd hidden below deck. Olivia Jensen might be mad about that, but an evening chill had settled in, making it too cool to ride outside.

Besides, Bryce didn't seem to want to manhandle me for the cameras tonight. He didn't even seem to register that I was sitting beside him.

I pretended to listen to Daphne, smiling and

nodding in all the right places, but I was distracted by my husband. More precisely, I was distracted by how distracted *he* was. He'd barely noticed my dress, which was sexy to the point of being ostentatious. Under normal circumstances, he'd either be pawing me or telling me to hide behind him, so no one else saw my outfit—or both. But there was no reaction from him, no connection.

It was as though our afternoon at the guesthouse had never happened. Had he really had me in handcuffs only hours before, my face planted into the bed as he rode me? I'd come so hard I'd seen stars. He'd exploded inside of me, calling my name... And now he acted as if I wasn't even there.

What. The. Fuck? Bryce was once again giving me emotional whiplash. The problem was that I might be too raw to be able to handle it this time. The pictures of Felicia online, the "spin" Olivia Jensen was putting on the whole thing, coupled with the fact that my father and Lydia had somehow dragged their sorry asses all the way to upstate Maine and had been talking to a lawyer about fighting me for Noah...

"Chloe," Daphne was saying, "are you even listening to me? We're here. Let's go!" She flicked her ponytail over her shoulder and smoothed her jumpsuit. Daphne looked very pretty, her eyes sparkling with tasteful

271

makeup, her lip gloss perfect. I wondered if she was shopping for a new baby daddy or perhaps Husband Number Two. Thinking about it made me feel tired.

"I'm listening—sorry, I spaced out for a second." I forced a smile. "Bryce? Are you ready to go?"

He frowned and put his phone away. "Do I have a choice? I don't feel like socializing tonight."

"Me either." I smiled at him, too, trying to show solidarity.

He didn't smile back, but he held out his arm. "Shall we?"

"Ooh, I'll take your arm, too. This'll look good for the pictures!" Daphne went to Bryce's other side. He grimaced, but he had the decency to let her hold on. Shaking off his pregnant mother-in-law was probably not a good look for the cameras.

Security went first, and we followed. As we exited the boat and started up the dock, it hit me. Daphne was excited and looking her best because of the paparazzi. The only reason Bryce was here, despite his crappy mood, was the same. Both of them wanted something from the exchange—some sort of advantage. They were both working the program.

Again, I was an accessory. I felt like a belt or some sort of handbag. Something to be posed with, flaunted, shown at a good angle in order to sell something. And I would be fine with it—I would do it gladly—if Bryce didn't seem so distant. Fear and insecurity crept up, making me feel crazy. *When was the last time he told me he loved me?*

He hadn't said it that afternoon. He'd just said that he *owned* me. And I'd been desperate to get him into bed, to get close to him because I wanted to feel connected. Having his big dick and his fingers inside me had been a connection, all right. And although I'd enjoyed it, it wasn't what I'd been looking for.

"All clear, Mr. Windsor." The head security guard came back after inspecting the party. "The paps are still out there on the water. I've already been in touch with the police, they're keeping an eye on things."

"Thank you." We reached the end of the dock, crossing under an awning of greens and twinkle lights. Kelli Nguyen had outdone herself again. Her backyard was lit with fairy lights; an enormous table faced the ocean, set with a white tablecloth and gorgeous, colorful pottery place settings.

Daphne leaned across Bryce's chest to talk to me. "Oh wow, she decorated with all the locals' work. You see those dishes? There's a potter in Northeast Harbor, she made those. And see the vases filled with sea glass?" She pointed to the table, where there were massive vases filled with colorful pieces of sea glass and bursting with flowers from Kellis' garden. "An artist in Southwest collects it and makes those arrangements. Isn't it stunning?"

"It is." Under normal circumstances, I would be charmed, or at least overwhelmed, by Kelli's decorations. But at the moment, I couldn't care less.

Because at the moment, Felicia Jones was staring at Bryce from across the party.

Bryce pretended not to notice. I stared at Felicia, taking in her black dress, shiny hair, and annoyingly gorgeous face. As usual, she didn't seem to register that I was standing there: she only had eyes for my husband.

I clenched my fists, ready to scratch those eyes right out.

"Oh boy. This is going to be a long night." Daphne disengaged from Bryce. "Do you want me to get you a drink, Bryce?"

His face showed no emotion. "Might as well."

"Chloe?"

"I'm fine, thanks."

I forced myself to look away from Felicia. The tabloids might love it if I launched myself at her, but I refused to give in to the temptation. She'd been after my husband all summer. If Bryce could ignore her, so could I. She acted as though I didn't exist—I should give her a taste of her own medicine. I didn't want to give her the satisfaction of knowing she'd gotten under my skin. *Screw her!*

Instead, I watched as Daphne strode across the party, all eyes on her. She seemed to light up from the attention, the fact everyone was talking about our family, and the whispers about her pregnancy and the state of her marriage. Daphne blossomed under these circumstances. She passed by Mimi and Michael Jones, her nose stuck in the air. Mimi Jones's face puckered with either hate, pain, or a combination of both. Michael Jones chugged his drink and looked anywhere but at Daphne or his wife.

"Why are they here, huh?" I asked. "And why is Felicia staring at us? Doesn't she have anything better to do?" Like go have hot sex with that famous guitarist, or better yet, go die in a hole?

Bryce took a deep breath. He looked uncharacteristically uncomfortable.

"What is it?" What's the matter?"

A long, heavy silence stretched out between us.

"Bryce? You're kind of freaking me out."

He was just about to speak when Daphne swept back and delivered his bourbon. "Enjoy! I'm off to mingle."

My husband clutched his drink and had a large sip.

"*What* is going on?" But at that moment, Kelli

Nguyen joined us. She looked fantastic as usual, with her long, tawny-colored hair loose over her shoulders and a sage-colored dress that skimmed her toned figure.

"Hi guys." She hugged Bryce, then me. "I'm glad you finally showed up."

"You've outdone yourself, Kelli," Bryce said quickly. "The place looks great."

She arched an eyebrow. "Well, since your people did it, you shouldn't sound so surprised."

An awkward silence settled over our group. I glanced at Bryce. He wasn't looking at anything in particular, and he definitely wasn't looking at me.

Kelli seemed confused by his reaction, so she turned to me. "How are you holding up, Chloe? I'm sure it's been a bit of a circus."

I nodded. "It has been, but I'm...fine."

"Fine?" She arched an eyebrow. "As in Feeling Insecure, Neurotic and Emotional?"

When I blinked at her, she laughed. "You've never heard that one before? Ah, I guess you're too young to have been in as much therapy as the rest of us. Do you want to come and try the appetizers? There's a sushi roll with local crab and seaweed—to *die* for. C'mon." Kelli put her arm around me and gently led me away from Bryce.

"Wait..."

But Bryce nodded, indicating I should go with Kelli. He drank more of his bourbon, almost draining it in one gulp.

"He's having a hard time, huh?" Kelli maneuvered me through the well-dressed crowd, who were all staring at me, Bryce, or Felicia, while pretending not to.

I shrugged. "He is, but he's not the only one."

Kelli nodded. "You're feeling like he's not supporting you. Am I right?"

"Sort of. I'm feeling like he's... Oh, I don't know." But the truth was, I absolutely knew how I was feeling. It just wasn't anything I could voice to Kelli Nguyen. *I feel like he's putting up walls. I feel like he's pushing me away. I feel used.* Not long ago, he'd fired me and sent me back to Boston. I needed to remember that he was all too capable of hurting me just like that again.

Why was he being so cold to me? What had I done?

I was prepared to give him everything, and he seemed more than willing to take it. But what if it was just a black hole, a vacuum? What if he took my love and never did anything with it—like return it or appreciate it?

"What did you say to him, back there?" I asked Kelli, shifting gears. "About his people decorating for the party?"

"I thought you knew. Me and my big mouth," Kelli sighed. "Gene Windsor reached out to me and asked me to throw this party. He donated a million dollars to my foundation so I'd say yes."

I almost spit out my crab roll, even though it was delicious. "He paid you a million dollars to throw a *lobster bake?*"

She shrugged. "I work in Hollywood. Let me tell you, this sort of thing is more common than you might think."

"But...why?" I shook my head. "Maybe I just don't understand people who are that wealthy. No offense."

"None taken. Billionaires are a different breed, that's for sure." She raised her hands. "I've seen it all. Like I said—I work in Hollywood. There's so much bullshit I need to bring a shovel to work every day. That's why I like you, Chloe. You're not jaded yet."

I sighed. "I think I might be getting there."

"Not just yet, kid." Kelli shook her head. "And as for why Gene donated a million dollars to have this party? It's because he's trying to save his company. Olivia Jensen has them all believing that a PR campaign is going to impact the possible charges against him. She believes the court of public opinion is what matters. I hope she's right—otherwise, things don't look good for the company. Gene's throwing everything he's got at this. And what he's got is money and influence."

She stopped talking and furrowed her brow, watching the party. I followed her gaze. Felicia Jones was crossing the lawn, heading straight for Bryce. "Stay here, Chloe." Kelli gently put her arm out to hold me back. "I have a feeling this is something that needs to happen."

"Oh God." I watched in horror as Felicia reached my husband. All eyes were on them. If only the earth would open up beneath me so that I could go die in a hole myself and not have to witness this...

The heiress wore a black tank dress with a huge slit up the side, showcasing the lightly tanned skin of her long, toned legs. Her glossy black hair was swept over one shoulder, and of course, Bitchface's makeup was perfect. I might hate her slightly less if she'd ruined her good looks with too much facial filler. Unfortunately, she appeared totally, naturally gorgeous.

She looked up at Bryce from beneath her lashes, a smile curving her lips.

"She really *is* a bitch, isn't she?" Kelli marveled. "I mean, *come on*. She just doesn't quit!"

It was a good thing Kelli was holding me back. Felicia smiling at my husband made my blood boil! But just when I thought things couldn't get any worse, just when I thought I'd hit my limit, there was a *new* all-time low.

Bryce smiled back at her, his eyes raking over her dress.

And in that moment, I was certain he had never loved me at all.

decoy

KELLI GLANCED AT ME, but there was nothing to see: I felt numb inside. My features were likely slack. I stuffed another crab roll into my mouth, chewing and swallowing without ever tasting it. I watched as Bryce and Felicia talked for a minute. There was a lot of mutual smiling. She continued to gaze up at him from beneath her lashes, which I decided then and there was a troll move if I'd ever seen one.

Finally, Felicia left to join her brother and another friend. Bryce finished his drink and then waved for another one.

"I'm going to go to the ladies' room. Okay, Kelli?" My voice came out small.

"It's in the barn—over to your right." Kelli motioned

toward a gray shingled building decked out in fairy lights. "Are you okay?"

I shrugged. "I'm fine. Thanks, Kelli. It's a nice party."

"My foundation helps wounded veterans if that makes me any less of a jerk." Kelli sighed. "I'm sorry, Chloe."

"You're not a jerk, and you don't need to apologize. I'm glad Gene's money is going to vets—I think it's awesome that you have a foundation that helps people."

I straightened my shoulders as I headed for the barn, keeping to the edges of the party. I didn't want anyone looking at me, feeling sorry for me. After all, nothing had happened. My husband had talked to his ex-fiancée for a few minutes, nothing more. The stuff on the internet—about Felicia putting the "ex" back in "sex"—it was all nonsense. It was manufactured by our team for the purposes of driving public interest. That was all.

If there were tears pricking my eyes, it was only because of my allergies.

I didn't look in Bryce's direction. I didn't want to see if he was chugging another drink, ignoring me, smiling at someone else, or all of the above. I took my time in the gorgeous barn bathroom, fixing my makeup and smoothing my hair.

Just as I was about to leave, Felicia Jones sauntered in.

Motherfucker! Could anything else go wrong tonight?

I almost tripped over my own feet. "H-Hey." It was only the two of us in there, it wasn't like I could ignore her.

She rolled her eyes. "Don't make a scene, okay?" She brushed past me and went to the vanity. She whipped out her expensive lip gloss and began dabbing it on her already glossy lips.

"What?" I clenched my hands into fists. "What do you mean, don't make a scene?"

She rolled her eyes, then kept glossing. "The last time I saw you, you chased me out onto my boat. Remember?"

"I was trying to talk to you."

"Whatever." The way she said it? It was like she was talking to someone else's annoying, ill-tempered child, who was about to have a meltdown.

Anything that can go wrong will go wrong...

"Can I ask you a question?" I teetered in my heels. Whether I was about to crumple into a ball on the floor or launch myself at her, I still wasn't sure.

She sighed. "What." She didn't make it sound like a question.

Why are you such a fucking cunt? "Why are you here tonight?"

"Because I was invited, silly." She rolled her eyes again, which nearly pushed me over the edge. "You really are just a decoy, aren't you?"

"Excuse me?"

Felicia finally whipped her head around and faced me. "I *said*, you really are just a *decoy*." She enunciated the words slowly as if I had a hearing impairment.

"I'm Bryce's wife." My voice came out small. "I'm not a decoy."

"Ha! If you say so." With one final pass of her fingernails through her glossy locks, she sauntered back out. Bitch took her time, too. Felicia Jones was making it *very* clear that she had nothing to fear from little old Chloe Windsor.

And I just stood there. I didn't launch myself at her, I didn't crumple up into a ball. I did nothing. I considered crying, but everyone would know. Felicia would know. Bryce would know. I straightened my shoulders and looked in the mirror. *Decoys don't cry.*

Someday, I vowed, *I am going to fuck Felicia's shit up.*

But not today. Not just yet. I needed... I wasn't sure what I needed. Courage? A backbone? A getaway car?

I left to go and find my husband.

"Where have you been?" Bryce was standing at the

edge of the party. "I've been looking for you everywhere."

I eyed his fresh bourbon. "Looks like you've been managing just fine."

"What does that mean?"

I took a deep breath. "I'd like to go home."

"We're not finished here yet."

"I am." It was about time I located my backbone. "I am very much finished with this party."

"We haven't eaten yet, we're supposed to stay for pictures—"

"You can stay if you want. I'm asking Captain Johnny to bring me home. You don't care if I speak to *him* alone, do you?" I wanted to laugh. Per the terms of our new contract, I wasn't supposed to talk to men one-on-one without a chaperone. But Bryce was the one who needed a babysitter.

"I'll go with you." He sounded pissed, which was fine by me. "Let me just tell Daphne that I'll send the boat back for her."

"I don't need you to come with me—"

"It wouldn't look good if you left alone." Bryce's voice was icy. "Just give me a minute, please. Stay here."

I did as I was told. Standing in the shadows near the edge of the forest, I prayed that no one noticed me.

But Mimi Jones staggered by. She was visibly drunk,

unsteady on her feet. She nearly tripped over a tree root, and I rushed to her side. "Mrs. Jones? Are you okay?"

"Ha! No, I am *not* okay." Her words slurred. "I lost my drink somewhere."

I sighed. "Maybe that's for the best. Do you want some water?"

"No." She straightened herself and smoothed her dress. She smelled like a hint of expensive perfume and a ton of booze. "I'd like a drink that starts with a *v* and ends with an *a*. If I can still spell it, I can still drink it, that's what I always say! So back off."

She jerked herself from my arms and almost fell over.

I didn't reach for her this time. "I'm not telling you what to do, Mrs. Jones."

"No, you wouldn't do that, would you?" She chuckled to herself. "You're too busy being paraded around like the town strumpet."

I wasn't sure what a strumpet was, but it had a certain ring to it that made it seem like a definite insult. I took a step back. "Are you sure you're okay?"

"What, aren't you going to say something nasty back to me?"

"No, Mrs. Jones." I suddenly felt very, very tired. "I'm not."

"Well, you don't have to," she snorted. "My husband's done enough. I mean, hey, why not? I've stayed by his side for years. Through the drinking, the DUI, and the first affair. I forgave him. Why not shit on me some more? I'm just so *accessible*."

She laughed, a bitter sound. "And now he has an affair with someone young enough to be his daughter— and she's pregnant. She's married to someone we've known forever. So why doesn't everybody just come after me with a pitchfork, burn me at the stake and call it a day?"

"I'm sorry, Mrs. Jones."

"Don't be sorry for me, honey. I've got more money than God. I'll show him someday. Someday..." Mimi Jones blinked and peered around. She suddenly seemed lost. "I'd really like to find the bar. Do you remember where it is?"

"Sure, I can take you there." I started toward her, but she waved me off.

"I'm fine—I've had lots of practice." She straightened herself again and smoothed her hair. "You know, I shouldn't take it out on you. You must be just miserable. They really are a rotten family, aren't they? I've known Gene since I was a girl, and he's always been a snake. Those boys aren't any better. Y'see the way Bryce is with my Felicia? Won't even look her in the eye. And now Gene has her doing all this press—"

I held very still, waiting for her to continue.

"—and I think she's doing it to get him back, but it's never going to work. It's like her father and me. Once you get hurt that bad, it's never better. Never." The bitterness in her voice was absolute, irrevocable.

She stumbled off. I ought to help her back to the party, but she seemed intent on weaving her way back by herself.

Mimi's words rang in my ears. *Gene has her doing all this press. She's doing it to get him back. Once you get hurt that bad, it's never better.*

But... Who had hurt who? The way Mimi made it sound, Bryce was the bad guy. Maybe she just didn't know the truth, that Felicia had been the one to cheat. But what about the rest of it? Was Gene Windsor behind Felicia's current participation in all the drama?

Did that mean Bryce was, too?

Bryce himself returned a minute later, still with a glower on his face. "Olivia's not happy that we're leaving. I just texted her."

"Tell her I feel sick," I said quietly. It was the truth.

Bryce waited until security had escorted us back to the boat and left us alone before he spoke. "What exactly," he asked as he poured himself yet another drink, "is the problem, Chloe?"

"I don't know." My eyes pricked with tears. "But I'm feeling upset that you talked to Felicia again. And you seem really... I don't know."

"So you don't know what's wrong with *you*, and you don't know what's wrong with *me*?" He glared at his drink.

"That sounds about right..."

"And yet you dragged me out of the party before my brothers arrived or dinner was even served," Bryce continued. "My father donated *one million* dollars to the Nguyen's charity so that they'd host this party at the last minute. How do you think he's going to feel that we only stayed for fifteen minutes?"

Normally, disappointing Bryce would make me want to cry. But his anger, coupled with the bourbon wafting from his breath, only made me mad. "Like I said, you didn't need to leave."

"But if I didn't, it would look bad."

"I think it already looked bad." I tried to keep my voice light. "But I'm sure that was all part of the plan."

"So what if it was, Chloe? I don't understand why you're acting like this."

"Maybe because you've been acting like a dick ever since you woke me up this afternoon?"

He sighed. "I think we should re-implement the no-talking rule. I say we start now—and this time, it applies to you."

"Fine."

"Fine." He knocked back the drink.

Where was my husband? This was the Bryce I'd met the day I'd married him—*Bad Bryce*.

I shouldn't say more, but I couldn't just stand there. Sadness bubbled up inside me, threatening to spill over. "I don't understand why you're treating me this way."

He paced near the windows for a minute, not looking at me. Another heavy silence descended upon us.

Just when I thought he would never speak, he said, "It's because I knew this was going to happen."

"You knew *what* was going to happen?"

He scrubbed a hand over his face, suddenly looking tired. "I knew you'd be upset, and there's nothing I can do about it."

"You can not talk to Felicia like you did tonight and make me feel like shit. You could be n-nice to me." My traitor eyes filled with tears. "There's no reason for you to treat me like this."

"Do you think that I want to do this? Do you think *any* of this is my idea of a good time?" He went and stood by the window, staring out into the darkness. "Christ, I shouldn't even be standing here. The fucking photographers will have this on the internet tomorrow."

"Why did you talk to Felicia tonight? You knew that would make me upset. Aren't the pictures of her already enough?"

He sighed. "Olivia wanted me to. It was staged."

Ugh. I sank down onto the couch. "Why didn't you tell me before we went? That way, I wouldn't have been blindsided."

"I wasn't supposed to. They *wanted* you to be blindsided, so they could get the shot. And I did what they asked." He poured himself another drink.

"Okay." The weight of what he was saying sunk in. His father had paid for the party so that it looked legitimate. Olivia Jensen had orchestrated the run-in with Felicia. No one had told me about it because they wanted me to be upset, and they wanted it to look natural. They wanted the story to stir up the public's appetite for Windsor family drama.

"They" meaning Gene Windsor, Olivia Jensen, and... Bryce himself.

He was choosing his company over me. There had never been any competition, anyway. That was the reason I was here. That was the reason he'd married me in the first place. That was the reason he'd brought me back.

"It's not really okay." He shrugged. "But that doesn't change anything. Ha. Turns out, I'm more like my old man than I ever thought. I'm just as bad as he is."

"That's not true." I hesitated for a moment. "So... Did your father ask Felicia to go to the party tonight?"

"I'm sure he did." Bryce went back to staring out the window. "I don't know about you, but I've lost my taste for the whole thing."

"Well... Hopefully it'll help. Hopefully the photographers got what they needed." *I* needed to keep my eye on the ball. Bryce had hired me for a reason, and I'd taken the job for a reason. Money.

Keep your eye on the ball, Chlo! Millions of dollars!

I was upset—hurt—but I couldn't implode now. I reminded myself how much money I was being paid and how much it would mean for Noah. I shouldn't be so selfish; this wasn't about me anyway. Bryce and his father had planned the whole evening. They'd wanted Bryce and Felicia to have a private moment together. They'd *wanted* me to be upset. Obviously, my feelings didn't matter to my husband—I was a prop, an accessory, a...decoy.

"I'm sorry I didn't tell you," Bryce said, surprising

me. "I shouldn't have thrown you under the bus like that."

I nodded. "I understand."

I did. I understood everything.

But that didn't make any of it okay.

fetch

WE WENT to bed without incident, that is, without touching. Even though Bryce had apologized, an iciness had descended upon us. More specifically, an iciness had settled over *me*. Maybe it was the encounter with Felicia in the bathroom, maybe it was the fact that Bryce had hidden the agenda from me, or maybe it was the residual nastiness from my encounters with Lydia, my father, Bryce, Felicia, *and* a drunk Mimi Jones throughout the evening.

In any event, I felt frozen, glacial. Who knew how long I would take to thaw? A hundred years, a million.

Bryce was sorry. He'd apologized, which I hadn't even expected. But the fact that he'd pushed me away again and held me at arm's length in order to *deceive* me hurt more than I could say.

Maybe I wasn't frozen inside. Maybe I was dead.

I slept fitfully, knowing full well what I had to face in the morning. My father and Lydia were just as bad as Felicia Jones, if not worse. Felicia made being bad look good because she made everything look good. But my father and Lydia were just depressing.

Bryce and I were both awake before the sun came up. It was awkward, being near him but not feeling close to him. This time, the distance was on my end. It was a strange feeling to hold back from him, to *want* to hold back from him. But it was as if all the wind had been knocked out of me. I had nothing left to say; I couldn't even catch my breath.

I waited until he'd gotten into the shower to grab my phone. I called the number Lydia had given me, but there was no answer. Like so many other people this fine July morning on Mount Desert Island, she was probably hungover.

Once Bryce was finished in the bathroom, he came and sat on the edge of the bed. "Chloe..." He hesitated, then seemed to choose his words carefully. "Apologizing isn't really my thing. I'm sure I did a crappy job of it, just like I did a crappy job of putting you first yesterday. That's why I was being such an ass all afternoon. I didn't want to lie to you, so I just didn't say much. I didn't say anything."

"I understand," I said again. My voice was flat.

He looked as if he wanted to say more but then just gave up. "Fine. I'll see you at lunch?"

"Sure." I tried to sound normal. I probably failed, but what else was new?

He didn't say anything more as he got dressed. He seemed afraid to say anything, to come near me. He stiffly kissed me on the cheek right before he left. I smiled at him. He smiled back.

Everything felt like shit.

As soon as he put on his suit and left, I jumped out of bed. I threw on leggings and a sweatshirt, tugged my hair into a ponytail, and brushed my teeth. Most of my mascara was still on from the night before, the upside of being too upset and lazy to take my makeup off. I checked my phone again—nothing from Lydia. She was probably snoring her face off, an empty big bottle of wine on her nightstand.

I could still go to Northeast Harbor and bang on her door.

I needed to deal with her before she came looking for *me*.

But how was I going to get to the mainland? It was true what I'd remembered last night—I was contractually forbidden from speaking to men unless I had a

Bryce-approved chaperone. I'd already gotten one captain fired; I didn't want to push Captain Johnny back into retirement by getting him fired, too. The contract term was *stupid*, and I doubted Bryce would really care if the older man gave me a ride, but that didn't make it any less binding. Akira Zhang had drilled it into my head: if I breached the contract, Bryce would have grounds to refuse me my payment. I needed to follow the terms to the letter.

I just needed a female chaperone, someone Bryce would approve of. But I had to find someone without asking Bryce himself. We were already on thin ice. He did *not* need to know that my step-monster and dad were on the mainland, threatening to sue me to get my brother back. Lydia kept threatening to 'fuck my shit up,' and my step-monster was, if nothing else, a little scary. She had nothing to lose. If Gene Windsor got wind of that—of *them*—I was dead. He would throw me off the dock and move Felicia Jones into my bedroom once and for all.

I had an idea, probably a very fucking stupid one, but it was all I had. I refused to drag Midge or Dale into this—I didn't want to get them fired. Hazel would be the *perfect* chaperone, and I'd be thrilled to get *her* fired, but Bryce's spindly little lap dog would tell him my plan before the words even left my mouth. No, I had to call someone else.

There was only one person who could help. Lucky for me, she was already doing Pilates at the crack of dawn, per her regular routine.

"Yes?" She sounded winded. "What the heck do *you* want at six a.m.?"

"Want to head off-island to go shopping?"

God bless her, Daphne didn't hesitate. "I thought you'd never ask."

It turned out we didn't even need Captain Johnny. "Gene has a Hinckley I can drive. It's down on our dock. C'mon." Daphne hadn't bothered to change out of her workout clothes, and for good reason: she looked great. Black leggings and a lavender crop top showed off her flat-as-ever washboard abs.

"Can you explain what you were saying to me before?" she asked. "About not being able to ask Captain Johnny to take you off-island? You sounded a little...paranoid."

"Oh, it's just this thing with Bryce. He doesn't like me being alone with the staff—he's weird like that."

"You mean he's *obsessed* like that." She sighed. "Ah,

to be loved. I remember when he fired that other captain for talking to you. And then he fired that waiter. It's kind of hot that he's jealous like that, don't you think?"

"Not exactly," I said, uneasy. "It's more like he's crazy. And hypocritical."

"What do you mean—are you talking about Felicia?" Daphne asked. "That whole thing was planned. It was so *obvious*. Trust me, you don't need to worry about her. I mean, *she* herself is a fucking pain in the ass. I just mean you don't have to worry about Bryce and her. He sees her for the cow she is."

"She doesn't see it that way." I frowned. "She accosted me in the bathroom."

"Did you hit her?" Daphne sounded hopeful.

"No, I chickened out. But she really *is* a bitch. Maybe someday..." I shook my head. I sounded like a drunk Mimi Jones! "Anyway, I wanted to go home after that. Sorry we stranded you."

"Oh, don't worry about it—I had fun." Daphne climbed aboard, undid the ties, and brought the bumpers up. She surprised me by seeming at ease being in charge of the boat. "Jake and Colby showed up right after you left. They were drinking a ton, so they made it fun. They actually got Kelli Nguyen to limbo."

"That sounds like a good time."

"It was! But what did Felicia say to you? She's probably upset about the way she's being portrayed by the media. She's being cast as the bad girl, and you're the good one." Daphne started the boat and backed it away from the dock.

"She does have black hair, and I *am* blond." I shrugged. "So it's no real surprise that she's getting the negative treatment. That and the fact that she's a bitch on wheels."

Daphne surprised me by laughing. "I didn't know you had it in you, Chloe Windsor! Why didn't you just beat her up last night? It's not like she doesn't deserve it. And for the record, not all girls with dark hair are bad girls. But most of us are!" She laughed again.

She seemed to be in a great mood as she navigated into the harbor, the island falling away behind us. Before I knew it, we were passing one of the paparazzi boats. They seemed to wake up as we drove out further. One of the guys yelled at the team, and they fired up the motor.

"Uh oh." Daphne glanced back over her shoulder. "We've got company."

"Crap." I sat down on the couch and pulled my hood up. I'd forgotten all about the photographers.

"Did you happen to clear this trip with Olivia Jensen? Because I didn't." Daphne bit her lip.

"Um, no. I didn't."

"We're not supposed to do anything off-script." But Daphne didn't seem concerned. "Whatever. We're just going shopping!"

"Right." I nodded, trying to be upbeat. "That's right."

"Why, exactly, are we going shopping at six a.m.?" She eyed me. "And more importantly, where?"

"Um, I thought we could grab breakfast in Northeast first. And then maybe you could show me that cute baby store you've been talking about? I also want to look for a new dress for Caroline Vale's wedding. Do you know what you're wearing?"

"Not yet! Ooh, there's a super-cute boutique we can go to—my friend owns it. This is perfect!" Daphne's eyes lit up. "I'm *so* glad you called me! I needed to get off that rock!"

"Me too." I smiled. "Me too."

Daphne docked the boat with ease, and we headed up to the parking lot to find her car. "Hey, I just remembered something," I lied. "I was supposed to pick up some paperwork from the dog trainer. I think he's staying at a motel over here."

I scanned the properties next to the lot, quickly finding the *Northeast Nights Inn*. I knew I'd seen it before. "I think he's staying there." I pointed to the inn.

Daphne wrinkled her nose. "What kind of paperwork? Can't he just mail it? I'm pregnant, remember? If I don't eat, I get heartburn! I thought it was a myth, but it's actually true!"

"Do you want to run up to the restaurant and get a table? I'll only be a minute."

"Sure." Daphne secured her sunglasses against her face. "Do I look all right? Those dudes in the boat are still taking pictures of us."

Crap! I'd been so nervous about getting to Lydia that I hadn't considered that the photographers were still following us. "You look great, Daphne. Strut up to Main Street, they'll love it."

"Ha!" But strut she did as she left my side, her long legs carrying her quickly across the lot.

I prayed that the photographers were engrossed in Daphne's firm buttocks, in full display in the leggings, and that they ignored me. Either way, I needed to be careful. I tried calling Lydia again.

"Hello?" she croaked. I'd woken her up.

"I'm here in Northeast," I said quickly. "Can I come to your room?"

"What time is it?" She cursed. "Seriously, you couldn't even wait till seven?"

"I'm sorry. I knew it was urgent—I wanted to get here as soon as I could."

Lydia cursed some more, muttering under her breath. I only caught the words *stuck-up bitch* and *selfish*. I sighed. This wasn't going well already.

"We'll come out in a few minutes," she grunted. "But we need coffee."

"Um...can I please just come to your room?" I nervously looked around.

"Were you *born* to be a pain in my ass? Jesus!" Lydia laugh-coughed. "Just get us two coffees, extra sugar and extra cream. We'll be down in a minute."

Motherfucker! I really didn't want to meet them in public. I would have to find a secluded spot for us to talk, but first, I needed to get them coffee. If Lydia wanted it with extra cream and extra sugar, I would fetch it for her. I would love to tell her to take it and shove it up her ass, but instead, I would do her bidding. I'd deliver her order with a smile on my face, ask her how much money she wanted in order to keep her from blackmailing me, and then go on my merry way.

Mother. Fucker. I stomped up the stairs from the parking lot to Northeast Harbor's Main Street. It was cute and quaint, with a restaurant, an art gallery, a small grocery store, and a cafe. I spied Daphne on the sidewalk, engrossed in conversation with a woman about her age. I ducked into the cafe without her seeing me. I got in line at the coffee bar; it was crowded, busier than I'd expected. But as it was the only place to get coffee in town, it made sense.

As I waited, I noticed several people stealing glances in my direction. I didn't recognize anyone in line. From all the flip-flops and *I Heart Maine* t-shirts, the customers mostly looked like tourists. Some of them nudged each other, whispering, glancing at their phones, then at me. *Weird.*

By the time I made it to the counter, I felt flushed. People were definitely looking at me. I placed my order. While one barista poured my coffees, the other one gaped at me.

"Is there something on my face?" I asked her.

"No—oh man, I'm sorry." She was a cute girl, about my age with curly red hair and a nose ring. "It's just that... You're Chloe Windsor, right?"

"Right." It was so weird to have a total stranger recognize me.

"Are you okay?" she asked.

"Yes. I mean, I think so." I leaned closer. "Why're you asking if I'm okay?"

She bit her lip. "Because... The internet."

"Ah, got it. Thank you," I said as I grabbed my coffees.

But I wasn't sure that I was really thankful, not at all.

thin ice

DAPHNE WAS STILL on the sidewalk, talking to her friend. It looked like they were having an intense discussion. After my encounter with the barista, I was worried it was about me. I hustled down the road and ducked into a little seating area on the sidewalk. I put the coffees on a nearby bench, turned my back to the road so no one would recognize me, and opened my phone.

I scrolled immediately to the gossip websites.

Brylecia Makes a Comeback at VIP Party

Felicia's Smirk Says It All

Chloe's Dramatic Bathroom Brawl — All the Details!

Brylecia? Seriously? No. Please, for fuck's sake, *no.* But what had I expected? I quickly went to the articles. They were, as usual, light on details and heavy on pictures and insinuation. The first link was multiple pictures of Bryce and Felicia at the party last night. She was looking up at him coquettishly, her chest stuck out. Bryce was smiling down at her. *Why* hadn't I scratched that bitch's eyes out last night?

It made me feel sick to look at the images. I closed the link and moved on.

The following "article" showed a picture of me standing next to Kelli Nguyen, my lips twisted, my face pale. *Chloe wore a form-fitting dress to the party,* read the caption. The next picture was of Felicia walking across the lawn, a smirk on her face. She looked high as a kite. The juxtaposition of the images said it all: even though I was in a hot dress, I was upset; Felicia was triumphant.

Then there were the bathroom photos.

Whoever the photographer was, he or she was very good at their job. They'd captured me walking in, a distracted look on my face. "A source from the party says they heard yelling from inside the lavish bathroom." Next, there was a picture of Felicia coming out, grinning—the cat who'd just pummeled the canary. She looked gorgeous, her tan leg flashing through her dress's long slit.

Then there was another one of me exiting the barn, looking as though I might cry. I was miserable, and I looked it. The final picture was a wretched one of Bryce and me back on the boat, leaving the party. He stared out the window, a grim expression on his face. I watched him, looking like I was about to burst into tears. The caption asked, *Are Chloe and Bryce Headed for a Split?*

Nice. All the dramatic details, indeed. How, exactly, was any of this helping Bryce's father avoid federal charges for insider trading?

I shoved the phone into my bag, grabbed the coffees, and hurried back down the steps. Daphne was still talking to her friend and didn't see me. Lucky for me, she *loved* to talk.

As I headed across the parking lot to the motel, I wondered where the photographers were. Were they watching me now? I couldn't let them see me with my dad and Lydia. That would be a disaster...

I glimpsed Lydia outside, hanging over the railing of the motel's second floor, smoking a cigarette. I didn't call to her or wave—instead, I scooted around the back of the property. There was an abandoned-looking pool with a unicorn inner tube floating on the water. Otherwise, it was empty. A forest of pine trees bordered the backside of the motel.

I texted Lydia. *I'm around back. Can you guys come out here?*

She didn't respond, but a minute later, she and my father rounded the corner. Lydia was still smoking. She looked the same as the last time I'd seen her—pissed off and hung over, her orangey-blond hair slicked back into a bun. But she had a new, large tattoo on the front of her thigh, the face of a lion. I bet Bryce had paid for that.

My father followed her. He was still handsome, but years of drinking had worn him down. His pants were sagging, his black T-shirt faded. His hair was sticking up, *Northeast Nights* bedhead.

Lydia took a drag off her cigarette. She seemed wired, shaky. My dad looked uncomfortable, like I was about to give him a root canal with no novocaine.

"Are those our coffees?"

"Oh—yeah. Sorry." I handed them over, then stood there awkwardly.

"So, I'm glad you're here. Even though it's too early" Apparently, Lydia was running the meeting. "Your father and I are very upset. We don't like the way we're being treated in all this. It's disrespectful."

I dug my nails into my palms. "I'm sorry that you feel that way," I said.

"Oh you will be, honey—you will be." She started pacing, drinking her coffee, and smoking. "I told you we got screwed at that casino, but Miss High-and-Mighty didn't have time for us, did ya? You sent that bitch of a lawyer, instead. And all she gave us was thirty thousand while you're living in a mansion!"

"Thirty thousand dollars is a lot of money," I said quietly. "Especially when you add it on top of the million that Bryce already gave you."

"Especially when you add it on top of the million Bryce gave you," Lydia mimicked, a scowl on her face. "Would you listen to yourself? Who do you think you are, huh? You just marry this guy out of nowhere, and now your shit don't stink? *Somethin'* sure smells."

I took a deep breath. I was not going to let Lydia get to me. I was *not* going to think about the fact that she'd called my dead mother a stuck-up bitch, I was not going to think about the time she'd screamed at Noah because he'd tripped and knocked her ashtray over, I was not going to think about the fact that she'd thrown us out on the streets because she was a lazy, selfish bitch and now she was trying to extort money from me. "I'm here because I want to help. What do you need?"

"Can you believe this?" Lydia turned to my father. "She's acting all sweet and nice as pie now! I'm telling you, it's an act!"

"It's not an act, Lydia. I just want to give you what

you need. Tell me what that is, and I'll see what I can do."

She turned back to me, a gleam in her eye. "We want three million dollars. Cash. Today."

I almost choked. "I can't do that! What are you, crazy?"

"Fine." My step-monster looked almost gleeful. "If you can't give it to us, someone else will. I'm sure either your husband or his dad will be happy to make a deal with us. Ooh, or the newspapers. I've been wanting to call them and tell them who you really are. It's interestin' that none of those articles talks about us, you know? It's almost like you're ashamed of your family. Ashamed of where you come from. Trying to hide something, aren't you?"

My heart started racing. A chill needled my back. This could *not* be fucking happening right now.

My dad stepped forward. "We talked to a law firm. We're being represented. I didn't agree to let you take your brother like that. That fancy Asian lawyer of yours tricked me into believing he was just coming up for the summer. She pulled a bait and switch—that's what *my* lawyer said."

"Dad?" I blinked at him. "Do you really think I'd try to trick you into something?"

"I don't know. But maybe I don't know you at all

anymore, do I? I think it's crazy that you married some rich guy, and now your picture's all over the internet." He raked a hand through his hair. "I *do* think you and your rich-ass husband took advantage of me. I *don't* think what's happening up here is great for your brother—"

"Since when have you ever cared about him, huh?" I surprised myself by hollering.

"You watch your tone. Don't you disrespect your father like that!" Lydia got in my face, a cloud of cigarette smoke, white-wine breath, and body odor.

"Are you fucking kidding me, Lydia? *Disrespect* him? Or you?" My voice kept rising. Help me God, I was losing it. "All you guys have done is treat us like trash! My brother doesn't deserve that!"

"See?" Lydia turned to my dad. "I told you she was a little bitch! You didn't believe me but it's true! *This* is what she's really like!"

"*Chloe.*" My father's voice was ice. "That's enough. Lydia said you've been being really rude to her. Like you don't know us anymore, or something. Now that it's convenient for you, you act like we're nothing. How's that supposed to make us feel, huh?"

"I'm supposed to care about your *feelings*? Lydia *threw us out of your apartment*!" All of a sudden, it was like a dam burst inside me. I couldn't stop myself from yelling. "And you didn't do anything about it! You took the money and you never even called him! You don't even care! You've never even cared! You're a shitty excuse for a father—you always have been!"

He looked like I'd slapped him. "That's enough," he said.

It was more than enough: it was the truth, and the truth hurt.

"Fine." I was shaking.

Lydia watched us with interest, a half-smile on her face. She was probably enjoying this: the final nail on the coffin of my father's relationship with me. I wanted to shake her, to tell her that it had been dead and buried a long time ago. But there was no point.

"I can't do three million. That's impossible." I took a shuddery breath. "I might be able to do one, but I have to call my lawyer."

Lydia put her hands on her hips. "I want three."

"Lydia." My father sounded exhausted. "One is plenty, so long as we don't go back to Foxwoods. Let's just take it—I want to go home."

I straightened my shoulders. "Are you going to fight me for Noah? Because if you are, I'm not giving you a dime."

"Depends." Lydia lit another cigarette. My father might be done with the conversation, but she seemed to be in no rush to end it. "I'm thinking there's more than a million available—especially if I ask your husband. Not only is he rich as fuck, but his family's also in a lot of trouble."

She blew out a cloud of smoke. "I'm thinkin' he might not want the press to know that you guys swindled Noah away from us. And that you tried to pay us off to go away."

"He offered you money in exchange for guardianship—Dad signed the papers in less than one minute! It's not like it took much convincing." I shook my head, disgusted. "How do you think that makes you look, huh? And now you're back and threatening to blackmail me for more!"

"The thing is," Lydia took another deep drag, "I don't care about my reputation."

She let that hang in the air, along with the cloud of smoke she exhaled.

I longed to rush her, smack the cigarette out of her mouth and yank her stupid orangey hair. Instead, I tried to gather what was left of my wits. I needed to get rid of her and my dad. I needed them to leave Northeast Harbor that morning and never come back. No matter how upset I'd been with Bryce, I knew one thing for sure: I didn't want to hurt him, not like this. If Lydia and my dad went after him for the money, or worse—went to his father or the press—it could be devastating. I couldn't do that to my husband.

"If you want to come at me and try to get more money—more than another *million dollars*—go right ahead." I looked her straight in the eye.

"I just might." She laugh-coughed again.

I shrugged. "Good luck pulling this with my husband or his father. They will fuck *your* shit up, Lydia. Compared to them, you're junior varsity at a shitty little middle school in the middle of nowhere. They've gone pro as first-round picks. They will eat you *alive*. But like I said, it's your choice."

My dad groaned. "Lydia... Let's just take the money."

"Fine." She narrowed her eyes at me. "But I'm not signing nothin' this time."

"You don't have to. Dad's the only one with legal rights to Noah." I turned to him. "If I give you this money, you have to walk away once and for all. If you come back asking for more or threatening me, I'm going to have my fancy lawyer go after you. You don't want to deal with that, trust me."

"Fine Chloe." He shook his head. "But what happened to you, huh? You used to be a nice girl."

"How would you know?"

My father didn't answer.

Sometimes, there was nothing left to say.

pinned

MAYBE IT'S TRUE, I thought as I hustled back to Main Street. *Maybe I used to be a nice girl, and now I'm not.* Perhaps protecting my brother had made me rabid. Maybe dealing with Gene Windsor and Felicia Jones had gotten under my skin worse than I'd even thought. Maybe I *wasn't* a nice girl anymore.

But... That didn't make me wrong. That didn't make my father any less of a deadbeat dad or make Lydia any less selfish. I might not be perfect, but I was still Noah's best shot at a happy life.

Right?

Daphne was pissed—and finished with her breakfast—by the time I joined her at the restaurant. "Where the hell have you been?"

I sighed. "The dog trainer wanted to talk about

Boss's pedigree or something. I barely understood what he meant, but he wouldn't stop talking! I should've gotten out of there sooner—I'm sorry."

"It's okay." Daphne shrugged. "I saw my friend on the way here. She told me the pictures from last night were pretty bad. Apparently everyone's talking about it, wondering if you and Bryce are having issues."

I sighed. "Did you look at them yet?"

Daphne held up her phone. "I had to do *something* while I ate breakfast alone."

"They *are* pretty bad." I absentmindedly played with my napkin. "I'm not sure how this is really helping Gene."

"Me either, but he's convinced Olivia Jensen's going to save the day." The couple at the table next to ours started whispering, and Daphne rolled her eyes. "Want to get out of here? The tourists are flagrantly staring."

"Sure."

She left cash on the table, and we headed outside. As soon as we hit the sidewalk, both of our phones beeped.

It was a text message from Olivia Jensen herself. *WTF, ladies? Did you ask if you could go off-island at the crack of dawn? The paps are all over your asses.* She sent a picture of Daphne and me on the boat, smiling and talking.

Bryce is pissed, she wrote. *What were you two thinking?*

"Honestly?" Daphne squinted at her phone. "Who died and left Olivia Jensen in charge?" She rapid-fired off a reply text. *We're shopping for wedding guest dresses!* She added a smiley face, even though her real-life expression was sour.

Sounds like a good photo opp. I'll meet you with a photographer in 30 minutes, Olivia replied. *Send me a link to the shop—security needs to clear it.*

"Jeez Louise." Daphne snorted. "She's really sort of a buzzkill, isn't she? I need to call my friend who owns the boutique—she'll open early for us, I know she wouldn't mind. That way, we can get out of here quickly. Did you notice how everybody's staring?"

She glanced over her shoulder at the tourists on the sidewalk. Some of them were, in fact, peering curiously in our direction. One guy was taking a picture of us on his cellphone. "Hey, cut that out!" Daphne snapped at him. She dragged me around the corner to a quiet residential street. "We don't need Average Joe taking pictures of us with his crappy cellphone. He might get a bad angle! Ugh, let me call my friend and see if she's in yet."

As she got on her phone, I got on mine. It wasn't safe

to talk, so I texted Akira. *Made another deal with my step-mother,* I wrote. *And by 'deal' I mean I gave them way more money than they deserve.*

Akira texted back immediately. *You can't keep giving in to their demands—they won't stop! It's extortion.*

Can you please disburse the money from my account? 1M, I wrote.

Chloe! That's crazy, she texted back.

I sighed, then kept typing. *I didn't have a choice. I need another agreement drafted. They can't ever come after Noah and try to get him back. Can you please help me? Can you put something in there that they can't come back looking for more?*

I'll do it, she wrote, *but nothing can stop them from being greedy. You're burning through your money and you haven't even completed the assignment yet. Does Bryce know about this?*

No, I replied, *and I'd like to keep it between us.*

Three dots appeared. Then, finally: *I'll reach out to Lydia. I don't like this, though.*

I didn't like it either. Still, paying them off—again—would hopefully make them go away once and for all. I didn't know what else to do.

"Let's go to the shop," Daphne said. "She's already there unpacking some big order. As soon as I mentioned the photos, she said we could come right over." She hustled me back around the corner to an upscale-looking boutique named *Aqua*. Her friend unlocked the door and ushered us inside.

"Hey Daphne!" She was an attractive older woman with white hair in a pixie cut, hot-pink lipstick, and an expensive-looking, wrinkly-on-purpose linen outfit. "And you must be Chloe."

She air-kissed us both, then inspected me. "You're much prettier in person," she said.

"T-Thanks."

"I'll just be out back unpacking," the owner called, hustling to the rear of the store. "There's a *ton* of new dresses on the floor—feel free to try things on. I just know you'll find the perfect thing for Caroline's wedding. Let me know when the photographers get here!"

"Thanks!" Daphne headed straight for the racks, motioning for me to join her. "I heard the bridesmaid's dresses are blue. Anything else is fair game!" Expert shopper that she was, she dove right in.

I didn't really have the stomach for gown shopping at the moment. It seemed silly after my run-in with Dad and Lydia. I *did* need to find a dress for the wedding— with everything going on, I'd forgotten all about it. Midge probably had something picked out, but since I was here, I might as well look. It was a way to pass the time.

I started looking at the dresses—the first one I picked up had a price tag of *three thousand dollars*. The next one was five thousand. I grabbed them both, along with one that cost seven. I wasn't even sure if I liked them! But I listlessly put them into a dressing room, then hunted through the racks for more.

Still, I couldn't get excited. I felt drained, frazzled. My thoughts zigzagged from the party last night, to Felicia, to how cold Bryce had been, to Lydia and my father. To the fact that I had just agreed to pay them a *million dollars—another* million dollars—because they were basically blackmailing me. There was also the fact that people had seen my pictures on the internet, and apparently, I looked much better in person.

It had been, absolutely, a crappy twenty-four hours.

More than anything, I missed Bryce. I'd felt so distant from him last night and this morning, but as I stood in the quiet boutique, dispiritedly looking for more things to try on, the pang hit me hard. *I miss him.* When things were right between us, I felt like I could handle anything. But now I was adrift, alone, and my circumstances felt insurmountable.

He'd apologized to me, he'd explained himself, but I'd still pushed him away. On some level, I didn't blame myself for that. It was painful that he'd planned the run-in with Felicia and had hidden it from me. Hiding things was lying.

He'd hurt me, and he'd known that he was doing it. That's why he'd seemed so removed after we'd made love at the guesthouse. That was why he'd pushed me away. It had been easier for him to keep me at arm's length when he knew he was about to wound me. But *that* had hurt me, too. His icing me out as he prepared to lie to me added insult to injury. The whole scenario was pre-meditated, ugly, and cold.

My mind wandered. What was it that Old Hazel had said about Bryce? Something about how he'd cried for his mother and his father had made him feel ashamed...

"After that," Hazel continued, "when he would get upset, he told everyone to go away and leave him alone. It was a coping mechanism, you see."

A coping mechanism. Hmm, maybe Hazel wasn't a hundred percent terrible, after all. Maybe just ninety-nine percent.

What Bryce had done was wrong, plain and simple. But he'd apologized for it. He'd owned it. Still, this wasn't the first time he'd turned on me. I'd made a pact with myself when I'd agreed to return to the island: I needed to be careful, to protect my heart. I needed to remember that he'd broken me when he'd fired me and sent me away.

People sure could be disappointing. I thought about Lydia, how she'd taunted me. I thought about my dad, who was a shadow of the father I longed for.

But then I thought about my mother. She had always had my back, been my rock. She'd loved me in a way that made me feel safe.

Not everybody's out to get you, Chlo. Some people were, that was for sure. But not everyone.

As I flicked past another designer dress, I knew something deep in my gut. Bryce was not a bad guy. He was, in fact, a surprisingly good guy. When things were calm between us, I felt protected and secure in a way I'd only ever experienced with Noah and my mom.

He'd hurt me, that was also the truth. But he'd done it for a reason. He was trying to protect his family, his business. As ill-advised as his choices were, he still wasn't coming from an awful place. He wasn't doing it to hurt me as the *goal*—the pain he'd caused me was a byproduct, the collateral damage. That didn't make it okay. But it was something to consider.

And I loved him. That was also something to consider. I didn't want to love him, it was painful, inconvenient, and scary to love him, but I did, in fact, love him. That was also the truth.

I should probably try to talk to him, tell him how I felt. That would be the mature thing to do. It would also make me...vulnerable. I shivered. With everything going on, I already felt pretty fucking vulnerable at the moment.

"Chloe?" Bryce threw the boutique door open and stormed inside. "What the hell are you doing off-island without letting me know?"

"*Bryce?*" I blinked at him. "What're you doing here?"

He was up on me before I had a chance to catch my breath. He was still wearing his suit, but there was nothing else professional about his appearance. His hair was mussed from the boat ride, he was breathing hard —like maybe he'd run to the store all the way from the dock—and his eyes were wild.

"You didn't have permission to leave. *I didn't give you permission.*"

"I didn't know I needed it!" I lied. "Daphne drove the boat over—I thought it was okay." That was at least true. "I knew I couldn't ask Captain Johnny or anybody else for a ride. We just wanted to go shopping. For the wedding," I babbled.

The way he was looking at me, I was in deep trouble.

"Bryce?" I squeaked.

Just then, Olivia Jensen, a photographer, and several security guards hustled into the boutique. "Oh, this is so cute!" Olivia gushed to the photographer. "We can get pictures of Chloe trying on different dresses. I was so pissed at them for going off-island, but this is going to work out great!"

She chattered on, and I gritted my teeth. I couldn't deal with Olivia Jensen at the moment.

Bryce glared in her direction. "I'm just about done with her ginger ass. Come on." He took my arm, guided me toward the dressing rooms, and then shoved me into the one where I'd hung the dresses.

Once he'd locked the door, he turned and glowered at me. "Speak. Now. And tell me the truth. What the hell were you thinking, leaving like that?"

"Bryce..." Ugh. I needed to tell him the truth, but this wasn't the place or the time. I couldn't risk someone overhearing us.

"You're still upset, aren't you?" He took a step closer, reaching for me. "I said I was sorry, Chloe. I shouldn't have done that to you yesterday. I should've gone with my gut, I should've told you the truth. I should have, would have, could have done so much better. But I didn't. I hoped that by doing what they asked, it would help things. But you know what? I knew last night it was a mistake. And as soon as I saw those headlines this morning, that confirmed it for me."

"It's okay, Bryce. You already said you were sorry. I just couldn't deal—I felt too raw."

"When you left this morning and didn't tell anybody..." He took a step closer. "I almost lost it when Olivia called me and said you'd gone and the photographers had followed you. Don't do that to me, babe."

"Do what?"

He closed the distance between us, pressing me up against the wall. His gaze roamed over me, hot and hungry. "Leave me. Make me worry." He swooped down and kissed my neck. "Make me crazy. Fuck, you're making me crazy right now."

"Bryce—" But his mouth claimed mine, possessing me, and suddenly nothing else mattered. Warmth bloomed inside my chest, opening me up. Here was the man that I loved. He wasn't pushing me away—he was pulling me toward him. Gone were the cameras, the ugly headlines, stupid Felicia Jones. It was just us.

He'd come for me. He was here with me. He still wanted me.

I was still his.

Bryce deepened the kiss, running his hands down my sides until they came to rest on my hips. He pressed himself against me, and I could feel him—all of him.

Fully erect, he jutted against my belly. *Unf.* We shouldn't be doing this, not in the dressing room with the security team right outside, not to mention Daphne and Olivia Freaking Jensen…

But the fire had already started. It was already consuming me; there was no way to stop the flames. I had to have him; it was inevitable. Our tongues connected, and then I was grabbing at him, ripping his jacket off, tugging at his tie, running my hands down the muscular splendor that was his chest.

Bryce didn't ask. He just took. He shoved my pants down, pushing my legs apart with his knee, while I fumbled with his belt and zipper. We shouldn't be doing this, we were in *public*, for Christ's sake, but his cock sprung out and thank fuck, he didn't hesitate. He notched it inside of me. "You're already so wet," he groaned.

He grabbed my ass, lifting me up, and I wrapped my legs around his waist.

He pinned me against the wall and entered me all the way, all at once. *Fuck. Oh, fuck.* "I'm not gonna last long, babe," he grunted.

His thrusts were so urgent, so deep, that I immediately cried out. He clapped a hand over my mouth and increased the already punishing pace. Deep strokes reached inside, all the way to my core. I felt the pressure building as I met him stroke for stroke. *So. Fucking. Hard.* Bryce was relentless, brutal. He was marking me as *his*, branding me with his body.

I ground my clit against him as he drove into me. *Fuck, fuck, fuck—*

"Bryce—*fuck!*" I screamed into the palm of his hand as I came, hard, riding atop his dick.

Once my cries subsided, he released my mouth and grabbed my hips. Bryce slammed me down onto him, chasing his own release. He did it over and over again until I saw stars. *Fuck!* He owned me once again. The pressure built inside me once more, and there were no words, no thoughts, only the intense pleasure of having him deep inside, stroking the places only he could ever reach. The cords stood out on his neck as he thrust, his hard length filling me. Time stopped as I bounced on top of him, once again close to the edge. His thrusts became savage, ragged, our desire breaking down the distance between us. "Yes Chloe, *mother-fucking yes*," he hissed as he emptied himself inside me. I convulsed against him, riding new waves of pleasure as he drove deep and released. My pussy sucked him greedily, wanting everything, wanting every last drop of him. When he came inside me, I felt complete. *Yes.*

Yes, Bryce, yes.

We shuddered against each other, holding on for dear life.

It was everything, but it was over in a moment. When we finally came to, clutching each other in the dressing room, Bryce's expression mirrored my thoughts: *Oh shit.*

I couldn't help it; I laughed.

"Shh." But he was laughing, too, as he pulled up his pants and attempted to straighten his tie. Bryce looked okay, but there was no hope for me. All I could do was fix my leggings, re-do my ponytail, and pray. I refused to even pray for anything specific, like my dignity to return. There was little hope for that.

We hid in the dressing room for a moment. It had gotten very, very quiet out in the boutique.

"Are you ready?" Bryce asked, straightening his tie once more.

"Yes," I lied.

When we walked through the door, Daphne and the boutique owner were studiously *not* looking in our direction. The owner looked pissed—her cheeks were red. Daphne looked as though she were apologizing. She also looked as if she might start laughing.

The security guards appeared to be very intent on checking security-related items. They also didn't look in our direction.

But Olivia and the photographer sprung out at us. A flash went off in our faces. "This is *awesome*!" Olivia clapped her hands together. "Reunited, and it feels *so* good!"

Before I even knew what was happening, Bryce was lunging for her.

direction

"Bryce? Woah, don't do it." I jumped in front of him, shielding Olivia. "Don't you dare take a picture of this!" I snapped at the photographer. He has the decency to put the camera down.

"I'm done with being a fucking puppet," Bryce spat out. His eyes were wild again as he peered past me at Olivia and not wild in a fun let's-do-it-in-the-dressing room kind of way. "Seriously, Olivia. What you're doing isn't helping. You know it's not."

"Bryce, please. Calm down." Olivia herself sounded surprisingly calm. Maybe she got threatened by her high-profile clients regularly? "I know this morning's been rough, but it's all part of my plan. I promise. Can you listen for a minute?"

"No." He still looked like he might lunge at her.

"Bryce, honey?" My voice was calm and soothing, courtesy of the intense orgasmic experience he'd just given me. I must be flooded with feel-good, peaced-out hormones. "We can listen for a minute. Can't we?"

Bryce took a step back and smoothed his jacket.

Olivia's expression softened. "I know what I've asked you to do might seem unconventional. It is. But I promise you, there's a method to my madness."

"Making it look like I'm having an affair with someone—that's helping my father avoid federal prison? Really? There's some methodology there that I just can't fathom?" Bryce scrubbed a hand across his face. "I can't believe I've let you take the reins like this, Olivia. You're running us into the ground. And I've been following your lead, just waiting for it to make sense. But I'm done."

He reached for my hand, tugging me to his side. "*We're* done. My shareholders are probably all ready to have heart attacks. I can't believe I signed up for this circus, let alone participated in it."

"Don't quit before we get to the good part," Olivia said quietly. "Because what I'm about to unveil is the redemption arc, where America *really* falls in love with you."

Bryce sighed. "I don't care anymore. My father's

probably going to prison, and no amount of PR can undo that. I'm going to be running what's left of the company. I'd prefer to do that honestly."

"And you will—*trust me*, although I know that's hard to do right now." Olivia straightened her shoulders and put her hands on her hips. "The thing is, Bryce? I do actually earn my fee. I know what I'm doing, even if it seems ugly. The public is going nuts, and I've accomplished that in *one week*. Every day people recognize you now. A week ago, the only Windsor people knew about was your father, and that was because he was being investigated. He was just another greedy rich guy. Now your family has a face. Your stock—emotional and actual stock—is on the rise."

"It's a parlor trick," Bryce said. "People will have moved on to the next drama in a week."

"Not necessarily. That was just the first phase. The next part is where we show you and Chloe reuniting, stronger than ever, and put those rumors to rest. Which is why I still need you to do that talk show, Chloe. People would love to hear from you after all this."

"She's not agreeing to anything right now—"

"We don't need to make a commitment today," Olivia interrupted. "But I want you to know where I'm going with this."

"I'm still listening," Bryce said, "but only because Chloe is making me."

"Hold on a minute." Olivia snapped her fingers and pointed at the boutique owner. "She needs to be NDA'd."

"What?" The woman asked, looking concerned. "I need to be what?"

"You need a non-disclosure agreement. Here." Olivia started tapping out something on her phone, then handed it to the woman. "Please review this and then sign. Daphne, can you take her out back and explain it to her? And let her know about the fee we pay. Also, we'll feature the boutique in our press release--and buy those dresses Chloe was just, uh, trying on."

At that, the owner perked up. Daphne steered her toward the back room, talking to her in low tones.

"Here's the thing," Olivia said once they were out of earshot. "I have some news I didn't tell you yet, Bryce. I wanted to keep the focus this morning on you and Chloe. I wanted to get a picture of you two reuniting— it's important for our next steps."

Bryce tensed beside me. "What's the news?"

"It's not great," Olivia sighed. "The settlement negotiations have stalled out. Legal has informed me that the government is playing hardball on this— they've decided to make an example of Gene. Apparently, the SEC has direct evidence your father participated in insider trading. Some sort of a recording or a document, hard evidence. No amount of PR can fix *that*, I'm afraid. I'm so sorry."

Bryce rocked back on his heels. I squeezed his hand.

"The SEC has decided to fast-track the case. I believe the next step is that he will be formally charged," Olivia continued. "As a result, the board has asked me to shift my focus."

We waited for her to go on. "They want me to start highlighting your strengths, Bryce. Your father has been adamant that we stick to the drama; I'm not going to lie, it's been effective. It was my idea to start with. But I've noticed that he's particularly devoted to the Felicia-Jones angle. Again, that was my idea, and it was a good one. The public has been eating it up. But polling still indicates that Chloe is the most relatable person in the Windsor family. You're second, Bryce. Your father hasn't wanted to share that information with the board, but as of this morning, I had to. Ultimately, my client is the business. I have a fiduciary duty to represent its best interests."

"Which means what?" Bryce arched an eyebrow. "Taking a picture of my wife and me after we have sex in a dressing room?"

"Well...yes." Olivia smiled. "Because of how I'm

going to frame it. We'll say that the rumors about Felicia are fabrications cooked up by the tabloids and that you two are basically drunk-in-love with each other. America's Sweethearts, that's where we're going with this. That's why I need Chloe to do the talk show, and I need you both at your cousin's wedding with your hands all over each other. Doesn't really seem like *that* should be a problem." She laughed.

"Once it's established that you two are solid, the news about Gene's indictment won't hit so hard. You'll seem like what you are—a reliable candidate to become interim CEO. Your company's forecast should stay on an even keel. At least, that's the hope. Gene isn't going to be happy, but then again, Gene's probably going to prison. So he doesn't get much say anymore."

"Are you sure about that?" Bryce asked. "Why didn't anyone from legal call me this morning?"

"Because they're scrambling. I finally marched into their office and demanded an update, that's the only reason I know anything. I had to meet with the board and decide on a strategy," Olivia said. "Gene isn't taking the news well. I'm sure he's very upset about all of this."

"He should be." Bryce scowled and looked out the window. "I can't believe the SEC just dropped this bomb on us. If they've come out and said they have direct evidence, that changes things. That changes everything."

"Legal was blindsided by this, let me tell you. We have to move quickly—very quickly." Olivia watched him closely. "Bryce, I know we've gotten off to a rocky start. I'm sorry I put that pressure on you and Chloe, but like I said, there was a reason."

"I still don't agree with how you approached all this. I'm embarrassed that I went along with it," Bryce admitted.

"You did what you needed to. You did it to protect your family." She tilted her head. "Can we agree to collaborate a little while longer? Your board really wants this to work out. You were right—several members were ready to have heart attacks over how the family was being covered in the press. They're ready for a change. It's only been a few days, but we've been hitting it hard. It's time to right the ship and let the drama go. Are you willing to give me one more chance? I promise I won't let you down."

Bryce turned to me. "Only if my wife wants to."

I hesitated. "I'd really like the coverage to be more positive. No more love triangle, fighting-in-the-bathroom type stories."

"We're done with the drama." Olivia stuck out her hand. "I'm answering to you guys now. It's a deal."

Holding my breath, I shook it. And so did Bryce.

Later, after Daphne and I had spent tens of thousands of dollars on dresses at Aqua in an attempt to keep the owner happy and, more importantly, on our side—we headed back to the island. Bryce insisted on riding with Daphne and me. He, of course, brought several security guards. Olivia rode in the other boat with Captain Johnny, and three skiffs filled with paparazzi followed us back.

It was the new normal—a typical day at the office.

Bryce kept his arm around me, and he wasn't just doing it for the cameras, I could tell. Our connection was back. Whether it was our encounter in the dressing room or the news that our drama-filled internet romp was coming to an end, I wasn't sure. But I was thrilled about it and very relieved. I leaned back against him, sighing happily as he wrapped his arms around me and held me close.

Daphne looked over at us from the boat's helm. "You two need to get a room. Oh wait—you already did! A dressing room!" she joked, cracking herself up.

"Very funny." Bryce glared at her.

She shrugged, still grinning. "I know."

I hadn't been able to tell her what Olivia had shared regarding Gene's impending indictment. I was told it wasn't my place. Olivia explained that Legal would sit down with her and Gene that afternoon to review the next steps. Olivia wanted Daphne to hear it from her husband and legal, not from us. I supposed that was fair, but I still hoped she would be okay.

When we got back to the island, Daphne and I parted ways. We made plans to go for a walk later. I wasn't sure if we'd technically become friends, but it felt like maybe we were moving in that direction. Funny, I hadn't expected *that*. But Daphne wasn't all bad. There was plenty of bad there, but she was sort of fun—in a dark-haired, scheming, pregnant-with-Michael-Jones' baby kind of way.

Bryce and I drove the golf cart back to the house. Once we got inside, I hesitated. "You have meetings all afternoon, right?"

"Yes. It's going to be a long day." He took my hands. "I'm glad I got so upset that I followed you to Northeast. At least I got to squeeze some...time...in with you."

I arched an eyebrow. "You squeezed in more than that!"

He chuckled. "I know, that's why I was making a joke."

"Is that what that was?" I teased him. "I'm never sure."

"Ha ha. Anyway." He bent down and kissed my cheek. "I probably won't be able to see you until much later. I'm sorry."

"It's okay." I twisted the cuff of my sweatshirt. I needed to tell him the truth about my dad and Lydia. I'd been so upset that he'd kept a secret from me about meeting Felicia Jones at the Nguyen's party—I would be a total hypocrite if I kept this from *him*.

"Actually, I was wondering if *I* could have a meeting with you really quick. I need to tell you something."

He immediately looked concerned. "What's wrong?"

"It's nothing bad—I mean, it's *bad*, but everything's okay. At least, I hope it is."

We went inside his office and sat down. Once again, being across the desk from him made my mind wander. There was that scenario where I was a naughty schoolgirl, and he was a glowering, dominant principal about to deliver my punishment... *Stop it, Chlo!* Jesus, what had Bryce done to me in that dressing room? I needed to go take a cold shower or something.

The thing was, what I was about to tell him was *so* not sexy. My mind was just stalling, spending its time on more pleasant things. I thought of Lydia and her enormous lion-leg tattoo. *Ugh.* No wonder I didn't want to think about it!

I took a deep breath. "I went to Northeast this morning because I needed to... I met with my father and stepmother." I talked fast, the words tumbling out on top of each other. "Lydia's been texting me for a while—I didn't tell you. I wanted to, but I didn't. She's a problem. They already blew through all the money you paid them, and they wanted more."

"They already spent a million dollars?" Bryce's eyes were wide.

"They were gambling at Foxwoods—that's a casino," I babbled. "The thing is, after they lost it, I sent them more money. But Lydia said it wasn't enough. She was really mad, texting me all sorts of threats."

"I'll rip her fucking thumbs off so she'll never text again," Bryce said, his voice matter-of-fact. "How's that for a threat?"

"Ha! It's good. It's perfect." I nodded, nervous energy bubbling inside of me. I hated lying; it was a relief to tell the truth, even if it was embarrassing. Even if Bryce was threatening to rip Lydia's thumbs off.

"But that's why I didn't tell you, Bryce. I didn't want you to freak out, I didn't want you to go after them, I didn't want you involved. You already paid them a ton of money. You have your own stuff going on—that's the only reason I hid this from you. I didn't want you to worry when you already have so much on your plate."

"Chloe... You have to be able to come to me with your problems. I'm your husband." He sighed.

"I know that! And I would have, I swear, under normal circumstances. But with everything going on with your father and the business, it just seemed like too much." I reached for his hand across the desk. "Do you understand that?"

He squeezed my hand, giving me courage. I continued, "They talked to a lawyer about getting Noah back. I made a deal with them, Bryce. I agreed to give them more money so they can't ever take him from me. From us. Akira's drawing up the paperwork and taking care of everything. We won't have to worry anymore. They won't be able to come back after this, I swear."

"Babe." Bryce looked into my eyes. "Why do I feel like you're apologizing? You didn't do anything wrong. Except give them more money, which they don't deserve. How much?"

I shook my head. "It doesn't matter. I took care of it. They're my family—my problem."

"Chloe. Do you hear yourself? What do you think you've been doing for me? Helping with *my* shit-show of a family."

"But that's the whole reason I'm here," I argued. "That's what you're paying me for."

"You know what I think, Chloe?" Bryce asked.

"What?"

"I think you'd do it for me even if I was broke."

My brow furrowed. "Why do you think that?"

He laughed. "Because I'd do it for you, and you're broke."

"Ha. That's...sweet." My lips twitched up into a smile. I felt so much better that I'd told him the truth.

"Everything's going to be okay. I have to take a call, but I'm here for you. I'm so glad you came to me with your problem. I want you to trust me, Chloe. I want us to be there for each other." Bryce came around the desk and kissed me on the head. "And I know you want to handle this on your own, but we're in this together. Except for the part where I rip Lydia's thumbs off—I'm doing that alone."

I couldn't help it: I laughed.

Then Bryce hugged me, and I hugged him back. He said he would have his personal attorney reach out to Akira so they could craft an agreement together, making sure it was airtight—making sure that Lydia and my dad never came after Noah again.

I left his office feeling ten tons lighter.

That is until I bumped into one of the maids in the

hallway. "Mrs. Windsor—I've been looking everywhere for you," she said, keeping her voice low, "I have a message for you."

"Oh?"

She nodded. "Mr. Windsor would like a word."

"Really?" I asked, confused. "I just left his office."

"The *other* Mr. Windsor," she said, her eyes wide. "And he said it was important."

THIRTY-FIVE

the other mr. windsor

T<small>HE</small> *OTHER* M<small>R</small>. W<small>INDSOR</small>?

My stomach dropped. "Does he want to see me right now?"

She nodded. "And you know, Mr. Windsor doesn't—"

"Like to wait," I finished for her. "I'm aware."

"He's waiting at the guesthouse," she said.

"Thank you for letting me know. I'll go now." I didn't have much choice. It would be lovely if I had a chance to change out of the clothes I'd worn to Northeast Harbor. Not only was I un-showered, but I'd also stood in a cloud of Lydia's second-hand smoke and had rocking, unplanned, explosive sex in a dressing room with my husband... Who happened to be Mr. Windsor's son.

But there was no time for showers or nice outfits. There was only time to panic and power walk. If Gene Windsor had summoned me, I'd best deliver my ass immediately.

I hustled across the grounds toward the guesthouse. Bryce would want to know that I was meeting with his father, but Bryce was in a meeting with legal. I couldn't interrupt him. In any event, it was best not to worry him —I was worried enough for both of us! I would tell him everything when I saw him later that night. After coming clean about Lydia and my dad, I would never keep anything from my husband again. Everything was better when he knew the truth. Everything was better when we were on the same page, close, and connected. I felt like I could handle anything with Bryce by my side.

Except, perhaps, for his father...

What did Mr. Windsor want with me? Maybe he wanted to again try and bribe me into getting an annulment, into leaving his son. He'd always thought Felicia or someone of her stature would be a better choice for Bryce.

I shook my head as I walked. It was probably better not to guess. Gene Windsor was crafty, always five steps ahead—a top-round pro pick to my sorry junior-varsity status. Whatever it was he wanted, I had better be on alert.

I knocked on the guesthouse door, and a guard answered. "Right this way, Mrs. Windsor." He brought me up the stairs to the living room, where Gene Windsor sat on the couch. He surprised me by smiling and standing up when I joined him. "Nice of you to come, Chloe." He sounded almost friendly.

Uh-oh.

"Would you like something to drink?"

I shook my head. "No, thank you."

He turned toward the kitchen and called, "Just a water for me, please." He turned back toward me, a smile on his face. "No bourbon for me—I need to stay sharp. Today's a big day for me."

Double uh-oh.

"Really?" I asked. "What's going on?"

"First of all," Gene sat back on the couch and put his loafer-clad feet up on the coffee table, "I'm being formally charged with insider trading soon. We've asked them to hold off until after the wedding to honor my niece's nuptials and her privacy, but I'm not sure the federal government gives a shit about that. So." He shrugged.

"Second, I understand that the board has asked Olivia Jensen to focus on my son. They want him portrayed as a source of positive stability during a rather tumultuous time." He had a sip of water. "It's unfortunate that we had to get to this point, but understandable. And as he's my successor of choice, I knew this would happen someday. Not exactly like *this*, but still."

I nodded. I didn't know what to say. But Gene didn't seem to think he needed to hear from me. He looked at me and said, "The thing is, Chloe, I need something from you."

"Oh...?"

"Olivia Jensen is very good at her job," he continued. "I hired her for a reason. That reason is her success rate. The thing about Liv is, she doesn't give a shit if she hurts your feelings. That's why she's good at what she does. She analyzes the data and understands what story she needs to tell based on that analysis. So she has data now, data about my family."

The way he said 'my family,' I knew he didn't mean me. "Yes, Mr. Windsor? I don't really understand where you're going with this."

"Of course you don't." He smiled, but it wasn't a nice smile. "That's my point."

He paused for a beat, all the better to let the insinuated insult sink in.

"I know you're testing well with certain segments. And I know that you and my son have a genuine affection for each other, which is baffling to me, but it's really none of my business. Bryce was emotional in the past, but he'll learn soon enough that he can't let that control him." He crossed his ankles together. "The thing is, I don't believe that you are what's best for my son. I've told you this before. He needs to be with someone who can understand the kind of world he lives in. If he's to be at the helm of Windsor Enterprises, that's even more crucial."

"He doesn't want to marry Felicia Jones." I was surprised by how firm my voice sounded, so clear. "I'm going to bet her parents don't want that either, especially after what happened with Daphne." I thought about what Mimi Jones had said. *I think she's doing it to get him back, but it's never going to work.*

"Felicia hasn't tested that well. I'm not tied to her as a particular outcome. She's still a candidate, but I'm not married to the idea." He laughed a little. "See what I did there? I made a pun."

I didn't dare tell him that his "joke" was neither a pun nor was it remotely funny. But I was shocked at how casually he was dismissing Felicia. He'd been her champion. He'd planted a phone with fake text messages in Bryce's room to convince me they'd been having an affair. But just like that—because she hadn't "tested" well—she was out?

"This is why Olivia and I got along so well. I'm ruthless, too. But now that she's abandoning me for the greener pastures of the board, I have to take matters into my own hands."

I swallowed hard. I had a bad feeling that he meant *me* when he said 'matters'—and I definitely didn't want to be in Gene's hands!

Gene regarded me. "The thing is, Chloe, it doesn't have to be Felicia. It just can't be you. You're not good enough for my son. That's not personal—that's an objective fact."

"Your son thinks I'm good enough." He was getting my hackles up. "Just because I wasn't born into a rich family doesn't make me 'bad.'"

"No, it doesn't. But being born into a family of low-class, lazy people who'd rather run a blackmail scheme than work a day in their life makes you a liability, that's for sure." He whipped out his phone, put on his reading glasses, and started tapping away. "See what I mean?"

He handed me his phone. There was a picture from that morning, taken behind the *Northeast Nights* motel. Lydia was gesturing at me with an angry look on her face. My father was inspecting his sneakers.

"My son can't be exposed to these people. He can't be vulnerable to them," Gene said quietly. "Whatever would the board say?"

"Where did you get this?" I asked.

"I hired my own private photographer to follow you. I've paid her very handsomely to report directly to me. Today she finally delivered something worthwhile." Gene smiled. "I haven't talked to these fine folks yet, but a picture tells a thousand words, doesn't it? I'm rich enough to have been blackmailed many times in my life. I can see it on their faces—they want your money, Chloe. They want *my* money. And I bet they're threatening you in order to collect. But what's the threat? Hmm, now what could an average girl like you care about? Let me see..."

He sat back, tapping his fingers together. "You might want to keep your past a secret. It *is* horrible, that crappy little apartment you all were living in. Or it could be something else about your past... Maybe how you met my son?"

He watched me carefully. As though my life depended on it, I didn't react. I didn't even breathe.

"There's something to that, I feel certain. But I'll get to it at some point. Once I start, I'm not going to stop."

I shivered. I didn't want my ruin to be on Gene Windsor's "to-do" list. *Fuck!*

"I'm thinking maybe there's something else you care about, too. Maybe your brother?"

I held very still.

"Maybe it's your sad, pathetic little brother, huh?

The one that no one loves? The one that your father abandoned? If you're all he's got in the world, he's *truly* fucked. Don't you think so, Chloe?"

I refused to look at him. I held my breath.

"It's not like he's ever getting his mother back." Gene chuckled. "No, young Noah's quite on his own, isn't he?"

I clenched my hands into fists. But I still wouldn't look at him. I wouldn't give him the satisfaction.

"I'm thinking the lady with the tiger tattoo is your stepmother—Lydia Burke," Gene continued. "I haven't had my investigator look into her yet, but I will. And that unshaven, ill-looking man must be your father. By the looks of things, they're in rough shape. I wouldn't want to give them custody, either."

Sweat broke out on the back of my neck.

"The thing is? If you don't do what I ask, I'm going directly to them. I will find out what they want, and I will give it to them."

"No! You can't do that." Despite myself, I finally found my voice.

"But that's not true," Gene said slyly. "Because I can do whatever I want. I've been doing it my whole life."

I tried to sound calm as I carefully chose my next words. "Enough with the threats, Mr. Windsor. I'm going to tell Bryce everything. If you threaten me, you threaten him. I might not be able to stop you, but he can."

"You don't want to do that, Chloe." Now Mr. Windsor's smile reached all the way to his eyes. "I've been thinking, you see. Now that it seems inevitable I'm going to prison, I am going to lose control of the day-to-day operations of Windsor Enterprises. Bryce has always been next in line. He almost lost his position, but then he fulfilled his trust terms by getting married. He vested when he married you—you know that."

He paused for a beat. "I told you before that you were not the intended beneficiary of that trust clause. I thought he would come to his senses and marry Felicia Jones, or at least someone like her. Someone from our class. But he didn't, and it seemed as though there was nothing I could do about it. Until now."

Gene had a sip of water, his eyes sparkling. "Once you have nothing left to lose, things become a lot clearer. Now that I'm going to prison, I can see that I need to take action. Bryce will be the face of my company—but not you. It was never supposed to be you. And I know all about the test markets, but I haven't worked my entire life to build my company just to hand it over to someone common. You're from nothing, Chloe, from no one. In fact, if these pictures are indicative of the type of people your family is, it's even worse than that."

A heavy silence settled over the room, and I knew he was about to go in for the kill.

"You love my son, I know you do. So do the right thing and let him go. If you don't, I'm going to change the corporate structure of Windsor Enterprises before I go to prison—I'll fire Bryce from leadership and give the reins to Colby or Jake. Probably Colby, because he at least calls me sometimes. And no one will be able to stop me, not even the board, because I can claim an 'executive exigency.' My lawyers just told me about it this morning, isn't that neat? It's a little-known privilege that allows leaders to make *unilateral* emergency changes to their company. So I don't need anyone's permission. If I claim that it's a necessary emergency measure in the best interests of the company, I can do as I like."

"You wouldn't do that." I licked my lips. "You've been doing everything you can to save your company, to make sure it stays alive even if you go to jail. Why would you blow it up like that? Even I'm not *that* bad."

"I don't agree with you," Gene said coolly. "The way I see it, I'm still saving my company. I have a new perspective on things. Like I said, desperation makes things very clear. I know what I want now. I want my company to go on the way it was intended. I want Bryce to run things the way he's supposed to. He needs to be focused and supported. And it has to be the *right* kind of support, Chloe. We're running an empire. We're very important people. He needs a partner who will understand him and protect him. Not expose him to trash like this." He held up another picture of Lydia. She'd just exhaled a cloud of smoke and was absentmindedly scratching her lion tattoo.

"You have a lot to lose. When I say that, I'm not just thinking of your marriage. I'm thinking of your brother." Gene didn't blink as he stared me down.

I felt like I was underwater, drowning. Gene Windsor had an army he could fight me with. He had *piles* of money, an endless supply. No doubt that even if his assets were frozen, he'd just hawk a fifty-million dollar painting or two and keep coming at me.

"I want you to leave, and it has to seem natural. My son cannot find out that I'm behind this. If he does, I'll make damn sure that you lose everything. *Everything.* And I'll make it ugly, Chloe. I'll make it hurt."

I couldn't catch my breath. I felt like an undercurrent had snatched me and was dragging me out to sea. The safety of the shore was disappearing; I was never going to get back there. *My brother, he was going to hurt my brother...*

"What do you want me to do?" I could barely get the words out.

Gene appeared to have no such angst. He sat back, grinning, and recrossed his ankles. His stupid, ugly, ridiculously expensive loafers mocked me. "I want you to do exactly what I say."

twinge

IT WAS the best of times, it was the worst of times. It was the best because I no longer had to sit across from Gene Windsor. It was the best because he hadn't hurt me, Bryce, or my brother—not yet.

It was the worst because I knew that he was going to. Unless I did precisely what he asked, Gene was absolutely going to take the company from Bryce. He would also absolutely do something terrible to Noah. He'd said he would make it hurt; I didn't doubt him for a second.

So I couldn't say anything. Not to my husband, not to anyone. If I went off-script, Gene would blow up my whole world—he would hurt the people I loved. I loved Noah too much to risk it.

I loved my husband too much.

I set about following his instructions. I called Olivia

and said I would do the morning talk show like she'd asked. I ordered a specific dress for the wedding. I called Akira Zhang to ensure that Lydia and my father agreed to the proposed contract and would sign it. Then we could send them the money, which would keep them quiet. At least for now.

I went through the motions of my day, dreading each second, sweating each detail. From that point on, I would be living a lie.

And I had to sell it as though my life depended on it.

Because it did. It absolutely did.

Lucky for me, Bryce was in meetings until late that night. He climbed into bed next to me. I pretended to be asleep as he slipped his arm around me and pulled me close. Tears pricked my eyes, but I refused to cry: there would be time for that later when I was alone again.

I clung to my husband and fell into a restless sleep.

When my alarm went off early, he was already gone. He'd left a note on my nightstand:

Meetings all day again. I'm going to miss you.
You're going to do great today—I'm so proud of you.
Love you.

xx

Bryce

It was better that we were apart. If I had to be around him right now, after everything his father had said to me yesterday, it might break me.

I got up, took a listless shower, and shuffled to my bedroom. "There she is," Midge said, but when she got one look at my face, she put a hand over her heart. "What's the matter, hon?"

"Oh, it's nothing," I lied. "I'm just nervous about taping this segment for the talk show. You know me—I don't exactly love being the center of attention."

"Oh honey, I know." Midge bought me to the makeup chair and started gently combing my hair out. "But I think with the new headlines, it's going to be a *lot* more pleasant. You'll see. It won't be so bad."

"What new headlines?" I'd been so upset, I hadn't even bothered to get on the internet.

"Ooh, you haven't seen them? This'll cheer you up." Midge grabbed her phone and opened it, scrolling to something before she handed it over. "*Much better* than that other crap. I'm loving the new direction."

I read the headlines linking to the various gossip sites.

Chloe and Bryce Fight Back on Cheating Rumors

Felicia Who? Bryce Only Has Eyes for Chloe

*Bryce and Chloe Can't Keep Their Hands off Each Other—
And It's So Cute*

I clicked on the first article. As usual, there was zero reporting. It was all pictures, but at least these were happy ones. They were shots from the boat ride back from Northeast Harbor, with Daphne at the helm. Bryce had his arms wrapped around me from behind. We were both smiling. There was even one of us kissing—I didn't even remember doing that, but the picture was cute. My heart twisted, remembering how happy I'd felt to be back in his arms.

I clicked on the following link. There was an uncharacteristically unflattering photo of Felicia. She was scowling at her phone, her shoulders slumped. I didn't know if it was a new picture or if the internet gods had dug it up from some old archive, but in any event, it sold the message: Felicia was upset. The next photo was of Bryce and I laughing, his arm thrown around me as we walked down the dock. We looked like we didn't have a care in the world—young, in love, living our happily ever after. The juxtaposition of these photos was crude but still clever. Felicia was losing. Bryce and Chloe were winning. I'm not going to lie, it felt much better being on the winning side of the "article."

The final piece had the money shots from inside the boutique. The crafty photographer had snapped one of us slipping inside the dressing room, an intense look on Bryce's face. "According to a source, they were locked in the private fitting room for several minutes." The next shots were of us coming out. Both of our faces were flushed. Bryce's tie was askew, and his hair was a mess. I *definitely* looked glowing, as though I'd been freshly fucked. We were both smiling. Bryce had his hand firmly on my ass.

We looked happy and in love. We looked like we couldn't keep our hands off each other—even in a boutique—and it really *was* so cute.

My eyes filled with tears. "Chloe?" Midge's voice rose in alarm. "What's the matter?"

I blinked back tears. "I j-just love my husband so much. I'm glad I don't have to read that nasty crap about Felicia anymore. This is so much better."

"It is. Those are nice pictures, hon. Don't be sad— you've got everything in the world to look forward to."

I wiped at my eyes. "Thank you, Midge. That means a lot." But sadly, it wasn't true.

Still, I vowed to hold it together. I had my husband to think about. My brother.

I let Midge go heavy on the makeup—I needed it for television. She smoothed my hair with a flat iron, making it fall in silky waves over my shoulders. The dress she'd chosen was another jewel tone, a deep sapphire-blue, which was fitted and flattering. Of course she insisted that I wear mile-high heels on the premise that they would make "my butt look awesome."

When I argued that I'd be sitting down, she only rolled her eyes and shoved me out the door.

Olivia Jensen waited at the landing, clutching her signature enormous iced coffee. She was no Bryce, but at least she smiled at me. "You look perfect, Chloe. That dress will crush it on camera. How are you feeling?"

"Nervous," I admitted once I reached her. "They aren't going to make me talk much, are they?"

"They're definitely going to ask you some questions." Olivia looked thoughtful as she led me through the house. The interview was being conducted downstairs, in the media room. It was on the lower level, a section I'd never ventured to. Apparently, it had excellent sound quality. The camera crew had come to the island in the middle of the night before the paparazzi would be awake to snap pictures. The network wanted this to be exclusive.

The morning talk-show hosts were going to interview me live from New York; I was set up for a video chat. They'd sent the production crew and an assistant to get me set up and walk me through the process.

"Let me talk you through it." Olivia opened the door to the media room, which was buzzing with the camera crew settling all the last-minute details. "They're going to want to know how you are holding up during the investigation and how Bryce is. They will probably ask you about the cheating rumors, even though I told them to go light on that. Finally, they might ask you about the upcoming wedding, what you're wearing, and maybe what it's like living in a giant mansion on a private island."

"Okay. That doesn't sound too bad—except for the cheating part." The only thing I had to remember, the one crucial detail, was Gene's instructions. *Make it seem as though you're crazy in love with my son.*

That shouldn't be too hard. It was the truth, even though the truth hurt.

The assistant, who wore glasses and clutched her clipboard as though her life depended on it, hustled over to me. "Are you ready, Mrs. Windsor?"

"Yes," I lied.

"You look *great*. That dress is perfect. I'm going to mic you, okay?" I held still as she clipped a small microphone to the collar of my dress. The assistant stood back and inspected me, an approving look on her face. "We might need to steal your hair and makeup person away. She's *terrific*."

That brought a genuine smile to my face. "Yeah, she is. I'll tell her you said so—except for the stealing her away part."

"Ha, fair enough. We're going to go ahead and get started, okay? Follow me." She brought me to a high, long table with a glass of water on it. "Stand behind here and face the screens. Let me show you what you'll be looking at."

She nodded, and a cameraman lit up several screens. There was a picture of a studio in New York, with two well-dressed women sitting in chairs facing the cameras. Behind them was a large window with an audience standing outside, smiling and waving. The other two screens were individual angles of each of the women.

"You're going to look like this," the assistant said, pointing at the final screen. My image popped up. I looked better than I should—I was miserable inside. This interview was the first part of Gene's plan, and I was dreading it. I felt like I was about to walk the plank. Once I started, there was no way back.

"Let's go, everyone! Live in five!" The assistant scurried away to the other side of the cameras. Olivia Jensen gave me a thumbs-up from the sideline.

I took a deep breath as they counted down. "Five, four, three..."

"Hi there, we're back after the break!" One of the pretty women on the screen said. "And our next guest is someone we're *all* excited to meet. It's Chloe Windsor, wife of billionaire Bryce Windsor."

The other host turned to her. "We've all heard about Gene Windsor, Chloe's father-in-law. He's the embattled CEO of Windsor Enterprises. He's been having a tough time lately, but it's so nice for the family that Chloe and Bryce seem to have been becoming more public. Bryce Windsor used to be really reclusive, didn't he?"

"M-hmm." The first host nodded knowingly. "And with a face like this, who wants to hide?" They laughed, and the image cut to several older photos of Bryce. He was dashing in each of them, with his handsome face and massive shoulders. The co-hosts sighed dreamily.

"Since he and Chloe married, the family's become much more public," the first host continued.

The second host nodded. "It's like they're our American Royals, you know?"

"Absolutely. We're all falling in love with them. So with that, let's bring on our next guest, Chloe Windsor!"

I could see myself on their screen. I felt frozen, but I forced myself to smile. Olivia grinned from her spot on the wall, all encouraging optimism.

"Hey there Chloe, it's great to see you!" The hosts waved to me, and I waved back. "You're coming to us from your gorgeous house in Maine, correct?"

"Yep!' I sounded peppy, happy. I smiled some more. "It's beautiful up here this time of year. We're in Mount Desert Island, near Acadia National Park. Have you guys ever been?"

"Yes, and *oh*, it is gorgeous! Much better than New York in July." The host fanned herself. "Woo, it's hotter than one of my hot flashes here! So Chloe, we were just chatting about your father-in-law, Gene Windsor. We know there's been some legal trouble—allegations of insider trading. We're sorry to hear it. How're you all holding up?"

"Thank you so much for asking. You know, it's been hard. Everybody loves Gene," I lied. "But we're also grateful for all the work the American government's putting into this investigation. We want everyone to know that we support them and have been cooperating with them fully. If any laws have been broken, we want to take responsibility. We'll do whatever it takes."

The hostess tilted her head, nodding. "I love that, Chloe—the fact that not only are you supporting your family but that you're openly supporting the government, too. These things don't have to be mutually exclusive. Good for you."

The other host leaned forward. "Okay, now it's *my* turn. How is that handsome husband of yours holding up?"

"Aw, thank you—he is handsome, isn't he?" They laughed, and I continued, "He's doing as well as anyone could expect. Bryce loves his father, and he loves his company. He's committed to doing the work. He gives his best every day."

"Wow." The hostess nodded. "That's wonderful. He's lucky to have such a loving wife."

"I'm lucky to have *him*." I started to choke up.

"Oh sweetie!" The first hostess put her hand over her heart. "That actually brings us to our next question. The elephant in the room—Felicia Jones." The image swapped out to the picture of Bryce and Felicia at the Nguyen's party, the one in which she was thrusting her chest out at him while looking up from under her lashes.

Both of the hosts frowned. "So what's the deal?

Rumor has it that she used to date Bryce. Can you confirm that?"

"Ha, way to put me on the spot, ladies!" I laughed, playing along. "But actually, I'm really glad you're bringing this up."

That got their attention. "You are?" asked the second host. "How come?"

"Well..." I took a deep breath. Gene had been very specific about this part. "Thank you for the opportunity to address this. Because it really hurt me—what everyone was saying about her and my husband."

The hosts looked at each other. My chin started to wobble.

"It's just that it's not true." My eyes filled with tears. "M-My husband loves me. He wouldn't ever do anything to hurt me. What the press said was lies. It was lies, but it still hurt."

A tear slid down my cheek. "I love my husband more than anything. I would die without him, just die. And I think the press doesn't get called out on these things enough. He never had an affair with that woman. But what was posted online still hurt me, you know? I'm human. I have feelings."

I was telling the truth. I *would* die without Bryce— that was why it was so easy for me to cry. Gene was going to make me say goodbye to him once and for all.

"Chloe, Chloe, Chloe!" The first host reached her arms out. "I just want to give you a big hug! Of course, you have feelings. We hear this from many celebrities—they feel that the laws around paparazzi and privacy need to be changed. You need to speak up for yourself. Because when you help yourself, you help others!"

"Oh, thank you." I wiped at my eyes. "That's really nice of you to say."

"Oh sweetie. I want to hug you, too." The second host clapped her hands together. "Let's end with some happy stuff. How does that sound?"

"Good." I blew out a deep breath. "That sounds really good."

"So!" The first host grinned at me. "The other big news is that there's an upcoming family wedding! Caroline Vale, Bryce's cousin, is set to marry tech-billionaire Eli Hazleton! Are you excited for the wedding?"

"I'm *so* excited. It's going to be amazing—they're getting married at a beautiful spot on Spruce Island. I can't wait."

"And what are you wearing?"

"It's a surprise—I can't tell you that!" I laughed. "But how about I text you a picture from the wedding? Then you can see for yourself!"

"I love it. Awesome!" The first host said.

"One final question, Chloe." The second host leaned

forward, eyes sparkling. "Girl to girl... What's it like living in a giant mansion with America's hottest billionaire?"

I grinned at her. "It's like a fairytale," I said. "It's every girl's dream come true."

The interview ended, and Olivia Jensen came over to me. She whistled. "That was amazing, Chloe. I can't believe you teared up like that, it was so emotional!"

"Did it go okay?" I asked.

"Are you kidding me?" Her eyes were wide. "After seeing that interview, no one on earth would doubt how much you love your husband. The love was just oozing out of you. *Oozing.*"

"Good," I said, even though it wasn't good.

It was, however, exactly what Gene Windsor wanted.

THIRTY-SEVEN

wedding bells

THE NEXT FEW days passed in a blur. Tons of requests rolled in for more interviews; I politely told Olivia Jensen to decline them. There would be no more press for Chloe Windsor. My ratings were favorable with the public, but that no longer mattered.

My ratings with Gene Windsor would *never* be favorable. What mattered was following his script, doing his bidding. What mattered most was protecting my husband and brother, the two people I had left in the world.

Akira had checked in. Lydia and my father had signed the contract and taken the money. They understood that there wasn't any more coming, at least in theory. My father had once again waived his legal rights to Noah. This time, Akira had him execute an agreement that she filed with the family court. She said it could take a while, but eventually, a judge would approve it. Then he wouldn't be able to fight me for my brother.

Not that he really wanted him. Not that he'd called to check in on his son—he hadn't. He and Lydia had probably cashed their check, hit the liquor store, and were having a good old time doing what they did best— getting fucked up and making a mess of things. They weren't aware of what they'd set in motion, how their actions had impacted me. They would never know because I would never speak to them again. They hadn't meant for Gene Windsor to take their picture and use their existence as the rationale to get rid of me once and for all. Once again, I was collateral damage—their poor choices had led to my downfall.

I prayed to my mom. *Don't let me get bitter.* But I was worried I was already halfway there...

A bright spot was my brother. Noah seemed as happy as ever. He played with Boss the puppy and fished off the private dock for hours. The troubles the rest of us were facing—the paparazzi, the pending charges, the blackmail—didn't trickle into his happy bubble. I was so relieved about that.

The thing that sucked? I was going to pop that bubble sooner rather than later. And I knew my brother would never forgive me.

Don't think about it, don't think about it, don't think about it! Because if I didn't do what Gene asked, Noah would face a lot worse. *That* was the thought I needed to keep front and center in my mind.

Every moment of every day, I needed to think about the people that I loved. I needed to keep my eye on the ball and forget everything else.

After the interview, Bryce sent me flowers. *I'm one lucky bastard,* the card read. *I'm so proud of you, babe.* I hugged the card to my chest as my eyes filled with tears. Bryce had no idea what was happening with me, what was about to happen. He'd been so busy with the board and legal that he'd barely slept.

It was better that he was busy. If I was around him too much, if we were close... I was pretty sure it would break me. I couldn't risk that. It seemed that fate was intervening, making Gene's plans come true. Everything was falling into place.

The government still hadn't announced the formal charges against Gene, but it was just a matter of time. Daphne wasn't taking the news particularly well. She was worried about how it would impact her, of course. "He told me that he's definitely going to prison. They'll probably freeze his assets—I don't know what that means for the baby and me!"

I wanted to comfort her, but I didn't know what to

say. When I asked Bryce about it in passing, he made me feel better. "Don't worry—we'll take care of her. She'll be able to stay in the house. It's not like I'm going to let her and her child *starve*." He was already assuming the leadership role, and I was glad for it. Bryce was a good guy. He would make choices that helped the people around him.

I was doing this for a reason.

I hoped Bryce's position would make Daphne happy, but then again, she was accustomed to a more lavish lifestyle. She'd been texting me all morning—not about her husband's impending arrest but about which gown to wear to the wedding. She'd sent me six different pictures, all with different "looks." *I still can't decide—help!*

At least Daphne's priorities were still intact. I had to give her that. I texted back that I liked the pink dress best. *You look pretty in that color.* Her husband was a snake, the devil, and a master manipulator all rolled into one, but she *did* look good in pink.

She responded immediately. *Thanks! See u soon!*

The wedding was that afternoon. I trudged to my bedroom so Midge could do my hair and makeup.

"Chloe Windsor!" Her tone was scolding, her eyes wide as she stuffed me into the makeup chair. "You did *not* tell me about that dress! It just got delivered today. Holy hell, it's a hot one!" She fanned herself.

"Oh...thanks." I actually hated the dress. It was red, the color of evil. Of course, Gene Windsor had picked it out. Maybe the color wasn't really the problem!

"We have to do stick-straight hair to go with that dress. I want it to swish. I want people to go bananas." She turned the flat iron to hot and let it sit for a minute. "Are you excited about tonight? I love weddings."

"Me too," I lied. All I did anymore, it seemed like, was lie. "I can't wait."

"Chloe." Midge furrowed her brow as she dotted some concealer under my eyes. "I'm not trying to pry, but you don't really seem like yourself these last couple of days. I thought you did so good on that talk show. I don't know—I thought you'd be relieved when it was over. And now there's no more pictures of stupid 'Bryle-cia' on the internet. But you seem more upset than ever."

I sighed. Midge was my friend; she'd gotten to know me too well. "I guess I'm still just feeling raw from everything, you know? There's a lot going on with the investigation. Bryce is under a lot of pressure. I feel like I'm hurting, not helping."

"What do you mean?" She applied my foundation with a pouffy brush.

"It's just that... I love him, you know? And I know the whole thing with Felicia seems like it's blown over, but... I don't know if *I'm* over it. It's still making me feel crazy."

"Okay. Tell Midge more—go on."

I needed to fine-tune this part. Gene had been specific, but Gene was good at being a dick and making money—he *wasn't* good at people and feelings. "It's just that she hurt me, you know? The press blew the whole thing out of proportion, but Felicia had a part to play. She wanted my husband—I'm worried she still wants him. And I know she's going to be at the wedding tonight. Ugh, it's making me feel sick that I have to be at an event with her."

"You have the hottest dress on earth," Midge offered. "So there's that. And if you see her, maybe just ignore her. There's nothing she can do to you, Chloe. Just be the bigger person. Let it go. She's not worth it."

I nodded. She *wasn't* worth it.

But that didn't mean I was allowed to let it go.

someday

I TOTTERED outside to meet the others. Bryce, Olivia Jensen, Daphne, Jake, and Colby waited on the dock. There was a large team of security guards, too—the wedding was going to be crowded. It was the event of the season.

Bryce stared at me, his mouth agape. I wasn't sure if that was good or bad.

Daphne was the first one to break the silence. "*Damn*, Chloe." She eyed my dress. "Are you trying to get arrested tonight?"

"Ha! Not exactly. Your dress is pretty, Daphne. I love you in pink." I managed to make it over to Bryce without falling off the dock, no small feat in my sky-high heels.

He continued to gape at me.

"You look too handsome in that tux," I finally said.

"You look..." His gaze raked over me. "I don't know. I might need you to put on my jacket, babe."

"Ha."

"I'm not kidding." From his tone, it was obvious that he was not, in fact, kidding.

"Don't be silly." I nudged him playfully. But the fact was, I wished I could wear his jacket. The "dress" Gene had chosen for me was several scraps of crimson material sewn together. The top piece was comprised of red triangles that covered my breasts; they tied together in the back like a bikini. The top connected to the bottom portion, a long, fitted skirt, by a tiny tab in the front. My back was entirely bare down to the top of my ass. My sides were also wholly exposed, my skin glistening in the late-afternoon sun.

Jake and Colby did not look at me, not once. "Hey guys."

"Hey Chloe." They both seemed really interested in staring at the ocean.

"That's quite the dress." Olivia Jensen was beside me, checking out the back, making me feel exposed under her curious inspection. "No offense, but it doesn't really scream 'wedding guest.' How come you chose it?"

I wanted to tell her the truth: Gene Windsor had picked out the dress because he thought it made me look like I was trying too hard. That's what he was going for, and that's exactly what he had achieved. The gown left nothing to the imagination. "Um, I thought it was pretty. And different, you know?"

"It's definitely different." Olivia herself wore a classy aqua dress that covered her shoulders. She looked pretty and understated, which was perfect for a wedding. Daphne's dress was a little more daring— formfitting, with a plunging back—but it was still rated PG.

My dress was R. Or maybe NC-17 if that was still even a thing.

"Anyway! Looking forward to this wedding. Should be fun," I lied again.

"I'm keeping you under my arm all night." He eyed the back of the dress. "And maybe in front of me."

"Ha! Sounds good to me." We filed onto the boat, and Captain Johnny headed out into the harbor. The paparazzi boats followed us, the photographers' zoom lenses pointed in our direction, but I no longer cared. Let them take pictures, let them take all the pictures. That was what Gene wanted, wasn't it?

The men were having drinks below deck. "When are they bringing the charges against Dad? I feel like this whole thing's been hurry-up-and-wait," Jake said. "I don't say this often, but I actually feel bad for him. It must be a lot of pressure."

"He's handling it as well as can be expected," Bryce said. "As soon as they bring charges, he's going to be taken into custody. I don't think he's in any real rush for that to happen."

"How is he doing with the transfer?" Colby asked. "I can't get him to talk to me—I don't really have a sense of how he's doing."

"He's not happy about it." Bryce had a sip of his drink. "But he knows I have the company's best interests at heart. He knows I'll do my best and that I understand how much it means to him that I keep growing our business. I'm really hoping that you two want to have a more active role."

"I'd love that," Jake said immediately.

"Me too. Wow, I'm honored." Colby raised his glass, and they all toasted.

Seeing Bryce with his brothers, and hearing their plans to work together, warmed my heart. *This* was why I wanted to protect his position with the company—because he was the right person to lead. He would be a great CEO. He would take care of his brothers. He would steer Windsor Enterprises through a difficult time, which would be better for everyone.

"*I* know why you picked that dress." Daphne sidled

up next to me. "It's because you know that bitch Felicia Jones is going to be at the wedding. You're going to show her up, am I right?"

"Maybe." I smiled at her. "If she says anything to me, hold my drink—I'm not going to take it anymore!"

"That's my girl." Daphne beamed at me. "She deserves it. But she probably won't say anything. I heard she's bringing that guitarist as her date. She's finally moved on!"

When my smile faltered, Daphne nudged me. "That's good news, right? Don't tell me you were looking for a fight."

"Ha! No, of course not." Another lie.

I was quiet as we reached Spruce Island, quiet as we climbed onto the enormous jeep-truck that chauffeured us to the venue, a gorgeous private estate overlooking the ocean. We went through security, had our pictures taken for identification purposes, and put our eyes up to some sort of retina scanner. "Very *Jason Bourne*," Colby said, impressed. Finally, we were allowed into the space where the ceremony would be held.

There was seating for four hundred guests across the gorgeous grounds, all in neat lines. The altar was at the front, the ocean rolling behind it. It was the perfect view. The sun was shining, and there was a breeze; it was literally the best day of the summer. I'd never been to a wedding like this before. I was overwhelmed by the sheer number of guests, everyone decked out in their tuxedos, the women in pretty dresses. It immediately became apparent that my dress was woefully out of place. The other female guests looked pretty; I looked vulgar.

I sat next to Bryce in our pew, relieved that he was shielding me. I didn't want to be exposed. I didn't want anything to do with this wedding, so I was happy to sit by my husband's side while I could.

"You're awfully quiet tonight," Bryce said. "I'm sorry that I've been so busy. I feel like I haven't talked to you in days."

"Don't be sorry." I rested my head against his shoulder, soaking up the feeling of being with him. I would pay for this later when I was alone—the indiscretion of letting myself feel my feelings. It was going to hurt so bad. But I was powerless to stop myself; I wanted to be close while I could.

"I'm so proud of you," I said. "I know you're going to do an amazing job as CEO. I know it's been stressful, but you're doing so good, babe."

"Aw... Thank you." A smile broke out over his face, and it was like the sun coming out. "I love you, Chloe."

"I love you, too."

I basked in his love, his attention, his warmth. I

vowed to remember this moment and savor it during the hard times, the times I knew were coming.

Out of the corner of my eye, I saw a flicker of long, dark hair. Felicia Jones walked down the aisle to her seat, hips swaying beneath her beautiful lavender gown. She was holding hands with a handsome guy in a black tux. He had a tattoo on the back of his neck, a cross. He said something to her, and she threw her head back, laughing, as though she didn't have a care in the world.

Bryce caught me staring. "She's dating Finn Ryder again. See? It all worked out the way it was supposed to."

"You're right," I lied again. "You're absolutely right."

THIRTY-NINE

crazy in love

CAROLINE VALE and her new husband, Eli Hazleton, were quite the couple. Caroline was tall, blond, and aloof; Eli was short, chubby, and never stopped smiling. They'd written their own vows; the ceremony was moving to watch. I found myself blinking back tears several times.

But that might have been for a variety of reasons.

I kept track of Felicia Jones throughout the ceremony and reception. Worried that I'd lose sight of her, I couldn't relax. Bryce kept his arm around me all night, trying to keep my dress under wraps, and also, he was being sweet. My husband seemed like he was in a great mood. For once, he was very social, chatting with old friends and family members he hadn't seen in a long time. He introduced me to everybody, but I couldn't for the life of me remember anyone's names. I just smiled and nodded, hoping that I appeared engaged.

I wasn't. I was starting to sweat. Gene Windsor had given me specific instructions; if I didn't execute them properly, he was going to fuck my shit up, as Lydia would say.

There were several bars set up around the property. Felicia and Finn Ryder worked their way through all of them, laughing and doing shots. I thought Felicia was sober, but that didn't appear to be the case. It seemed that the guitarist was quite the partier, and she kept up with him. Finn talked easily to everyone, keeping his hand firmly on Felicia's toned ass all night. They looked like they were having a great time. It was going to be challenging to get her alone.

But where there was a will, there was a way.

Bryce and I followed his brothers to the same bar where Felicia and Finn were hanging out, ordering yet another round of shots.

Colby got the bartender's attention. "Who wants what—Bryce, Jake? Another round?" He turned to me. "Do you want anything?"

"I'll have a shot of...tequila," I said.

Bryce's eyeballs almost popped out of his head. "You're drinking?"

I shrugged. "It's just a little drink, right?"

"A shot's pure alcohol." Bryce looked at me like I'd sprouted three heads. "And you don't drink alcohol."

"I do tonight." I smiled at him, hoping I sounded like I was trying to be fun. What was *really* happening was that I was scared shitless. I prayed the tequila, whatever it tasted like, would somehow help. I knew firsthand that people did crazy shit when they'd been drinking. I needed an excuse. So what if I hated alcohol? I'd made a deal with the devil, and I was about to do the devil's work. I might as well take a sip from the devil's cup while I was at it...

Colby handed me the shot, and I knocked it back in one sip. It burned and made my eyes water. My stomach roiled. People actually *liked* this? It was awful! "I'll have another one," I told Colby.

Bryce practically had steam coming out of his ears. "Chloe—"

"Aw, come on." Colby patted his shoulder. "Let her have some fun."

He handed me the second shot; this time, I held my nose while I drank it. Colby laughed. "Classy, Chloe. Really classy."

"Ha! Thanks." The tequila instantly gave me a weird feeling. I felt hot, then chilly. But after a moment, it passed.

Felicia and Finn were only a couple feet away,

talking to another attractive couple. It was getting dark out. Soon, we'd have to attend the sit-down dinner and listen to speeches and toasts. *Game time.*

"I think I need one more." I winked at Colby while Bryce fumed.

"You're going to regret this," he said.

I nodded. "Probably." I downed it anyway.

Now I felt sick. And dizzy. And not at all like myself, which was precisely the point.

"I need to go to the ladies' room," I mumbled.

"I'll take you." Bryce reached protectively for my arm.

"I got it, silly." I smiled at him, but I felt woozy. "Be right back." I tottered away, and I heard Bryce curse.

"She'll be all right," Colby said. "And if not, we'll just go get her. Let her relax a little. You guys have been through a lot."

Bryce cursed again.

I ignored him. I ignored the fact that I said I was going to the bathroom. I ignored the fact that there was a buzzing in my head, a pit in my stomach.

I made a beeline for Felicia Jones.

I staggered up to her little group and joined them. I noticed I was still swaying on my feet even when I stopped walking. *Uh oh.* I was sloppy, a mess.

It was probably for the best.

As usual, Felicia ignored me. She was talking about something to her friends, probably her apartment in Paris and her aversion to carbohydrates. I stood there, swaying and blinking until it became obviously uncomfortable. Finn Ryder nudged her.

"What, babe?"

He pointed in my direction, and she rolled her eyes. "Ugh, what the hell do you want now?"

"Can I talk to you?"

"About *what*?" Her lip curled in a sneer. "I don't know what your problem still is—seriously. Everybody else has moved on. You need to get a life!"

It would have been better, I thought, if I had just hit her in the bathroom at Kelli and Kenji Nguyen's house. She had deserved it at that moment. Now she was still being a total bitch, but she had a point. It was over between her and Bryce. It was yesterday's news. Coming up to her now was like my vulgar dress—it was too much. Still, I needed to follow my orders.

I conjured up my past hurt and worked from that.

"You shouldn't have sent my husband pictures of you in a bikini," I slurred. "Only trolls do that."

"Can you hear yourself?" Felicia asked. "You're *drunk*. And what's with that dress? You look like a waitress at a freaking gentleman's club—and not the upscale kind, more like the cheap handjob kind."

"You would know."

"You would know," she mimicked me. "Seriously? You sound like a fourth-grader!"

"You *look* like a fourth-grader." I probably should have worked on my lines.

"Get *away* from me. You're a fucking idiot. I'm glad Bryce ended up with you—that's exactly what he deserves."

"Don't you talk about my husband like that!" I raised my voice. Now people were looking at us, which was what I wanted, even though, in reality, it was the last thing I wanted.

"Okay, Miss, you need to go now." Finn Ryder had a British accent.

"I'm not going anywhere. Not until this bitch apologizes to me for talking to my husband behind my back. And for being a snob."

"You want me to apologize for talking to my ex —*talking*—and for being a snob." Felicia's eyeballs looked like they were about to pop out of her head. "Seriously? Go home, Decoy. You're drunk."

"What did you just say to me?" But it didn't matter. I wasn't capable of saying anything witty enough to provoke her further. I was just going to have to get it over with and fuck the bitch up!

I launched myself at Felicia, pulling hair, yanking

her stupid dress, and wrestling her. She was in better shape than me, but I was pissed.

I heard Finn Ryder curse in his stupid British accent as I wrangled Felicia to the ground and jumped on top of her. *Then* I heard a litany of curse words, strung together with phrases like: *only trolls text married men!* and *how does it feel like to be beaten up by a decoy, you smug fucker?*

It wasn't as good as I'd imagined it. But it wasn't that bad, either.

don't say a word

"WHAT THE HELL, Chloe. What. The. Hell." Bryce paced our room.

"Can you please stop yelling at me? My head hurts. Ow." I pulled the pillow over my face.

"I'm not yelling at you." Bryce lowered his voice. "I'm just trying to understand why you went after Felicia. The MDI police just called—they might bring you up on assault charges, Chloe."

"Ugh." That was actually helpful, even though it was awful. "I'm so sorry."

He sank down onto the bed. "You don't have to be sorry... But can you explain yourself to me? That wasn't like you. That dress wasn't like you, the drinking... You don't drink, Chloe. And you certainly don't fight. You weren't yourself tonight."

"I think... I don't know, Bryce. I think it was something I had to do."

"Okay." His brow furrowed. "But why now?"

"I don't... I don't know."

His phone rang, and he cursed. "Fuck, it's Regina Hernandez from the board. This isn't going to go over well. I'll be back." He put the phone to his ear and marched out of the room.

I lay there, feeling dead inside. This was it. This was the last act of the crappy play Gene had cast me in. My starring role was about to come to an end...

I had to act fast. Gene Windsor had told me, in no uncertain terms, that I was to leave as soon as the wedding was over. Otherwise, he would make good on his promises. He would cut Bryce out of the company and do God-only-knew-what to my brother.

I needed to leave, but I needed help getting off the island. I had waited until the last second to organize my exit because I couldn't risk anyone knowing what I was up to. I crept from the room, then hurtled down the back staircase to the staff's living quarters. I knocked on each door, waking more than a few employees up until I found who I was looking for.

"Hazel—hey."

She tightened her bathrobe against her. "Yes, Mrs. Windsor?"

I took a deep breath. "I know how much you care about Mr. Windsor. You're the only person I can turn to. I need your help. *Now*."

I explained what I needed—my brother woken up and packed lightly, his things brought immediately to the boat, a promise from Captain Johnny to get us to Northeast Harbor. Money for two bus tickets and a hotel room, enough to last us until tomorrow, when I could call Akira Zhang. Gene Windsor hadn't given me anything, and I hadn't asked: I'd been too afraid.

Hazel listened to everything and didn't say one word. But just as I turned to run back upstairs, she cleared her throat. "Mrs. Windsor—wait."

I stopped dead in my tracks.

"May I ask you something?"

"Sure." My heart was pounding; I needed to get going. "What is it, Hazel?"

"Why are you doing this?"

I took a deep breath, and then I told her the truth— at least, a part of it. "Because I love him. I love him very much. And I'm not good enough for him, Hazel. I've never been good enough." That was as much as I dared to tell her.

She nodded, and I knew she'd help me.

I ran back to the bedroom and ransacked it,

throwing on clothes and stuffing some toiletries into an overnight bag.

Bryce came back in. His face turned ashen as he watched me scrambling. "Chloe? What the hell are you doing?"

"Bryce... I don't know how to tell you this." I could still smell the tequila on my own breath.

Crazy. I had to seem crazy, which felt pretty fucking close to true at the moment. That was the angle Gene wanted. He wanted me to act jealous and crazy. He wanted me to make myself a liability to Bryce so my husband would understand why I had to leave.

My devotion had to be so great, Gene posited, that it was driving me to do crazy things. I was no good for Bryce—I couldn't be trusted. He had to let me go.

It was going to kill me. Leaving him was going to kill me—but if I stayed, I would destroy *him*. And I loved him too much.

"I've been thinking about what you said before—when you ended things with me."

"Okay...?" Bryce raked a hand through his hair, making it stand up. "I thought we'd gotten past that. I thought we'd moved on."

I nodded slowly. "We had. We did... But with everything that's happened, I'm starting to see what you meant. You said I made you vulnerable, exposed. You said having me in your life made you lose control."

"Why are you throwing this back in my face? I told you I was sorry. I had you come back, Chloe." Pain crept into his eyes, making me hate myself.

I had to stay strong. Bryce's future depended on it. So did Noah's. This might break my heart—it might be the thing that undid me, once and for all—but I would sacrifice myself for him. I would choose the people I loved every time.

"I'm not throwing it in your face. It's that I love you, Bryce. I need to protect you." Tears filled my eyes, and they weren't an act. "Do you remember what you said? Having a wife makes you vulnerable, and you don't do vulnerable. You're about to take over as CEO of Windsor Enterprises. Now, more than ever, you need to be in control. You need to be safe."

"You make me safe, babe. I *love* you."

"But you shouldn't." My voice was gravelly, full of despair. "Look at what I did to you tonight. I *humiliated* you. In public. Drunk and fighting, that's Chloe Windsor. Jealous and crazy. You can't be married to someone like me, Bryce. Look at me! I'm no better than Lydia and my father. The apple doesn't fall far from the tree, I guess. And an apple like me has no business being the wife of a billionaire CEO. Your company needs you, Bryce. They need you to lead. Otherwise, you're going to lose everything."

"If you leave me, I will lose everything."

"That's not true. I'm your hired bride, remember? I'm nothing, no one."

"That's not true, Chloe. Fuck! Don't do this. Please." He took my hands. "Think about my father. He'll cut me out of the company if I'm not married. You can't do this to me. That's not why I want you to stay, but think about it."

I shook my head. "We're not getting divorced tonight. You haven't breached any terms yet. And once he hears that I want out, he'll be more than happy to change the terms. He hates me, Bryce. Always has."

"Then what about your brother? If you leave, you'll destroy him. He loves it here, Chloe. Think about him— that's the whole reason you took the job in the first place. To give Noah a better life."

"He'll be fine," I lied. "I want to go, Bryce. After tonight, it's undeniable that I don't belong in your world. I don't belong with *you*. So let me go. Go and live your big life. Leave me to my little one. That's what I want. That's where I belong."

I rose to go, to leave. To leave *him*. "I quit, Bryce. I'll make sure that Akira returns the money she's holding in trust. I'm so sorry. I never meant for any of this to happen."

Before he could say a word—before he could beg or plead—I grabbed my bag and fled the room.

I was leaving him with nothing... Except for the future he'd always dreamed of.

The only thing that would be missing was me.

Note from the Author:

OMG, I know, *I know!* The final book in the trilogy, **THE FOREVER VOW,** is available now! You can find it here:

www.amazon.com

Love you guys!

xoxo

Leigh

USA Today and Amazon Top-10 Bestselling Author Leigh James is currently sitting on a white-sand beach, watching the sunset, dreaming up her next billionaire. Get ready, he's going to be a HOT one!

Just kidding! Leigh is actually freezing her butt off in Maine, USA, where she lives with her awesome husband, their great kids, and her BFF Choco the chocolate lab. But she promises that billionaire is REALLY going to be something!

Leigh also writes Young Adult Paranormal Romance as Leigh Walker. Her smash-hit series *Vampire Royals* was previously optioned by Netflix. Her books have been translated into German, French, Italian, and Portuguese.

Thank you for reading. Lots of love to all of you!

www.leighjamesauthor.com

Want to be the first to hear about new releases, free books, and other exclusive giveaways?

SIGN UP FOR
MY NEWSLETTER!

LEIGH JAMES

USA Today Best-Selling Author
LeighJamesAuthor.com

also by leigh james

The Escort Collection

Escorting the Player

Escorting the Billionaire

Escorting the Groom

Escorting the Actress

Escorting the Royal

My Super-Hot Fake Wedding Date

Silicon Valley Billionaires

Book 1

Book 2

Book 3

The Liberty Series

Made in the USA
Las Vegas, NV
15 September 2024

95297817R00236